the
DEATH
of
HER

Also by Debbie Howells

The Bones of You
The Beauty of the End

the DEATH *of* HER

DEBBIE HOWELLS

MACMILLAN

First published 2017 by Macmillan
an imprint of Pan Macmillan
20 New Wharf Road, London N1 9RR
Associated companies throughout the world
www.panmacmillan.com

ISBN 978-1-5098-3464-8

1 3 5 7 9 8 6 4 2

A CIP catalogue record for this book is available from the British Library.

Typeset by Palimpsest Book Production Ltd, Falkirk, Stirlingshire
Printed and bound by CPI Group (UK) Ltd, Croydon, CR0 4YY

Visit **www.panmacmillan.com** to read more about all our books
and to buy them. You will also find features, author interviews and
news of any author events, and you can sign up for e-newsletters
so that you're always first to hear about our new releases.

For Georgie and Tom

If there is any wisdom running through my life now, in my walking on this earth, it came from listening in the Great Silence to the stones, trees, space, the wild animals, to the pulse of all life as my heartbeat.

Vijali Hamilton

I know you from your words, the images you share. What touches you, makes you laugh, what angers you. The network of your friendships; a chequerboard of happy, bland avatars, no more or no less readable than your own is. Your latest haircut; shorter than I remember, the ends lightened by the sun.

It's in your eyes, the turn of your head, the secret you're smiling. Familiar to me, because you were always there; not yet centre stage, but in the margins of my life. Lost amongst others, waiting for your moment.

But moments pass. And now, you pretend you're safe. You don't know, do you, that no one can hide forever?

I am in the shadows, where you can't yet see me. You will, though, in the dark corners, the silences, before the blurred edges of reality close in. There's no stopping what will happen. One day, you'll understand the power of destiny. How some things are inevitable; that even shadow-dwellers like me have a purpose in this life.

You'll get that, I know you will. But then I know you well. You are my friend.

1

Charlotte

I hear the helicopter just seconds before it looms overhead, its dark shape low enough that I can feel the downforce from its rotor blades, whipping up my hair, mixing it with the spray flying across the sand.

I turn to watch it, the sun briefly dazzling me, and then just as quickly it's gone. Retrieving my towel from where it's been blown across the beach and shaking the wet sand from it, I'm only idly curious. Around here, it's not uncommon to be buzzed by a low-flying helicopter, on its way to rescue an inexperienced climber or injured surfer. There are any number of beaches along this stretch of the north Cornwall coastline, many not easily accessible by road. I turn my attention back to the waves, just in time to see Rick catch a glassy barrel, then gracefully ride it to shore. Picking up my board, I go to join him.

2

It's not until a couple of days later that Rick tells me more.

'Oh yeah, I forgot to mention . . . This girl was attacked. On one of the farms. Lower Farm, I think.' His hair is wet from the shower, his eyes bright after a morning surfing. 'A couple of Jimbo's lot were running. They found her in the middle of a maize field.'

I'm all ears. Jimbo runs an overpriced boot camp for tourists, and surfs with Rick when he can get away. The surfers' grapevine is notoriously reliable. It's all that time together, floating on their boards, as they wait for the perfect wave.

'What happened to her?' This is rural Cornwall. Nothing like this happens here.

He shrugs. 'Not really sure. It was bad, though. They thought she was dead at first.'

'When did it happen?' I'm frowning, thinking of the low-flying helicopter, wondering if the timing is coincidence or if she was airlifted to hospital.

'A couple of days ago. Maybe three?' he says, vaguely.

I'm amazed it's taken this long for word to get around, the

4

surfers' grapevine being what it is, or maybe Rick didn't think to mention it.

'Oh yeah,' he adds. 'Some of us are meeting at the Shack later. Around six – there may be some waves. You should come. With any luck we could get an hour before dark.' In an unusual display of affection, he plants a kiss on the top of my head.

The Shack is OK; a scruffy locals' bar on one of the beaches a short drive from here that sells Cornish beer and looks nothing from the outside, but inside is all bare wood with surfboards hanging from the ceiling, sand walked inside coating the floor. It'll be full of Rick's mates and wannabe tourist types, dressed to blend in, except you can spot them a mile off, because they don't.

If I'm going to drag myself out on a chilly evening, I prefer a bit of glamour – a cosy restaurant or warm, dimly lit cocktail bar. 'I'm good,' I tell him, stifling a yawn. 'I'll probably have an early night.'

For the most part, Rick and I lead separate lives – we sometimes drink together, smoke a joint or two, have sex. We're not star-crossed lovers; what we have is undemanding and convenient. Physical contact is like food – a basic human need. I should know. I've gone long spells without so much as the brush of a hand. And big, empty houses can be lonely.

After he goes out and I hear his Jeep drive away, I open a bottle of wine and start scrolling through Netflix, listening to the wind rattling the sash windows, knowing it'll whip up some waves. Only they'll be windblown, messy ones, rather than the clean, head-height barrels Rick will be hoping for. But it won't faze him. Nothing does. No matter how many forecasts, swell charts, wind maps you follow, the ocean will always surprise you, he's told me many times.

'Why do you drink so much?' I'm still in my pyjamas, nursing a hangover, when Rick picks up the empty wine bottle from last night. By the time he got home, I'd finished it then started on another, before falling asleep on the sofa.

'I really don't.' I'm irritable, not in the mood for one of his holier-than-thou lectures on how my body is a temple. I know my body better than he does. 'You probably had just as much and drove home, which is far worse.'

'Two pints,' he says, shortly. 'You do this every night. And it's usually more – we both know that. By the time you know you've fucked up your liver, it'll be too late.'

'Yeah, yeah . . .' I get up to go back upstairs, because I've heard it all before. It's not like Rick to be confrontational, but this time he grabs my arm.

'You take it for granted, don't you?' His eyes glitter angrily. 'Always so bloody sure of yourself. Do you have any idea how lucky you are?'

I stare just as angrily back at him, wondering where this has come from. 'It's a few glasses of wine, Rick. What the fuck's wrong with you?'

But he doesn't answer, just lets go of me and shakes his head as he walks away.

I don't like being spoken to like that, especially not by Rick. Even less do I like the spike of truth in his words. But better a shorter life lived to the full than the dragged-out mundane ones so many people cling to for as long as they can. Whether you live twenty years or sixty, unless you save the planet or cure cancer, what does it actually matter?

Upstairs, I pull on jeans and a hoody, glancing out of the window to see Rick stride across the garden then stand with his back to the house, gazing out across the bay. I've no idea what's eating him, but clearly something is. Taking a deep breath, I go outside to join him.

'Not surfing today?' As I catch him up, my tone is light, conciliatory, but he's still rigid as I slip my arm through his.

He shrugs. 'Maybe later.'

'Look, is something wrong?' I remove my arm, turning to face him. 'Because you're being shitty, Rick.'

He's silent for a moment, still looking out to sea, then he turns to face me. 'You really want to know?'

As I nod, I'm aware of an unpleasant prickling sensation.

'I don't get you. All this time we've been together, and you spend every day in that house, not really doing anything. You don't work. You were going to paint – but all you do is make excuses. Don't you have dreams? Places you want to see? People in your life?'

'Of course I do,' I say quietly, trying to contain the seething anger welling up inside me. I know exactly what I want from life. I don't have to share it with him.

'We all think we have forever.' His jaw set, he's on a roll. 'Only none of us do. We live in the most beautiful part of this country, where nothing bad happens, and then a woman gets attacked on our doorstep. Nearly dies. Doesn't it make you think it could happen to anyone? Like you, even?'

'I'm not going to walk around thinking I'm in danger,' I tell him. What's the matter with him? 'Things happen all the time, Rick. Bad things. People fuck up, even in pretty places like Cornwall. It's no different to anywhere else.'

When he looks at me, there's an expression of disgust on

his face. 'You know what? That's it, in a nutshell. You don't care. You're not shocked or even sad it's happened. You just accept it. And most people are just like you. Except I'm not.' He's silent for a moment. 'I don't know . . .' He breaks off. When he looks at me, I can't fathom the expression in his eyes.

But I've had more than enough. 'You know what, Rick? I'm going for a walk.'

I walk away from him, through the gate and onto the coast path, hugging my arms round me in the cool air, trying to keep warm. In my head I continue my conversation with Rick – angrily. It's a couple of hours later when I get back to the house, less angry, but the absence of Rick's Jeep still fills me with relief.

In the kitchen, I fill the kettle and turn on the radio. The brightness of the sun through the large window belies the temperature outside. I sit at the kitchen table and turn on my laptop. With a mug of strong tea in front of me and classical music playing in the background, I start searching for a local supplier of artist's materials. Rick was right about one thing – I've been making excuses not to paint.

I find what I'm looking for, and I'm jotting down the address when the radio news comes on. I'm only half listen-ing, until one of the items makes my ears prick up.

'*Police are looking for information about a woman who was found injured four days ago. The woman was discovered unconscious on farmland in a remote part of north Cornwall. Police are keen to establish who may have seen her any time during 24 September. They are also seeking the whereabouts of her three-year-old daughter. Anyone with information should contact Devon and Cornwall Police. More details are available on our website.*'

I sit there in silence. The fact that a local mugging has made national news somehow gives it more gravity. I check the station's website, and there it is. The police are seeking information after the woman, known as Evie Sherman, suffered severe head injuries in a brutal attack that left her unconscious on farmland in north Cornwall. They are also investigating the whereabouts of her three-year-old daughter.

Underneath, there's a photograph of the woman. It's hard to tell how old she is. Her face is an unhealthy grey, mottled with red-black bruising, and there's a dazed expression in her eyes. It looks as though she's in a hospital bed. Studying her more closely, I frown. There's something familiar about her.

I click on Devon and Cornwall Police's Facebook page. As I scroll down, there are several recent posts of a more trivial nature – a gun amnesty, a spate of burglaries, road traffic accident – none of which hold my interest. Then, further down, the same photo. The brief paragraph mentions how she was airlifted to hospital after being found unconscious. It gives her name again, and asks anyone who recognizes her to contact Truro police.

Further down still, there's another photo. I study it, deep in thought, then hunt around for my phone. The police are wrong. Her name isn't Evie. It's Jen.

3

'Babe? There's someone at the door. Can you get it? I've just got out the shower.'

Even if he hears me above the sound of the guitar he's playing, Rick doesn't reply. I feel a flash of irritation and wish I could be as oblivious, as self-absorbed, when someone asks me to do something. The doorbell rings again and, quickly pulling on some clothes, I run downstairs to answer it.

'Yes?'

The woman on the doorstep looks puzzled. She's probably one of those tourists who think they can rock up to any old place just because it's Cornwall and they think they've seen it on the television.

'Are you Charlotte Harrison?'

Oh God. How does this woman know me? 'I'm sorry . . .' I turn away and start to close the door, but something's in the way. When I look down, it's her foot. When I look up again, she's holding out a police badge.

'Detective Inspector Abbie Rose. Please don't close the door.'

'Why didn't you say? I'd completely forgotten you were coming.' I swing the door open and let her in.

I lead her through the hallway into the open-plan living area. She looks around, at the whitewashed Cornish-stone walls and the views that, even after a year here, still take my breath away. The house is perched above Epphaven Cove, which was one of Cornwall's best-kept secrets until a national paper ran a feature and ruined it.

She walks over to the north-facing window. Not many people come here, but I enjoy watching their reactions when they see the view for the first time. As she turns round, she glances at the paintings and the furniture; to the uneducated eye they might look incongruous, but to those who know, they're utterly wondrous. I wonder if DI Abbie Rose knows what she's looking at.

'Do you live here alone?'

'Some of the time.' A guitar wail comes from a distant corner of the house. 'That's Rick. He follows the waves.' He does, literally, follow them around the globe, coming and going like the swallows under the eaves, only less predictably.

'Won't you sit down?' I gesture towards the cerise velvet sofa. Pink's my favourite colour, as anyone who knows me will tell you. I have a pink bathroom, pink Jimmy Choos, a big American fridge full of pink champagne.

'Thank you.' She perches on the edge of the sofa, then reaches into her bag for a notebook.

I sit in the oversized armchair near the window. 'How can I help, Detective Inspector?'

'I understand you recognized the woman who was attacked, from the photo on our Facebook page.'

'Yes. With all that bruising, it's hard to be completely sure, of course, but I think so . . .'

'When you called the station yesterday, you said you knew her as Jen Russell. Is that right?'

'Yes. We were at school together.'

'Which school?'

'Padstow College.' I watch her write it down. 'Have you found her child?' Since the police posted her details on Facebook, there's been the typical, gushing public outpouring of condolence and shared grief – and a few haters. I've checked once or twice, curious to see who else crawled out of the woodwork.

'Not yet.' Abbie Rose isn't giving much away. 'How well did you know her?'

'We were in the same year,' I tell her. 'We weren't close friends. We moved in different circles that overlapped from time to time . . .' Cliques, is more accurate. The usual bitchy girl gangs who shagged each other's boyfriends behind each other's backs, is how I remember it.

'When was the last time you saw each other?'

Now there's a question. It's been a long time. Too long or not long enough? But then, we're not the same people any more. 'I suppose . . .' I frown, trying to remember, as someone thunders down the stairs and slams the front door noisily. I glance outside. 'Rick,' I say, by way of explanation. 'There's an offshore wind. Good for waves, if you catch the tide at the right time. There's a brief window of opportunity – at high tide, the beach here is completely submerged.' As I'm speaking, Rick jogs across the lawn, surfboard under one arm, the top half of his wetsuit unzipped and flapping behind him. 'Do you surf, Detective Inspector?'

She shakes her head.

'I'm sorry.' I pause. 'You were asking me about Jen. I suppose we last saw each other about ten years ago. Someone's twenty-first . . . I can't remember whose.'

'So that would have been after Leah Danning disappeared?'

Maybe I shouldn't be surprised that the police have already linked Jen's name to what happened. Since before I left Cornwall, all those years ago, it's the first time I've heard Leah's name mentioned. Three-year-old Leah, who Jen used to babysit – until one day, in broad daylight, she disappeared. It rocked everyone round here, more so because the police never discovered what happened to her.

4

I hesitate. 'Do you think this is connected to what happened to Leah?'

Abbie Rose gives nothing away. 'We've no idea. But at this stage, we have to look at everything.'

'Of course.' But it still surprises me. It must be fifteen years since Leah disappeared. 'Poor Jen. I don't know how you ever get over that. I mean, losing someone's child when they're in your care . . . You didn't have to know her well to see the change in her, after. And now her own daughter is missing . . .' I imagine guilt layered upon guilt, at the same time as I wonder how Jen's coping with what must be unbearable.

Abbie Rose doesn't comment. 'And you haven't seen her since then?'

'Like I said, the last time we saw each other was at that party.' I get up and walk over to the window. On the beach, I can just about make out clean, barrelling waves and, floating beyond them, the lone dot that must be Rick.

'Do you remember much about that time? When Leah disappeared?'

'God. It's not something anyone could forget in a hurry. It was awful.' I watch Rick catch a wave, wishing I could surf as well as he can. 'No one could believe a child could just disappear. It was like a black cloud over everything – it changed our lives. Everyone's parents became overprotective. And people gossiped . . . Eventually it died down, but at the time, it was like the world had ended.' Turning to face her, I add, 'Sorry, Detective Inspector. I don't mean to sound indifferent. It was terrible. It destroyed Leah's family. Did you know that?'

'Did you know them, Charlotte?' Abbie Rose's eyes linger on me.

'Not when it happened.' I'm not sure what to say, wondering what it will do to Jen right now, to have the police asking about another missing child, particularly one that was never found. 'I knew *of* them. I was good friends with Leah's older sister for a while, but that wasn't until later.'

'Do you know what happened to them?'

'I heard her father left. Her mother was really strange – I think she had a breakdown. Casey died – only a year or so ago. I think she suffered the most.'

'Casey was Leah's sister?'

'Yes.' I don't say it out loud, but I'm remembering how it was for Casey – the hardest of lessons, having to haul herself out of the darkest place. It was either that, or give up. Life makes no concessions for the bereaved. It goes on regardless, mercilessly, ruthlessly. 'Did the police ever find out what happened to Leah?'

'No.'

'It's still hard to believe something like that could happen. Especially here. It's so quiet . . .' Apart from the influx of drunken teenagers in the summer, it's true. That's why, as soon as they're old enough, most young people can't wait to move away. *Yet here I am, back again,* I muse, *not far from where I started.* So, it seems, is Jen.

Abbie Rose nods. 'I wanted to ask you if you'd come and see Evie – Jen, I mean. The attack has left her memory badly affected. Seeing a familiar face could really help.'

I don't answer straight away. I'm wondering how it would be for Jen. Too much of a reminder of the past? 'Are you sure it's a good idea? Of course I'd like to see her, but I wouldn't want to make things any worse for her.'

'To be honest, I'm not sure things could get much worse.'

My ears prick up. 'Really? How bad is it? It must be awful for her.' I look at Abbie Rose quizzically, but her face is blank. 'I could see her tomorrow morning?' I add. 'Say, around ten?'

'Thank you. I'll tell her you're coming. She's in the Royal Cornwall hospital – in Truro.' She hesitates. 'You wouldn't happen to know if she has family nearby?'

I shrug. 'I'm out of touch. But I remember her aunt's house. It's out in the sticks – near Bodmin. We went there sometimes during the school holidays,' I say, vaguely. 'You know, gangs of girls camping in the woods. Being so remote, Helen's place was perfect.' I try not to smile inappropriately. 'All our parents thought camping was such an innocent, idyllic thing to do, which it was – until we got older, of course. By then, Helen was deaf as a post. She had no idea what we really got up to.' I pause. 'Just teenage stuff – nothing bad,' I add quickly, thinking of drunken nights and the boys who used to join us but remembering I'm talking to a police officer.

'You don't by any chance remember the address, do you?'

I pause again, thinking not so much of the cottage, but the woods where we used to camp. 'Not off the top of my head.'

But then I remember something. 'Actually, I think her aunt's full name was Helen Osterman.'

Abbie Rose writes it down. 'That gives us something to go on.' Then she gets up. 'I better get back. Thanks for your help. I'll see you tomorrow.'

But I'm still puzzled about something. 'Why have the press been calling her Evie?'

'It's what she calls herself. From what you've told us, it looks as though she changed her name, though we don't know why. I'm hoping a face from the past might trigger her to remember something.'

'OK.' I shrug. It's understandable – maybe she wanted to break any association with what happened to Leah. Jen, Evie; it makes no difference as far as I'm concerned. 'Whatever. At least I know.'

Abbie Rose walks over to the door. As she opens it, she pauses, a quizzical expression on her face. 'Up until that time you last saw each other, do you happen to know if Jen was ever pregnant?'

'Shouldn't you be asking Jen that?' After talking about Helen's place, I'm uncomfortable all of a sudden. It was years ago. Why is she so interested in the past?

'She can't tell me much about anything right now.' Abbie stands in the doorway. 'I'm trying to help her build a picture of how her life was.'

I hesitate, not sure what to say. Not sure either why Abbie Rose wants to know. 'There was a rumour . . . but I'm fairly sure that's all it was. Probably spread by a couple of girls who had it in for her. She didn't look pregnant – certainly not when I saw her. I don't know if she's still the same, but she was skinny back then. I can't imagine she'd have been able to hide it . . .' I frown. 'But there was a time she wasn't around for a while. And no one knew why. I'm sorry, I don't really know any more than that.'

Abbie Rose frowns. 'Why would those girls have had it in for her?'

I shrug. 'The usual reasons. Because she was thinner and prettier and smarter than they were. Plus, everyone liked her.' Meaning boys, in particular, but Abbie Rose seems smart enough to work that one out.

'I see.' Abbie Rose pauses. 'There isn't any other reason?'

I shake my head. 'Nothing comes to mind.'

'Perhaps we can talk more tomorrow. You can always call me if you think of anything else.'

She hands me a card, and then I follow her outside to her car. After she drives away, I wander around the side of the house and onto the grass, which needs cutting again, feeling annoyed by the shrieks of children floating up from the beach below. The beach may no longer be a secret, but most holidaymakers are too lazy to walk the half mile down the stony path from the road, then clamber down the rocks. It's not for the faint-hearted. Other than the occasional lunatic like Rick, who carries his surfboard down there, those that venture all the way to the shore are few, and an irritation I'm forced to tolerate.

He's still out there, the water flat between sets as he waits for the next wave to roll in. Rick has his own philosophy, about how the universe brings us what we need. I learned from him when he tried to help me surf bigger waves; how to clear my mind as I sat on my board, to feel the rhythm of the ocean.

Nothing is by chance. A wave is the culmination of many factors. There's the swell, the wind, the shape of the coastline, the ocean floor. It shows the divine timing to all things, because you can't hurry the perfect wave. He's taught me the need for patience as you see a set coming, the importance of relying on your judgement. The perfect wave will come when the time is right.

I stand there watching him as he deftly rides a wave to the shore then, instead of paddling out against the tide, catches the rip. Its powerful flow is an easy ride out past the waves, when you understand the forces at work, as Rick does. When you don't, it's an easy way to die.

5

It's overcast as I drive to the hospital, drizzle painting the landscape a dull grey. On the way, I stop at the art shop in Truro I'd found online, which is overpriced but convenient, thinking it will save me a trip to Wadebridge, but half of what I want is out of stock. I leave with paper and a limited palette of watercolours and ask them to order the rest, irritated because it means I have to come back, then carry on to the hospital.

Walking along the corridors to the critical care unit, I'm overtaken by apprehension. Jen and I were acquaintances rather than friends. I haven't seen her in years. If I was in her position, I'm not sure I'd want one of my old classmates turning up out of the blue. But if there's no one else, maybe she'll be pleased to see me.

The quiet of critical care is broken by electronic noise and low voices. Everyone's busy, but eventually I catch one of the nurses.

'I'm here to see Jen,' I tell her. When she looks at me blankly, I add, 'Evie? Evie Sherman?'

'Can you wait here?' She walks briskly away through some

20

swing doors, then comes back a minute or so later with Abbie Rose.

'Thanks for coming, Charlotte.' Abbie Rose looks drawn, as though she was up half the night. 'I wanted to have a word with you before you see her.'

'Sure.' I frown, wondering what's on her mind.

'Earlier, Evie – Jen – got quite upset. Frantic, actually. She's beside herself about her daughter. I'd hoped to talk to her about Leah Danning, just to see if the name triggered any memories, but she's far too fragile. She's been given a sedative, but I wanted to ask you to bear that in mind. It's probably best not to talk about anything that could upset her further – at least for now. Hopefully, as her memory comes back, it will be easier.'

'Of course.' I try to imagine how it is, to lose all sense of your life. To not remember who you are.

'I'll show you where she is.' Abbie Rose starts walking back towards the swing doors.

I hedge. 'Are you sure this is a good idea? I mean, if she's upset?'

Abbie Rose pauses. 'There's a three-year-old child missing. Right now, we have to try everything.'

Her words remind me that this isn't just about Jen. She has to explore every means she can to find out more about Jen's missing daughter. I follow her through the doors and along a short corridor of private rooms. Outside one of the doors, the presence of a police officer somehow surprises me. But after an attack of the severity Jen's survived, I guess it's standard procedure. As we reach the room, Abbie Rose pauses. 'Evie's in here. It might be best to keep calling her Evie – for now.'

The room is small and white, and the high ceiling and large

window give it an airy feel. The woman on the bed doesn't move. It's definitely Jen, only a pale shadow of the girl I remember. Her eyes are closed and her face is turned away from us.

I'm too hot all of a sudden. I take off my jumper and drape it over a chair near the door. 'Maybe I should come back another time,' I say uneasily. 'I don't want to disturb her.'

Abbie Rose takes a step towards the bed. 'Evie? Are you awake? There's someone here to see you.'

I watch the slightest flicker of Jen's eyelids, indicating she's heard, before very slowly, she turns her head.

Abbie Rose glances at me. 'It might be easier if you come round here, where she can see you.' Then she turns to Evie. 'Charlotte's here, Evie. She remembers you. You used to go to the same school.'

'Hello.' I move closer, watching as her eyes focus on me. 'I'm Charlotte. Harrison. Do you remember me?'

Her face is skeletal, with dark circles under her eyes, her hair lank and unwashed. But it's not just Jen who's changed. My hair is short and bleached blonde instead of dark and ridiculously long, which is how it used to be. I've put on weight, too. As I watch, Jen – Evie – blinks. I can't tell if she tries to nod. The movement of her head is barely perceptible as her eyelids close again.

'Just talk to her,' Abbie Rose says quietly. 'The sound of your voice might trigger something.'

I look around helplessly, not sure what to say. 'Do you remember camping at your aunt's cottage? There were a few of us who used to – in the summer.'

I wait for a flicker of recognition, anything that suggests

she's heard what I'm saying. But as I take in the machines she's wired to, how still she is in the hospital bed, I know she hasn't.

'Evie? Did you hear what Charlotte said?' Abbie Rose tries to rouse her, then glances at me. 'I don't think we're going to get anywhere today. Sorry. I'll walk out with you.'

'Thanks for coming here,' she says, once we're away from Jen's room. 'I'm sorry it was such a waste of your time.'

'It's fine.' I'm still thinking of how fragile Jen looked, as though she's hanging on to life by the finest thread.

'It's probably the sedative. If it's not too much to ask, could we try again? Maybe in a day or two, when she's stronger? We're trying to find her parents, but right now, you're the only person who's come forward who knows her.'

I nod – reluctantly. It's one thing to spend a few minutes with her to see if it jogs some memories, but another altogether to get more involved.

'I may be going away in a few days,' I lie, just because I don't want to commit to anything. 'But perhaps I can see her before I go.'

When I get home, Rick's there.

'Where were you?' He's less angry with me, but there's still something eating him, I can tell.

'You know that woman who was attacked? The one you told me about? It turns out I used to know her.'

Rick looks astounded. 'How on earth did you work that out?'

'Photos,' I tell him. 'Devon and Cornwall Police Facebook page. So I called them. I wasn't sure at first, but it's definitely her. I've just been to see her.'

'Where is she?'

23

'Truro – in hospital. She's very weak and she's lost her memory. The police wanted me to see her, to try and help her remember.'

'And did she?'

I shake my head. 'They'd sedated her, but they're desperate. Her child's missing. They've asked me to go back in a couple of days.'

'God.' Rick's silent for a moment. 'Makes you wonder what sick bastard would do that to someone. I mean, a child, for Christ's sake . . .'

'I know.' I nod, numbly, and then a tear snakes its way down my face.

Rick sees it. 'Hey, are you OK?'

I nod again. 'Seeing her brought back memories, that's all.'

He comes over and puts his arms round me. 'Have you thought about talking to someone?' His voice is softer. 'About your parents? It might really help.'

He's referring to the little I've told him about my parents – a father who threw me out and a mother who stood by and let him make her daughter homeless. It's why I stayed away from here for so long. 'Maybe.' But I'm saying it to keep him quiet, instead of what I want to say, which is that it's too late, and no amount of talking can change what happened to me.

I'm hoping it's a truce between us. When he sees the painting materials I've bought, I can tell he approves. But he doesn't explain why he's been so mad at me. The mood passes, a large block of ice slowly thawing while I consider whether we've had our time, sooner than I'd reckoned on. But then we're transient, Rick and I. We always will be.

The truce lasts for twenty-four hours. I come in from a walk to find Rick standing there with a face like thunder.

'Were you going to tell me?' he says angrily.

'Tell you what?' I've no idea what he's talking about.

'Don't fuck with me, Charlotte. You tell the police you're going away in a few days, but you don't bother to tell me. Where are you going?'

Rick calls me babe. He never calls me Charlotte. 'How do you know what I told them?'

'You left your jumper at the hospital. One of them very kindly dropped it off. He said that normally they wouldn't have, but you weren't answering your phone and they'd hoped to catch you before you left.' He stands there with his arms folded. 'So? Are you going to tell me?'

I consider telling him the truth for a moment – that I didn't want the police to get too reliant on me – before bloody-mindedness kicks in. 'None of your fucking business,' I spit back, sick to death of how he's suddenly on my case about absolutely everything. 'You don't tell me everything you're doing, Rick. Why should it be different for me?'

'You are goddamned selfish,' he shouts. 'For a moment there, you almost had me fooled. I'd actually started to believe that there's another side to you. That you wanted to help your old school friend—'

'She's not really my friend,' I interrupt. 'I just knew her. I don't owe her anything.' It's not how I meant it to come out.

Rick stares at me, then when he speaks, his icy calm makes my skin prickle. 'That's just it with you. It's all about you. You don't owe anyone anything, do you?'

'It's not that simple.' I'm shaking my head. I care about Rick – to a point. But people always take advantage of you. This is supposed to be a year for me.

'It really is.' His voice is flat. 'It's dead simple. Life's about people, Charlotte. You know what? I'm going away for a bit. See if you can work it out while I'm gone. And if not . . .' He starts walking towards the stairs.

'If not, what?' I shout after his back. 'Don't you dare bloody walk out like this.'

He freezes. When he speaks, there's a hint of menace in his voice I haven't heard before. 'I'll do exactly as I please.'

6

Rick doesn't tell me where he's going – or who with. I wonder if he's met someone else. It might explain why he's behaving like this. But the clock is ticking, our relationship slipping through my fingers like grains of sand, the independence that once drew him to me now pushing him away.

After he's left, I get drunk. Not just drunk enough to numb my anger with Rick and the sense of insecurity creeping over me. I get blind, falling-over, forget-everything, throwing-up drunk.

It's midday when I wake up with the mother of all hangovers. Desperately thirsty and unable to keep even water down, I spend the rest of the day in bed, not even bothering to open the curtains. Screw Rick. If he doesn't want me, he can go to hell. My mobile buzzes once. Half asleep, I let the call go to voicemail, imagining a repentant Rick anxiously checking up on me, then wake hours later to find it wasn't Rick at all. It was Abbie Rose.

Wishing I'd never told the police I recognized the person in the photo, I play her message back, then with a heavy heart, call her back.

'I was hoping you'd have time to see Evie again – before you go away.'

'I'm not going. Change of plan,' I tell her. Why did she have to remember? A hangover is no place to lie from.

'Oh, OK. Well, when would suit you?'

Never, I'm thinking. Then, not knowing when Rick will be back, I suggest, 'Tomorrow? Afternoon?'

'Can we say three o'clock?'

'I'll be there.'

'Thank you, Charlotte. I really appreciate it.'

I mumble something into my phone before dropping it on the floor, lying back, staring at the ceiling and silently cursing.

As I drive to Truro the following day, I'm thinking about Rick. A year's a long time and we were never destined to be long term. But I still don't really know why he's so angry with me. I know I'm selfish, but I've spent a lot of time alone. It's a form of self-preservation. When no one looks out for you, the only person you can rely on is yourself.

But as I walk through the hospital, it occurs to me that being here, as well as trying to help the police, is the perfect way to show Rick he's got me wrong. Walking faster, I smugly imagine his surprise, his apology. No one speaks to me the way he did and gets away with it.

As I reach the nurses' station, I see Abbie Rose deep in conversation with another police officer. When she sees me, she stops talking.

'Charlotte. Thanks for coming back again. This is PC Miller. He's helping with this case.'

I glance at PC Miller. He's younger than Abbie Rose, with brown hair and clear, pale-blue eyes which hold mine a little longer than necessary.

'How's Jen today?'

'More awake, but still very unsettled, as you can imagine. She's been able to give us some more information about her daughter.' She looks at PC Miller. 'You may as well go, Dan. I'll let you know if she says anything else.' As he walks away, she turns back to me. 'Come with me, Charlotte.'

There's a different uniformed officer outside her room today. The police are clearly not taking chances. As we walk in, Jen's head turns towards us. Her eyes are agitated, worry written all over her face.

'Evie? Charlotte's here again.' As Abbie Rose says my name, I see it register with Jen, and she glances fleetingly in my direction.

'Hello.' I say it as gently as I can. 'I hope you don't mind me coming? The police thought seeing me might help you remember.'

Jen's eyes are wild as she glances from me to Abbie Rose, then back to me again. 'We were at school together – remember?' I persist. 'We weren't good friends, but I saw your photo and I recognized you.'

Wondering if I'm saying the right kind of thing, I glance at Abbie Rose. She nods.

Jen whispers something I can't make out, then she reaches out one of her hands towards me. 'Have you seen Angel?' Her voice is hoarse, her eyes pleading with me.

'Her daughter,' Abbie Rose says quietly.

Slowly I shake my head, then say, as sympathetically as I can, 'I'm so sorry.'

Jen's eyes close as her head falls back on the pillow. I turn to Abbie Rose.

'We found an address for Evie's aunt,' she tells me. 'Jessamine Cottage – on the edge of Bodmin, just as you said. We've been round, but the house is empty.'

But as she mentions Jessamine Cottage, Jen's eyes suddenly open. Then she's trying to pull herself up in bed. 'My . . . house . . .' she manages to say, her face contorted with pain, as one of the nurses hurries in.

'I'm sorry, but can you give us a moment?' Turning her back on us, the nurse attends to Jen. 'Evie, you need to rest. Let me help you get comfortable.'

Abbie Rose looks at me, nodding towards the door. Walking ahead, I wait for her outside.

She's right behind me. 'So far, we haven't found anything obvious at Jessamine Cottage. There's an old Peugot parked nearby which presumably could be Evie's. Can you think of anyone else who might know her?'

I shake my head. 'I completely lost touch when I moved away. I only came back here about a year ago. I suppose you could ask our old school? She was in the sports teams and stuff. She was good.'

Abbie Rose nods. 'We're doing exactly that.'

I'm frowning. It seems incredible that I'm the only person who's recognized Jen. Surely she has to buy food and fuel for her car. 'Angel's father . . . What about him?'

'We're doing our best to locate him.'

I hesitate. 'It makes you think, doesn't it, if no one's missed her, and no one's come forward after seeing her photo, either she lived somewhere else – miles away – or she was hiding.'

I can tell from Abbie Rose's face that she's thinking the same thing. But who or what was Jen hiding from? And why?

•

7

Whether it's because of the problems in my own life, or her link to my past, Jen's attack haunts me. Her face fills my mind as I find myself trying to imagine what she's going through.

I think about Leah, too. It seems incredible that she was never found. But there's no CCTV in the woods and fields. It's an easy place to disappear. Then I think about Rick and his cryptic remark before he left. *See if you can work it out while I'm gone.* Work what out? But I'm uneasy. It's not so much what he said as how he said it.

I'm intending only to go food shopping but I've no plans for the day, and idle curiosity, as well as the desire to impress Rick when he returns, draws me to the hospital. Abbie Rose looks only slightly surprised to see me.

'It's good timing, actually. I've a photo to show Evie.' I notice she's holding a brown envelope. 'It might be helpful that you're here.'

She's clearly read more into our friendship than I intended her to, not that it matters. 'Oh?'

Abbie Rose isn't giving anything away, not yet at least. 'Shall we go and see her?'

I follow her down the corridor to Jen's room. 'Has she remembered her real name?'

'We haven't pushed it. But the photo might mean we have to tell her. We'll see what she says.'

Jen's door is ajar. Abbie Rose knocks, then pushes it open.

'Hello, Evie. How are you today?'

Jen nods. 'OK.' An anxious expression flits across her face and I realize she's waiting for news of her daughter, yet knows without asking that there is none. Good news arrives in bright eyes and smiling faces, not brown envelopes.

'We found a photo in your aunt's cottage.' Taking the photo from the envelope, Abbie Rose passes it to Jen. 'Do you recognize him?'

Jen stares at the photo, then she turns to Abbie Rose. 'Yes . . . No . . . I think so?' Her flat, detached air of calm makes me think she's sedated again.

It's a photo of a man; facing the camera, unsmiling, an appraising look from eyes which seem to stare right through you. Jen studies it closely. 'I think so,' she says again, but she sounds far from sure.

'His name is Nick,' Abbie Rose tells her. 'At least, that's what it says on the back.' She gently takes the photo from Jen and flips it over, to show the words 'love from Nick' written there. 'Is it possible he's your husband?'

She swallows. 'I don't know.'

I try to imagine how it is to look at a photo that could be of your husband and not be able to tell. I watch her closely for the smallest sign of recognition.

'Could he be Angel's father?'

'*I don't know,*' she cries. Then she studies it more closely. 'Maybe I do know him . . . I was trying to see if Angel has his eyes.'

It's the most I've heard her say.

'Does he remind you of her?' Abbie Rose's voice is sharp.

Jen pauses again. 'I think so.' She falters. 'Slightly . . .'

'There's another photo.' This time, Abbie Rose hesitates before handing it to her. It's of the same man, only his hair is slightly longer and he looks more carefree somehow. Jen takes it, turns it over, then as she reads the message on the back, her face turns even paler.

To Jen, with love, Nick.

Jen drops it on the bed. 'Who's Jen?' Her reaction makes it clear that she has no idea; that she thinks Jen is either an old girlfriend or someone her husband was having an affair with.

'You don't know?' Abbie Rose is feeling her way, trying to push for answers, knowing that pushing too far, too soon, could be too much for Jen.

Staring at the second photo, Jen shakes her head, looking confused. 'No.' Whispering it, as if frightened to say it out loud.

Abbie Rose gets up and walks over to the window, making a call. 'We have a potential name of the father of Angel Sherman. Is Miller there?'

She's silent for a moment, then she goes on. 'His given name is Nick. I suggest we look for Nick Sherman – see if it turns something up. Call me if you find anything.'

She comes back over to Jen's bed. 'We've been trying to establish if anyone in the area knows you and Angel. We've checked with local preschools in case she's registered anywhere. So far it looks as though she isn't, but that doesn't really tell us anything. She's only three. You might not have got round to it yet. But we've also checked with local surgeries. So far, you don't seem to be registered with any of their practices, either.'

Jen looks at her blankly.

'There's something else.' Abbie Rose hesitates, and I see what she's doing – waiting for a subliminal, unspoken message to register, before the actual words deliver their shock.

It seems to work. I watch the look of unease come over Jen's face.

'There's no easy way to tell you this, Evie. Someone saw your photo on our Facebook page. We've been checking out the information we were given. But right now, from everything we know, it looks as though your real name is Jen Russell.'

8

A mixture of emotions comes over me as I watch Jen's reaction. Firstly, relief that Abbie Rose didn't tell her it was me who had identified her. I hope she knows what she's doing. It's a huge shock to deliver to someone.

'No.' Jen pushes herself up, her arms clutched tightly round her body. 'Who told you?'

Abbie Rose hesitates. 'It doesn't matter at this stage.'

'No! They're wrong. I'm Evie Sherman. I live here with my daughter Angel and my cat. You know I am. I'm not called Jen.'

'You have a cat?' Abbie Rose frowns, trying to deflect her panic.

'Yes.' Jen's tearful, then she's frantic again. 'Why would I have another name?' She's desperate, needing answers.

'It explains the photo,' I say to her quietly. Abbie Rose is silent. 'The inscription on the back.'

'No.' Jen shakes her head. I recognize her denial, however irrational. It's too much for her to take in. She turns to me.

'We were at school together, weren't we? Please tell Abbie I'm Evie . . .'

But I can tell she isn't sure. I meet her eyes, then look away.

'The school has photos,' Abbie Rose adds quietly. 'You were captain of the school hockey team. A very successful team that competed nationally. It seems you were the pride of your school – they have photos everywhere, even now.'

'I don't understand.' Jen's hands are shaking.

'People change their names all the time, Evie. For all kinds of reasons. It explains why we haven't been able to trace any records of you. What we'll do now is check for records of Jen Russell and Angel Russell. From the photo, we can assume that Nick knew you as Jen.' She pauses to let Jen take it in.

'It doesn't make sense.' Her voice is dull. 'Why did I remember my name as Evie? Wouldn't you think I'd have remembered Jen?'

'I don't know. Memories can play the strangest tricks. Maybe you'd been calling yourself Evie for some time, wanting to forget your real name, for some reason. So much of what's happening suggests you were hiding. If you're right and you were living in your aunt's house, there's the fact that no one's looking for you. You must have lived alone and avoided people . . .'

Including her husband, I can't help thinking.

'And what about Angel? What if I've changed her name too?'

'We don't know at this stage. But we have her description and that's the important thing. Until your memory comes back, we have to keep an open mind . . . But it doesn't stop us from looking.' Abbie Rose hesitates again, looking at her more intently. 'What was going on in your life, Evie?'

Jen's hands are clasped tightly, her nails digging into her palms, as she stares silently at Abbie Rose.

'It may not feel like it, but with all of this, you must be getting closer to what really happened,' I offer, wanting Jen to hear something more positive. And it's true, surely. 'You have to trust the police, Evie.'

From a place where nothing makes sense that must feel impossible to her, it's all she can do. Trust – in the police, even in me. That people are doing what they can. It's her only way through this.

'I need to make a call. Can you stay a little while?' Abbie Rose is looking at me.

I nod. 'Of course.' This time, she goes out to make the call. When she's gone, I turn to Jen. 'Is there anything I can do?' I don't know what else to say to her.

Her eyes blank, she shakes her head. I strain my ears to hear what Abbie Rose is saying on her phone, but she's too far away.

'Charlotte?'

I turn back to look at Jen. Caught in her fragmented world, she looks frightened witless.

'Thank you . . . for being here.'

'It's OK . . .' I'm flustered, not sure what to say, because there's nothing I can do to help her. Then Abbie Rose comes back in.

'Evie? Someone at the station found a press cutting.' Abbie Rose pauses, as though trying to gauge Jen's reaction. 'It's about Jen Russell's – your – engagement. Sara's emailing it to me as we speak. Constable Evans,' she adds, noticing my frown. 'This is probably it now.' As her phone pings, she scrolls down to find it. 'Here. It says you were engaged to a man named Nicholas Abraham. It was announced in the local paper – six years ago. I'll read it to you. *"Mr and Mrs Nigel Russell announce the engagement between Nicholas Abraham and their daughter, Genevieve . . ."'*

Genevieve. Jen. Evie.

'It explains the name you chose.' Abbie Rose is thinking the same thing.

But tears are streaming down Jen's face. 'My parents?' she whispers, her eyes searching the policewoman's.

'Sara's trying to find out more, but your father's dead, Evie. We're trying to locate your mother,' Abbie Rose tells her gently. 'But at least now we should be able to find Nick.'

9

'It's not particularly relevant right now,' Abbie Rose tells me
as we go outside, when I ask her why she hasn't mentioned
Leah Danning. 'There's a balance between pushing Evie just
enough but not too much. The Leah Danning case was years
ago. Until Evie's stronger, I'm not sure reminding her is going
to help.'

'I guess not.' I'm deep in thought. I already know that when
they're investigating crimes like this, the police look up similar
past cases. I'm wondering if there's something she's not telling
me.

'Are you sure I'm not keeping you?' Abbie Rose looks at
me.

'It's fine – now that I'm not going away.' Slightly ashamed,
I remember Rick's outburst, then airily wave a hand. 'I was
going to see a friend for a couple of weeks but she cancelled
– something came up.' I lie because I don't want her to know
how empty my life is.

'Do you work?' Her interest seems genuine.

This time I tell her the truth. 'I used to work in PR but I

was made redundant. I'm taking a sabbatical while I figure out what to do next.'

Back home, I unload the shopping and tidy the house. There's no evidence that Rick's been back, which ordinarily I wouldn't think about, but the circumstances of his departure are still rattling me. At one point I almost call him, but something stops me.

Wrapping up in one of his sherpa hoodies, I make a cup of tea and take it outside, sitting at the table at the far side of the garden. After an afternoon at the hospital, I'm glad of the solitude. I listen to the sound of the waves as the last of the light fades, until the drop in temperature seeps through my clothes, making me shiver.

I'm thinking of Jen, then Leah, then Casey – all of them victims and only one of them still alive – wondering if Abbie Rose has found a new link between them. After picking up my mug, I head inside, aware of an odd restlessness.

At this time of year, Cornwall is quiet, but not so quiet that when I drive to Truro to collect the paints I've ordered, I'm not astounded when I recognize Nick, talking on his mobile as he walks away from the same car park I've just pulled into. His photos had flattered him. In real life, he's smaller, his lips narrow and his chin weak.

He's not friendly either, when I catch him up.

'Excuse me . . .' He ignores me as I jog after him. 'You're Nick, aren't you?' The sound of his name gets his attention. 'Sorry.' Catching my breath, I stop beside him. 'I recognize you from your photo. I know Jen.'

He frowns, the line between his eyebrows deepening. 'And you are?'

'Charlotte,' I tell him. 'Harrison. I identified your wife from the photo the police put on Facebook. We were at school together.'

He hesitates for a moment, then nods. 'They mentioned you. But you clearly don't know Jen well if you think she's my wife.'

'Wife, partner, whatever . . .' I shrug. 'Why would I? I hadn't seen her in years and Jen can't remember anything. Have you been to see her?'

'Briefly. She was off her head on some cocktail of painkillers.' He sounds resentful rather than sympathetic. 'Same old Jen. Always the victim.'

I stare at him. 'She *was* attacked.'

'Yeah. So she says.'

Is he for real? 'You'd have to be a contortionist to self-inflict those injuries,' I say, sharply.

He sighs. 'Sorry. I've spent the last two hours being bombarded with questions by the police.'

'Abbie Rose,' I offer.

'Yes. Her – and this young sergeant. Jen and I parted somewhat acrimoniously. Excuse me if I'm less than sympathetic. I never expected to see her again, but then I get dragged into yet another of her dramas.'

The picture of Jen he paints doesn't sound at all like the confident, controlled girl I remember from school. 'What about your daughter?' I ask, trying to deflect him.

An odd look comes over his face. 'As I told that policewoman; as far as I know, there isn't one.'

I feel the blood draining from my face. 'You're kidding.'

But he's clearly not. 'Look, I've had a long drive and a difficult afternoon. I'd really like a sandwich and a coffee. Do you know anywhere?'

We walk down a couple of streets to a little cafe I know that does good coffee. He orders a double espresso and a cheese sandwich while I order a skinny latte. Sitting at the small table, he's less aggressive.

'So, let me get this straight.' He looks directly at me. 'You knew Jen at school, you obviously know nothing about me, yet you're going to see her and now you're sitting here with me.'

'When you put it like that . . .' I hesitate, slightly awkward at his directness. 'It probably sounds strange, but the thing is, people don't get attacked round here. Cornwall's safe. It makes what happened more shocking. I suppose, also, I've lost touch with everyone from my past. Seeing Jen again has stirred up all kinds of memories. But the main reason is that Abbie Rose thinks seeing me might help her,' I add, as the waitress brings our coffees over. But I'm still shocked at what he said about Angel. 'And apart from you, I'm the only person who's recognized her.' I change the subject. 'You said you don't have a daughter. After what Jen's said, I'm not sure what to think.'

'I couldn't believe it when the police told me. But thinking about it, I suppose she could have been pregnant when we split up, or got pregnant shortly after – I wouldn't have known. If it was mine, you'd think she would have told me, but like I said, we didn't part on good terms. Jen doesn't give a fuck about anyone other than herself. I've told the police that if – when – they find the child, I want a DNA test. But there's another possibility.' He stares at his mug, frowning. 'She had a late miscarriage a few years ago. It really upset her. She was six months pregnant – it was a girl. With her injuries and obvious amnesia, I wouldn't be surprised if she's confused.' He pauses. 'Anyway, I've told the police about it. It's up to them who they believe.'

His callousness leaves me flabbergasted. 'She's been through so much. If she has a daughter, and the police seem to believe she has, then this attack after the miscarriage, on top of what happened to Leah all those years ago—'

He interrupts me. 'Leah?'

'Leah Danning.' I stare at him. The entire country knew what had happened to her. It was in the national papers, on the TV news, for weeks. 'She disappeared in broad daylight from her garden – while Jen was looking after her. Leah was three.'

For the first time, he's lost for words. His mouth opens and closes again. 'I think I remember it. I'd never been to Cornwall so I didn't pay too much attention, I suppose. But . . .' He shakes his head slowly. 'Why the hell didn't she tell me about it?'

I shrug. It's a good question, and I'm amazed Abbie Rose didn't mention it. Maybe she's saving it for another day. But it's hardly a secret.

'She hinted that something had happened – in the past.' He's thoughtful. 'Jen had a habit of glossing over what she'd rather not talk about. If I pushed her, she got angry. She said that things happen to people – not always good – but that was life. If you couldn't change them, there was no point obsessing over them. It was better to move forward.'

I remember, dimly, how Casey used to hide her past. But life was really cruel to her, while Jen had led a charmed life –

or so it seemed to everyone else. After Leah disappeared, Casey hadn't been able to move forward. It seems unfair that, eventually, Jen had.

I change the subject. 'Are you staying long?'

'No longer than I have to,' he says firmly. 'I'm planning to leave after I've been to the hospital tomorrow. If necessary, I can always come back.'

'What went wrong between you?' Sitting back, I stare at him, curious.

'Too many differences. I thought we wanted the same things. It turns out we didn't. Nothing was ever enough for her – not me, not the farmhouse we moved to . . . not even being pregnant. She's one of those people who's always searching for something, only she hasn't figured out what it is.'

He makes no reference to the trauma of Jen's miscarriage – or the fact that she must have been unhappy. He's clearly one of those men who can see things only from his own point of view. Maybe Jen hadn't got over Leah, after all, but wasn't able to turn to him. I can understand that, now that I've met him. 'Relationships can be tough.' I raise my eyebrows. 'Speaking from experience. But it must have been good between you once. You were engaged.' I add, by way of explanation, 'It was announced in the local paper – the police found it. It's how they learned your full name.'

He stares at me, then shakes his head in disbelief. 'We were going to get married. We'd decided we'd move first. We looked at dozens of houses, but nothing was right. We knew exactly what we were looking for . . .' He glances at me. 'You don't want to hear all this.'

'No, go on.' I wait for him to continue.

'I'd found this rambling old place in the country. Our

forever home.' He says it sarcastically. 'We were living in London, so it was a big change for both of us. I was going to commute, and Jen was going to work from home. We were excited about it. Jen got pregnant – sooner than we'd planned, but it didn't matter. We decided to put the wedding off until after the baby was born. Then she had a miscarriage.' He falls silent.

'That must have been terrible – for both of you.'

He shrugs. 'Jen was devastated. She didn't really think about how it affected me – it hit her really hard. It didn't matter what I said, she cut herself off from me. I don't know . . . Maybe she had some kind of breakdown. Whatever, she was impossible. It was all downhill from there.' His voice is bitter. 'When someone shuts you out like that, it's the final nail in the coffin.'

So there were other nails – I wonder what they were. 'Was that why you split up?'

He laughs, cynically. 'To this day, I don't really know. She never tried to talk it through or explain. I came back from work one day to find she'd turned the house upside down and moved out. It was the last straw. I couldn't get through to her. In the end, I let it go.' He shakes his head. 'I didn't have much choice.'

What he's saying doesn't ring true. He doesn't seem like someone who'd give up that easily. 'When are you planning to see her?'

'The police suggested tomorrow morning. Suits me – I'll have plenty of time to drive home.' He looks as though he can't wait to get away from here. He frowns at me. 'I'd stay away from her, if I were you. She's bad news.'

I glance at the clock on the wall. 'Look, I'm sorry, but I have to go.' Pushing my chair back, I get up, leaving a few coins on the table for my coffee.

'You're off?' He looks surprised at my rapid departure.

'Places to go, people to see,' I say dismissively, pulling on my jacket. 'It's been nice meeting you, Nick Abraham. See you around.'

As I walk away, I'm trying to imagine him and Jen together – and failing. He's cold, with an anger under the surface that he doesn't hide very well. I hope Abbie Rose has seen that side of him. But I also wonder just how well he keeps his anger under control.

'It just seemed like the thing to do,' I say to Abbie Rose the following afternoon, when I go to the hospital. 'I came to pick up some art materials and happened to see him walking along the street.' I'm talking about Nick, wanting to find out what she thought of him. She already knows we've talked. 'We had a coffee. I felt a bit sorry for him.'

It's true. He wore the jaded bitterness of someone who didn't know how to roll with life's punches. What happened with Jen had clearly stayed with him – unless he'd always been like that. 'You can't tell, can you?' I add, looking at her.

'Tell what?' She looks confused.

'About Nick. Have you thought, Detective Inspector, that he could say absolutely anything about her and we wouldn't know if he was lying, because Jen can't remember a thing.' Personally, I don't trust him an inch.

Abbie Rose frowns. 'What exactly did he say?'

I shrug. 'Not much. Just that she lost the plot after she miscarried at six months. He made some remark . . .' I pause, trying to remember what he'd said. 'Yes. "Same old Jen.

Always the victim." Those were his words. And that he didn't know he was a father.'

'It's possible he isn't. And it's only one half of the story,' Abbie Rose says. 'That's the problem.'

'I thought after what she's been through, he'd have a shred of sympathy for her, but there was none. Not a shred. How is Jen?'

Abbie Rose stares at me, a frown on her face. 'After Nick left, she was quite upset. She might be pleased to see a friendly face. But it's probably best not to stay too long today. She's tired.'

'Sure.' I pause. 'Isn't it confusing for her? I mean, Nick calls her Jen, but we're all calling her Evie.'

Abbie Rose's eyes meet mine. 'Maybe you should ask her which she'd prefer.'

10

Abbie Rose is right. Maybe it's because of the visit from Nick, which I can imagine was anything but friendly, but Jen's pleased to see me.

'How are you feeling?'

She looks up at me with anxious eyes. 'Tired. Frightened. Unsure about everything. There's this voice inside me that tells me to trust no one.' Her voice wobbles.

'I bumped into Nick,' I tell her. 'I recognized him from the photo. We talked for a bit.' I don't tell her how angry he seemed, nor do I tell her I know about her miscarriage.

A haunted look comes over her. 'I don't know why he had to come here,' she whispers.

'I think the police hoped he might know where Angel is.'

'I never told him about her.' Jen looks petrified.

'So he said. But why?' I'm intrigued. Maybe my misgivings about Nick are warranted.

'He's bad, Charlotte. He would have taken my baby away.'

'But he couldn't. You're her mother.' I can't believe she'd

even think that. You can't just take a baby from its mother. I wait for her to go on, but her eyes are wide with fear.

'You don't know Nick. He'd tell the doctors I wasn't a fit mother. What if he'd found us? What if he's the one who's taken her?' Her voice is becoming more and more frantic.

'I don't understand . . . Why would he do that?'

'I had a breakdown. I had a miscarriage, Charlotte. I was six months pregnant.' Her voice wavers and her eyes glitter with tears. 'I gave birth to my dead baby . . .'

I swallow the lump in my throat. 'You've told the police this, haven't you?'

She nods.

'You mustn't worry. They'll check him out. You have to trust them. They know what they're doing.'

'They want to talk to his mother.' Her voice is unsteady.

'Is that a bad thing?'

'You don't know her. She'll say anything to make him look good. She hated me, Charlotte.'

'Look, let the police worry about Nick's mother. They won't be fooled for one minute.' I pause. 'Can I ask you something else?'

She nods.

'I know Nick calls you Jen, and I remember you as Jen, but would you rather be called Evie?'

She nods, but at the mention of Nick, fear flashes across her face again. 'That's why you changed your name, isn't it?' I say slowly. Having met him and seen his aggressiveness for myself, suddenly I get it. 'You didn't want Nick to find you. You were hiding from him.'

★

On my way out, Abbie Rose catches me up.

'Charlotte, I wanted to ask a favour. Evie seems to trust you and I need to have a difficult conversation with her – probably tomorrow. Would you be able to come back? Only if you're not busy, that is.'

'I could . . . What's it about?'

'I'd rather keep it for tomorrow, if you can come back then?'

I nod. 'What time?'

She thinks for a moment. 'I'll try to get over here by two.'

I turn to go, but then I hesitate. I wonder if Abbie Rose saw the same fear in Evie that I did, just now. 'You do know she's frightened of Nick? She said she was hiding from him.'

Abbie Rose hesitates. Then she says, 'I'm sorry, but I can't really discuss this right now. But rest assured, we've talked to him. I'll see you tomorrow?'

Irritation flares up in me; she wants my help, yet she's keeping me at arm's length. I don't answer, just turn away.

I drive the long way home, taking the road along the coast to Padstow, detouring towards the beaches, keeping half an eye out for a Rick-like figure. He could be anywhere. The roads are quiet. Out to sea, the sky is monochromatic. The grey clouds rolling in make for a dramatic landscape.

Driving this way takes twice as long, but I'm not in a hurry. It's a part of the coast I've always loved. In summer the wide beaches are filled with tourists, but at this time of year the sands stretch wild and empty.

By the time I get home, the last of the light is fading and the house is in darkness. I hadn't planned to get back so late, and as I go inside I'm aware for the first time of how empty it feels. It's a big house for one person. Reaching into my pocket,

I pull out my mobile to call Rick, pausing for a moment while I think about what I want to say. I dial his number but, whether by accident or design, the call goes to voicemail.

The following day, I think about not going to the hospital. But in the end, I go, for a number of reasons – because of Jen, and because it'll make Rick see me differently when he comes back. But also, I'm driven by my own curiosity. I don't know what the police are thinking, but surely, after what Nick said, Angel's existence is suddenly questionable. But then, even after a head injury, you couldn't invent a daughter – *could you?*

It's two thirty when I reach the critical care unit.

'So sorry,' I say to Abbie Rose. 'I got held up.'

'I need to talk to her,' Abbie Rose says, as we walk towards Jen's room. 'We've had some forensic reports back and I'm not sure how she's going to respond.'

She doesn't elaborate. There's another new police officer I haven't seen before outside Jen's door as Abbie Rose knocks, then pushes it open. 'Hello? Evie? Charlotte's with me.'

From over Abbie Rose's shoulder, I see Jen turn towards us.

'How are you today?' Abbie Rose asks.

But Jen doesn't answer. Abbie Rose walks over to the hospital-issue plastic chair in the corner, pulls it close to the bed and nods towards another beside the door. 'Why don't you get that, Charlotte?'

As if she senses something, Jen glances at me, then back to Abbie Rose, as I pull the chair over and sit next to her.

'Evie, there's another case we need to talk to you about. Another little girl, who disappeared. Fifteen years ago.'

'What does it have to do with Angel?' Jen's face is pale.

Suddenly I'm dreading what this newest revelation will do to her.

'We don't know if it's connected, but at the moment, we have to consider the possibility.'

'Why? What happened?' Jen's voice trembles.

'She went missing from her home on a Saturday morning. The police were called straight away. Dogs were brought in, an extensive search carried out. It was only a few miles from here, on the road to Chapel Amble.'

The Dannings' family home was a Cornish farmhouse about a mile from Chapel Amble, up a long track with a rambling garden that backed on to trees and farmland. I can just about picture it; slightly shabby and unloved. Casey rarely had anyone over, and by the time we were friends, all she wanted was to escape. I wonder if Jen remembers it.

'How long before they found her?' Jen's hands are clenched, her knuckles white.

It's the question she was always going to ask. I've no idea how Abbie Rose will handle this, because Jen's already fragile. The more she learns, the more her fear visibly escalates. Abbie Rose pauses, then takes a deep breath. 'They didn't.'

'No . . .' Jen's mouth falls open as she breathes the word. The reality is too much for her. 'They must have. You said they had dogs. She couldn't just disappear.'

'We never got to the bottom of what happened.'

'How old was she?' What little colour Jen has drains from her face.

'Nearly four.'

Jen's eyes are riveted to the policewoman's, her voice tiny as she says, 'Tell me.'

Abbie Rose speaks slowly, quietly, and Jen flinches at each

sentence. But even if she hadn't asked, Abbie Rose would have had to tell her, trying to trigger a hair's-breadth memory of the smallest detail that might be relevant. 'It was a Saturday. A teenage girl was babysitting while the child's mother was at work. It seems the little girl let herself out of the garden, which backed on to farmland. She could only have been out of sight for minutes. The babysitter saw the open gate and went running after her, but there was no sign of her. The most likely explanation is that someone abducted her, but it was never proved.'

I watch Jen closely, but her only thought seems to be what this means for Angel, and her shock appears genuine. Either that, or she's a supremely good actor.

'That doesn't mean it's happened to Angel.' She shakes her head, refusing to let herself go there.

'There's more I have to tell you, Evie,' Abbie Rose says quietly. 'There are press cuttings, extensive police reports and witness statements. They all say the same thing. The name of the teenager who was babysitting when it happened was Jen Russell.'

It's as though Jen's been given an electric shock. '*No!*'

Abbie Rose gives her a few seconds. 'I know this is upsetting, Evie, but—'

Jen's shaking her head. 'It wasn't me . . . I couldn't forget something like that.' But as I watch her, doubt flickers across her face. Her eyes swing round to me. 'Charlotte? You must have known about it. Tell her, *please* . . .'

Her eyes are pleading with me to back her up, to tell Abbie Rose that this is a terrible mistake. I shake my head slowly, glaring at Abbie Rose, hating that I've been put in this position.

'No . . .' Jen keeps saying. 'No. This is proof. Don't you see? Proof that I'm not Jen, and that I just look like her. You have to believe me . . .' She looks from one of us to the other.

'I have a photo of her.' After removing it from an envelope, Abbie Rose holds it out to Jen. 'This is the little girl you were babysitting. Her name was Leah Danning.'

Jen looks at the photo, then puts it on the bed. 'I don't remember any of what you're telling me . . .' She thumps her fist weakly on the sheets, a look of desperation on her face.

Abbie Rose looks strained. 'We have a Genevieve Russell on our records. There's a photo.' She pauses. 'There's the fact that Charlotte identified you. I've been to your school, Evie. All the evidence confirms that you and Genevieve Russell, who was babysitting that day, are the same person. But like everything else, right now you can't remember.'

Jen stares at her, speechless.

'I have something else I need to tell you,' Abbie Rose says quietly. 'PC Miller's had the initial forensic reports from your aunt's house, which is where you think you've been living. It's clear someone's been living there, and your aunt has been dead for some time. But . . .' As she pauses, I look at Jen, wondering how much more of this she can take. 'There are clothes there, that look as though they might fit someone your size. They've found fingerprints that match yours. But there are no children's clothes. No toys or books. Evie, there's no sign a child ever lived there.'

'There must be . . .' An anguished look crosses her face. 'Surely you saw Angel's room. It's at the top of the stairs. Her name's on the door. Everything's pink.' She stares at Abbie Rose.

The policewoman looks uncomfortable. 'As I said, right

now, it isn't as you remember it. Maybe she was staying some-where else. Maybe you both were. I don't know how else to explain it.'

'I – we – live there . . . It's our home.'

'There are more forensic reports to come. Maybe they'll show something.'

'And if not?' Jen whispers, terrified, Abbie Rose's silence telling her that nothing is certain, how little the police know. 'Who's doing this, Abbie?' she cries desperately. 'Who's trying to hurt me?'

'I don't know.' Abbie Rose looks troubled. 'Evie . . . If Angel lived there, Forensics will find something.' She speaks gently. 'But at the moment, there's no record of her anywhere – no birth certificate, no medical records. There's the fact that no one seems to know either of you. Even if we later rule it out, we have to at least consider the possibility that the trauma's brought back the memory of what happened fifteen years ago, when you were babysitting a little girl who matches the description you've given us of Angel.'

Jen gasps, as the reality hits her. 'You don't believe me.' She stares aghast at Abbie Rose. 'You don't think Angel exists.'

'No. That's not what I'm saying.' Abbie Rose is firm, but her eyes don't quite meet Jen's. 'I'm really not. But I think it would help you to talk to a counsellor. The person I'm think-ing of is an expert in memory loss. She may recommend a scan, too. I was talking to her this morning.' She breaks off, trying to be diplomatic. 'Evie, you've suffered a serious head injury. There's no disputing your memory has been affected.'

'But what I've remembered *is* reliable,' she cries. 'It's what's missing that's the problem.' Judging from her face, she knows that isn't true.

'There's too much that doesn't add up, Evie. Right now, we can't be certain about anything. We have to question everything.'

It's clear from the way Evie looks at Abbie Rose that she doesn't trust what the policewoman is saying. But I can see the DI's point – all there is to go on are two subjective accounts, the first being Evie's, fragmented and unreliable, the second being what Nick told the police. Is he any more reliable? There are no photos, no evidence whatsoever, that proves Angel exists.

'Abbie . . . please, please don't stop looking for her . . .'

'The search is still going on.' There's a note of uncertainty in Abbie Rose's voice – I wonder if Jen catches it.

Then Jen does something that catches us both off guard. As she picks up the photograph of Leah Danning, an uncontrollable wave of emotion seems to sweep over her. Doubled over, she clutches the photo to herself as a terrible noise comes from her. Somewhere, deep inside, she remembers.

'Oh God . . .' She's moaning, distraught, as Abbie Rose gets up to call a nurse.

Leaning forward, I take one of her hands in mine. 'Evie, it's OK.'

But she doesn't hear me. 'Oh God, oh God . . . It was all my fault . . .'

The nurse comes in and we're immediately ushered out into the corridor.

'Was that necessary?' I say angrily to Abbie Rose. 'You've told me enough times how fragile she is, and look what you did to her.'

Abbie Rose shakes her head wearily. 'Believe me, I got no pleasure out of that. But there's a child out there. We've no leads. The only person who knows anything about her is Evie herself. I had no choice.'

She looks exhausted as she has a word with one of the nurses, then walks away, leaving me standing there. Uncertain as to whether I should stay, I catch the nurse as she comes out of Jen's room.

'Is she OK?'

'I've given her something to calm her down, but it might be best if you come back tomorrow. Are you a friend?'

'Not really. I knew her a long time ago.' I look at the nurse. 'But I suppose, right now, I'm all she has.'

11

It's clear that Abbie Rose's brutal reminder of Leah's disappearance has taken its toll on Jen. When I see her the next day, she seems to have regressed, hardly saying a word, her eyes blank. But there's something I want to talk to her about.

'Evie? I've been thinking. I want to help you, but I need to ask you something.' I wait. Still silent, she turns towards me. I go on. 'Since you moved into your aunt's house, the fact that no one knows you, and that you didn't tell Nick, suggests you may have been in hiding. But what if someone saw you – and you didn't know. I'm not thinking of Nick . . .' Concerned she's having trouble keeping up, I pause for a moment. 'It might sound far-fetched, but maybe the same person who took Leah? Leah's disappearance was never solved. Maybe, locked away in your subconscious, you know something. Something that could lead the police to whoever took her.'

She stares helplessly at me. I don't want to frighten her, but I've been giving this a lot of thought. What if I'm right? What if Jen knows something?

When Abbie Rose turns up, she drip-feeds more details

about Leah Danning to Jen, about how she used to babysit on Saturday mornings, while Leah's father played golf and her mother worked in an estate agent's. Some of it seems to resonate with Jen, and I imagine her briefly reliving the heart-stopping moment she noticed Leah had gone; recalling the agony of the police search; the anguish that must have gone on for months after that terrible day. The end of life as she knew it – but far worse for Leah's family.

'I've brought the photos I told you about, of the hockey team. Your old school lent them to me.'

But Jen seems miles away.

Abbie goes on. 'Here.' She passes them to Jen. 'Your teachers spoke highly of you. You were sports captain, form captain, brilliant academically, well-liked by staff and students alike . . .'

It's clear from Jen's face she doesn't trust a word Abbie Rose is saying. I wonder what's coming next.

'After Leah disappeared, it all changed.' Abbie Rose frowns. 'It seems as though you had some kind of breakdown. I've looked back at your medical records.'

'You mean Jen's.' Her voice is flat.

'OK. After Leah wasn't found, you – Jen – spent a few months in rehab. It looks as though you tried to take an overdose. And after . . .' She trails off, which means whatever she's about to say isn't good. 'Understandably, I think what happened affected you really badly. You weren't yourself. A number of referrals are listed in your medical records—'

'I don't remember.' Jen's voice is a whisper. Then she folds her arms, moaning quietly, rocking herself. It's a step too far for her, and suddenly it's as though we've lost her. She's taken the only way out she can, retreating into herself as the fight goes out of her and she slumps forward. Giving in.

I walk with Abbie Rose out to the car park. 'You have thought, haven't you? That whoever attacked Jen might know she's in the hospital, with a police guard. But if her memory is coming back, it's just a matter of time. When she goes home, what if they're just waiting for the right moment to finish what they started?'

'Has she said anything to you?' Abbie Rose sounds irritated.

'Look, she hasn't. I'm just trying to help, that's all. And it seems to get further than bullying her.' I didn't intend for that to burst out the way it did, but it's true. It does seem as if Abbie Rose is bullying her.

'Charlotte –' there's a steely tone in her voice – 'I know you're trying to help, but we know what we're doing.'

'If you say so, Detective Inspector.' I shrug. 'Like I said, I'm only trying to help.'

She pauses, straight-faced as ever. 'I appreciate what you're doing.'

I shrug again. 'Whatever.'

By the time I get home, I'm regretting getting so involved in the police investigation, but at the same time, I find myself oddly gripped by Jen's background. After a sunny afternoon, the air is cool and damp and the wind has picked up. Drawn by the promise of a sunset, I pull on a coat and running shoes and head for the coast path.

As I walk towards the setting sun, Jen's attack, the hospital, Abbie Rose, they all suddenly seem a world away. Breathing in the salty air, I'm thinking of Rick again, wondering when he's coming back. My call will have shown up on his phone, but he hasn't returned it.

Ducking under a fence, I leave the coast path behind me, crossing the rough grass towards the cliff edge. Standing there, I feel a sense of exhilaration as I listen to the waves below crashing against the rocks. Danger too; from the wind buffeting against me, from the knowledge that there are only inches between me and the long drop onto the rocks below. As the sun slowly disappears below the horizon, I step forward, poised on the edge, raising my arms towards an orange-streaked sky, and in the invisibility of darkness, I scream.

I hear it echo as I spin all the way round, not caring if anyone hears me. A madness grips me, a sense of liberation from the frustrations of the day, from how I've been drawn into the police investigation. I scream again, revelling in the feeling, as the last of the sunset fades and night falls.

Casey, 1998

I remember dusk and gasping for air. Swimming against the tide of disapproval and criticism, my parents' expectations always out of reach. Waves of anger, crashing over me, dragging me down.

My mother's words. 'At last we'll be a proper family.' As she speaks, dusk darkening around me by another degree. She was pregnant, preparing the way for the child who was to come, because I wasn't enough. I never had been. I saw it in the mirror, epitomized by white skin and dull eyes that stared unblinkingly back at me, hiding the turmoil that lay beneath. I was the invisible child, even before my sister was born. Born to be silent.

In an environment that's joyless, when the light is perpetually fading, all you can see are shadows, but did you know shadows have their own dance? At night, as I lay in bed, I'd watch them, obscenely summoning other shadows in a grotesque *danse macabre*. Closing my eyes, I'd give them faces and shrill, terrifying voices, which they'd silence as they loomed close to me. Then they'd smile, holding out shadow-hands towards me. It was a world that beckoned me to join it. Without realizing, I'd crossed a line.

Maybe my mother knew. She didn't guard me with her life, the way mothers are supposed to. No one guarded me. And when the baby was coming, she sent me away.

'You're going to stay with Auntie Maureen.'

I remember telling her I didn't want to go. How even my agitated cries failed to move her, just angered her. Even when I screamed, she just yelled over me. Not even thinking to ask why I was so upset.

I felt another shade of darkness settle. The shadows danced for hours that night, keeping me from sleeping. When eventually I closed my eyes, they were there too, dancing on the inside of my eyelids. Only after sunrise could I sleep, wakening to my father's loud voice, his hand shaking me. There was no rest, no respite. There never was.

The darkness followed me to school, lingering all day, until the end, when I was kept back by my form teacher, standing in front of her with burning cheeks, as she went through it all over again. How I'd upset my mother; how I was old enough to know better; how I should grow up; how no one liked a jealous child. How when it arrived, I'd find out I really loved having a baby brother or sister.

I just stared at the floor in silence, listening to the horseshit spouting from her thin lips, waiting for her to finish. All of them knew I was upset. My mother, my father, my teacher. They had called me selfish, jealous and a dozen other things, but not one of them had asked me to explain.

The baby got the best room, previously reserved for the use of guests only, which I kind of knew would happen. Not for me a room that smelled of paint and was full of sunshine – the primrose yellow on the walls, the light pouring in through the sash window. My room was on the other side of the house, which lay in shadow.

Nothing in it was new. When I'd seen the spare room being painted, I'd asked if mine could be painted too.

There was nothing wrong with my bedroom, my mother had told me. I wasn't special enough for a new one. The baby-pink was perfectly fine as it was.

She didn't understand how that felt. The more I thought about it, the more it got to me, adding to everything else that wasn't right; the baby, who wasn't even here yet; my mother saying how lucky it was that I could stay with Auntie Maureen. How could my own mother not know how I felt? It was like she was talking about a stranger, not me.

I started picking at the wallpaper in my room, peeling tiny, narrow strips where the edge had already lifted, then making marks where the wall was exposed underneath. And if I didn't pull the curtains really carefully, the little plastic hooks that held them to the rail would snap off so the curtain drooped, but that wasn't my fault. They'd been there so long, they'd worn out. Anyone could see that.

But my parents didn't see anything the way I saw it. There was a framed Disney picture on my wall, of looming Minnie and Mickey Mouse faces. It was childish; the kind of picture I'd liked once, when I was about three. One day it fell and the glass shattered. My mother was furious.

'Pictures don't fall off walls on their own,' she snapped. 'And don't think I haven't noticed the wallpaper.'

'But it wasn't my fault,' I argued.

My mother didn't believe me. 'The wallpaper didn't come off on its own, Casey.' Completely forgetting we were talking about the picture, not the wallpaper. I already knew she'd stopped listening to me. All she wanted to talk about was the baby.

My parents were always cross. They didn't understand how that made me feel. How angry I got, how upset I was. How unworthy I felt. They didn't know either that when my fingers picked away at the wallpaper, if I did it right, sometimes it came off in long sections and, for a while, my anger would go away.

'Don't think I'm redecorating in here, too.' My mother's voice, like glass that I wanted to hurl a brick at and smash. She didn't care how I felt. 'Don't you think I have enough to do, with the baby coming?'

The baby again. It was always the baby. But there was still the possibility that the baby wouldn't come, I started to hope. That maybe it would die inside my mother's body and she'd die too. I didn't want horrible thoughts about the baby, but I couldn't stop them just appearing in my head. And the worst thing still happened, because just before the baby came, I had to pack some things to take to Auntie Maureen's.

No one listened to my cries of protest. No one cared enough to listen. My parents acted like I wasn't there. That's when you know you're destined not to become someone, because no one sees you.

Even when I clung to her, begging her not to send me away, my mother didn't ask why I was so upset. She just told me I was being naughty, when I was actually frightened. 'Please, please, I don't want to go there. Don't make me go there. Please . . .'

In the end, I ran upstairs, slamming my bedroom door, sobbing as I hurled myself onto my bed, the tears pouring out of me until there weren't any left.

I hated, hated this baby, so much. It was the baby's fault I had to go to Auntie Maureen's. Auntie Maureen's son Anthony would be there, who was older and made me do horrible things I didn't want to do. I hated Anthony as much as I hated the baby. If I didn't do what he told me to do, he said he'd get me into trouble. There was no point telling anyone, he told me. No one would believe a stupid little girl.

After the last time I'd stayed there, I'd had nightmares where I was walking up a staircase that went on and on, further and further from my parents. When I got to the top and looked down, the stairs had gone and there was no escape. I was trapped there. Then I could hear someone coming. Someone bad. Someone I knew. I started screaming.

'I can't see . . . I'm frightened . . . I want him to stop . . . I want him to go away . . .'

It was just a dream, my parents had told me when I woke up and found the light on and both of them standing there. Only a dream. I should try to forget about it.

'Close your eyes and go to sleep.' My parents' words, wishing me back into the nightmare.

I tried to tell them that part of it was real, too, but all I could think of was what Anthony had told me. No one would believe a stupid girl.

And he was waiting, when my father drove me to Auntie Maureen's house. My own father delivering me to the monster, whose ugly, leering face watched out of an upstairs window. I couldn't say good-bye to my father, just watched him drive away with a scream inside me, which instead of bursting out of me, stuck in my throat, choking me.

When people betray you, it turns you into someone else. Someone with locked-away feelings, who can't be hurt. It was my parents' fault and Anthony's fault. But it was the baby's fault, too. If it wasn't coming, I wouldn't be here.

12

Jack

While he'd been away, the dark, faded greens of late summer had given way to autumn's red and gold. Nature's attempt to lull everyone into a false sense of security before the sheeting drizzle and endless grey of the Cornish winter swept in.

In Spain, he'd left behind the heat of the sun and a parched landscape scented with pine and rosemary. Scents that had soothed his soul and allowed the faintest hint of hope to take root, hope that he'd been determined to bring home with him. Hope that had been lacking in his life. Because life had to go on. Now he was back, however, he could already feel it slipping.

Not that he didn't like living here. It was just that life had served up several types of shit, the kind that dragged you down and held you there. Hence the fortnight in Spain, to break away, change the record. Ordinarily, Jack would spend his time off walking the coast path with Beamer, his black Labrador. He was never short of things to do when he wasn't working. There was the house, which always needed some-thing or other done to it. The pile of logs that needed sawing and splitting, then storing in the porch until he needed another load for the wood-burning stove that he kept burning all winter. The garden – an acre and a half, mostly woodland, which at this time of year dumped leaves like the clouds dumped rain in winter.

It was a long time since Jack had been happy. There were too many ghosts in his life. His son, Josh, who had died after a car accident. Since then, his wife's affair and their more recent separation. No doubt divorce, given time – she'd given no indication she'd had second thoughts. It was something else to look forward to. Jack wasn't a cynic, but sometimes it felt as though life pushed you to see what you were capable of, only all of this felt a step too far.

Closing the back door, he walked towards his battered Land Rover, breathing in the damp air and feeling a pang of loss for Spain, allowing it to linger for a self-indulgent moment as he let the dog jump in, before he slid inside and started the engine. He needed to get his shit together and focus. He didn't want to be the sad git, always surrounded by some kind of tragedy. While he was away, his wife had picked up the rest of her things. It was the start of a new chapter, he kept telling himself. Better to be alone than with someone who didn't want him. Time to move on.

Autumn wasn't so bad. In the fading light, the leaves were still vibrant and even the stubble fields had stayed a pale gold. *Only until the rain starts*, he mused. Then it took mere minutes before everything got muddied to grey.

He'd left it rather late for a walk, but after two weeks away, he wanted a blast of sea air on his skin and the sound of waves crashing in his ears. In Spain, the sea had been a millpond, except for one night when there'd been a storm. As he'd listened to the waves pounding on the shore, he'd felt a flicker of nostalgia for Cornwall. And it didn't matter that it was getting dark – he could find his way round here with his eyes closed. He'd walked this coast most of his life, knew every twist of the path, where it narrowed and where the edge crumbled towards the sea.

Beamer was pleased to be back here, too. Jack watched him, a shadow lost amongst other, darker shadows, darting ahead of him. They'd made it just in time, minutes before sunset. Around the sinking sun, orange streaked the sky. He stood for a moment, taking it in. His last night's solace before he went back to work. *Probably a good thing*, he mused. Too much time alone made him introspective.

In an ideal world, Jack would be happy not to work, but being in his mid-forties he was too young to retire. Besides, the part-time hours he'd been offered since Josh's death were a compromise that suited him. And by the looks of it, he was going to be busy for the foreseeable future. After he got back from the airport, he'd briefly checked his emails. While he was away, a woman had been attacked and her child had gone missing. He'd been shocked. It was the kind of crime that happened rarely round here. By and large, Cornwall was peaceful. Most of the trouble happened in the height of the tourist season. Petty crime and drunken brawls – so many incidents could be related back to alcohol, though most towns had clamped down and it was less of a problem than it used to be. Things still happened, though.

The email he'd read had set all kinds of alarm bells ringing in his brain, before he'd turned off his laptop and silenced them. Work could wait until tomorrow.

Here, on the coast path, listening to the wind picking up

and the waves, he managed to salvage the flicker of hope he'd found in Spain. You had to believe things could get better. Otherwise, there was no point in going on.

His thoughts were interrupted by a scream. An animal? His heart quickened. It was human, he was sure. Whistling to Beamer, he turned in the direction it had come from, breaking into a jog, surefooted even in the fading light.

Hearing another scream, he started to run. What was going on? It was a raw, piercing sound that came from close by. Then ahead of him through the dusk, silhouetted against the glimmer of the sea, he made out the figure of a woman. At least, he thought it was a woman. There was something about the shape of her, or maybe her hair blowing in the wind – the way she was standing, her arms thrust towards the sky. She was wearing a silver coat, the colour caught briefly in the light from the dying sun.

Was she the one who had screamed? Or maybe she was one of the sun-worshipping hippy types they got round here from time to time and the scream had come from someone else. She must have heard it, though – and she was dangerously close to the cliff edge. He was about to call out to her, but before he could speak, she'd turned and run off into the darkness.

13

'Sir! How was your break?'

Jack's heart always sank slightly when he saw Sara. She was an adequate police constable, but that was the point. Adequate was functional, it wasn't inspiring. And she was nice enough, though irritating as hell, he tried to stop himself thinking. *Be charitable*, he told himself. Who knew what was going on in Sara's life? As he knew only too well, you never knew what lay behind the mask.

'Good. Thanks.' He was about to ask if he'd missed anything, but for once Sara was ahead of him.

'DI Rose wants to see you. She's in her office.' Sara pulled a face, as though she and Jack were in cahoots, and Abbie was the bad guy, which she wasn't. It was inappropriate – and typical of her – but Sara and Abbie were chalk and cheese. Jack pretended not to notice.

'Right,' he said, surprised. Abbie was here? He hadn't seen her much since she'd become a DI. She must be on the assault and possible abduction case. He muttered a thank you to Sara and wandered through the door into the familiar corridor.

There were half a dozen small rooms leading off it, but these days only three of them were used as offices. Devon and Cornwall was a huge area to cover, but even so, policing levels had shrunk to their lowest ever.

Standing outside one of the offices, he could hear Abbie talking on the phone. After knocking quietly, he pushed the door open and watched her face light up.

She held the phone away from her face. 'Give me a minute. I'll be right with you.'

Leaving her to it, Jack carried on to his office. Unusually, he'd had the same one for years. This wasn't due to the fact that he was a detective chief inspector; he'd kept it even after a major restructuring was carried out and a number of police stations closed and officers were forced to transfer. The restructure had happened as his personal life imploded, meaning he hadn't wanted to move away. In short, Josh's death had granted him privileges he detested. No one wanted to be treated differently because their son had died. In the same way, he hadn't wanted everyone's sympathy. It was nothing to do with them. Everyone died at some point. Yes, it was tragic when it happened to a teenager, more so when it could so easily have been avoided. Jack swallowed. He couldn't let himself go there. The bottom line was, you got on with it. You didn't have a choice.

Sitting at his desk, it was as though he hadn't been away. The memory of Spain had already merged into his past. He switched on his laptop just as there was a knock at his door.

'Jack?' It was Abbie. 'How are you?'

She was alluding to more than his holiday, Jack knew that. In spite of his efforts to keep his private life to himself, word had got around, but he didn't want to talk about the end of his marriage. 'Hey. Good, thank you. I wasn't expecting to see you here, but I've heard there's more than the usual going on?' By the usual, he meant the occasional break-ins or traffic accidents that occurred, neither of which merited the presence of a detective inspector.

Abbie nodded, coming over to his desk and taking a seat as she placed a file in front of him. 'Afraid so. A brutal attack that almost killed a woman, and a missing three-year-old child – her daughter.'

There was to be no gently easing back into work, then. Jack took the file. 'Is she local?'

'We think so.' Abbie hesitated. 'She has amnesia. What she does remember isn't reliable. We've found her ex-partner, who was somewhat unsympathetic. He said they weren't in touch and he didn't even know about the daughter. So far, only one woman has recognized her. But we've managed to locate where we think she was living and we've just found her mother. She's flying over from Italy. Apparently she lives there . . .'

Jack was frowning. 'Forensics?'

Abbie shook her head. 'That's the thing. They haven't been able to find any trace of a child in that house. It starts getting more complicated, because—'

She was interrupted by a knock on the door.

'Sorry to intrude . . .' It was Sara. 'We've just had a call. Someone's found a body in the middle of a field.'

Jack got up. 'I'll go. Are you coming?' He glanced at Abbie.

'I'm due at the hospital.' Looking at her watch, she got up. 'I should have left. I'll catch up with you later.'

Maybe the absence of the quiet Monday morning Jack had hoped for wasn't such a bad thing. It meant his head was filled with work instead of his train wreck of a marriage. Sara's directions took him along the main road to Wadebridge, then along narrower roads towards the coast.

He passed the single track he'd driven down to walk Beamer last night, then carried on through the handful of cottages that was Port Quin, then up the twisting narrow lane until he came to another police car pulled up in a layby.

Parking on the bank, he watched the officer in the other car get out. It was DS Underwood. He was thorough and reliable. Jack got out of his car, relieved. But there were so few of them these days, you almost always knew who you'd be working with.

'Do you know where we're going?' He addressed Underwood as they climbed the stile into a field.

'I think so. The guy who called in was working on one of the farms. David West – he's a contractor. He was cutting maize with another farm worker when they saw this woman running across the field towards them. She'd come up from the coast path. I think we should head over there.' He pointed towards a field in the direction of the coast.

They walked in silence across the field. It sloped steeply. *Winter grazing for sheep*, Jack was thinking. The surroundings were breathtakingly beautiful; the land edged with stone walls, the sun on the faded straw of the stubble fields, soon to be turned to brown earth when ploughing started. Ahead of them, endless miles of cerulean sky and sea.

As they crossed into the next field, the land flattened out.

'I reckon that's them.'

Underwood pointed to one of the stubble fields, where a couple of giant forage harvesters had parked near each other.

'It must be. There's nothing else round here.' Jack picked up the pace, feeling the wind on his face. As they got nearer, he could make out three people. Two men and a young woman, who watched them as they drew closer.

'DCI Jack Bentley.' Holding out his police badge, Jack glanced at his colleague. 'This is DS Underwood. I understand you've found a body?'

'She found it.' One of the men nodded towards the woman.

'Can you show me where?'

She hesitated, then nodded. 'It's over there.' She pointed towards the remaining area of uncut maize, then started walking. Jack followed, leaving Underwood with the farm workers.

'What were you doing here?'

'I was walking. On the coast path – I live a couple of miles away. I quite often walk here. Only it was windier than I expected so I decided to head inland.'

'The footpath is . . . ?' Jack was querying what had brought her so far off the beaten track.

'Oh God, the footpath's way over there.' She flapped her arm somewhere indiscriminate. 'But I knew something wasn't right. It's why I came over.'

'What do you mean?'

She stopped in her tracks, spinning round to stare at him. 'It's the birds. Look at them.' Jack followed her gaze to above the uncut maize, where the birds were circling, every now and then dropping down and disappearing into it. 'It's as if they're following the plough – only there is no plough.' She shook her head and carried on walking. 'At first, I thought there must be a dead animal. A large one, like a deer, that had been shot but not killed, and had run into the maize before dying there.'

She sounded matter-of-fact, but then if you lived in the countryside, you were constantly reminded of the impermanence of life. The pattern of the seasons, the preying of foxes, the slaughter of farm animals.

He watched a large crow swoop down, dropping below the tops of the tall spikes of maize, before it reappeared. It briefly flew towards them before veering away, but not before Jack spotted something hanging from its beak. Straining his eyes, he tried to make out what it was as it flashed momentarily in the sun.

'Did you see that?' The woman stopped for a moment. 'It looked like a pendant.' She carried on walking.

Jack had thought so too. As he watched, the crow dropped it. His eyes fixed on where he thought the object had fallen and he ran across the field.

'Can you see it?' The voice came from behind him – the woman had followed him. 'It must be here somewhere.'

It would be a miracle if they found it – it was the proverbial needle in the haystack – but then, a few feet away, a metallic glint caught his eye. Reaching down, he held it dangling from his fingers. It was small, heart-shaped, made of silver.

'Good work.' The woman looked impressed.

As they walked back towards where the body was, he wondered where the other attack had taken place. He'd have to read up on it as soon as he got back to the station. A maize field was a perfect environment in which to hide a body; seasonally it was almost impenetrable, especially now, while the crop was taller than he was and just about to be consumed by monstrous forage harvesters, which devoured everything in their path. If the woman hadn't seen the birds, the harvesters would have gone through, leaving nothing. The thought stopped him in his tracks.

'You might have been hurt.' Once lost in the maize, the

woman would have been invisible to the drivers of the harvesters.

She shrugged. 'Well, I wasn't. I think it's this way – it's
where most of the birds are.'

Glancing up, he saw that she was right. The maize was
dense around them as they found their way through, pushing
aside the woody stems, every now and then glancing up at the
birds circling above. Up close, Jack was astonished at how
many there were.

In front of him, the woman stopped suddenly. 'It's just
through there. I'll wait here.'

Apprehension had replaced her previous air of self-
assurance. *Understandably*, Jack thought, as she stood back to
let him pass her. He nodded. 'Of course.'

Just a few metres on, the maize started to thin out. Then,
as he glanced sideways through the leaves, he saw a hand.

14

'At first, I thought it was the child who was missing. But she's too old.' The woman's voice came from behind him. He didn't reply, just took in the full horror of the scene that lay before him as the stench of rotting flesh reached his nostrils, making him gag. A small section of the maize had been cleared – an area that measured no more than about ten feet square. In the middle of it was a girl's naked body – or what remained of it after the birds had found her. She'd been brutally murdered, her throat obviously cut, the remains of her blood dried into a darkened crust on her skin. The hand he'd seen had been severed, left on the ground a few feet from the rest of her.

She wasn't much more than a child. Or maybe a teenager – she was tall, with thick red hair made darker by congealing blood. He felt a sense of relief that he didn't recognize her.

It had been a long time since he'd been on a scene like this one, of carnage, decay, the rotting flesh a breeding ground for thousands of flies.

They'd need Forensics in here. And a painstaking search through what was left of the maize – though thanks to the harvesters, any evidence had most likely been ground up and lost for good. Quickly, he took a few photographs. Then he went back to find the woman. Her face was pale as she watched him come into view.

'Do you know her?'

Jack shook his head. 'Let's go back to the others.'

'I've got these two's details,' Underwood told Jack. 'I'll just make a note of yours.' He glanced at the woman.

'I'm Charlotte Harrison.' She was very self-possessed, Jack couldn't help noticing. Especially considering she'd just stumbled across a dead body.

Then Underwood said, 'Charlotte Harrison? The same Charlotte Harrison who recognized the photo of Evie Sherman?'

The woman looked irritated. 'That's me.'

'I took the call.' He looked at her oddly.

'Small world,' she said blithely. 'But I suppose there aren't that many of you round this neck of the woods, are there? Do you think this has anything to do with Jen – Evie? I'm not sure which name you're giving her?'

Underwood turned to Jack. 'Evie Sherman was the woman who was attacked and found in another maize field – it happened while you were away.'

The case he'd seen mentioned in emails and that Abbie had started telling him about. As Underwood took her details, Jack looked around. 'Who does this land belong to?' He was addressing one of the drivers.

'Jim Bellows. He owns about as far as you can see.' He pointed in a westerly direction. 'Lives at Lower Farm . . .'

Jack paused. 'How long had you been working in this field?'

'We started yesterday – around lunchtime.'

'And did you see anything strange?'

They both shook their heads. 'Don't think we saw anyone, did we? Not until today, when she ran across the field,' one of them said. They looked at Charlotte.

Jack turned back to the woman. 'Did you notice anything out of the ordinary, before you found the body?'

'No.' Charlotte shook her head. 'I was walking. It was only the birds that made me think something wasn't right . . .'

Jack frowned. 'That's quite a conclusion to draw from a flock of birds circling.'

She stared at him. 'After what's been going on? Do you really think so?'

She seemed touchy. 'It's just as well you did, in any case.' Jack didn't want to antagonize anyone.

The girl thawed slightly. 'It's just that after Jen – Evie – was found in a maize field, and with her daughter missing, my imagination went into overdrive. Anyway, like you said, it's just as well.'

He glanced at Underwood. 'Have we got everything?' Underwood nodded. 'That's all for now,' he told them. 'We need you to leave your farm machinery where it is I'm afraid. We'll be in touch when we're ready for you to move it.'

The men looked less than pleased. Charlotte stood there. 'That's it?' she asked.

'For now.' He nodded. 'Someone will contact you soon, to take a more detailed statement from you. Unless there's anything else you can tell us?'

She shrugged. 'Not really.' She turned and started walking away, leaving Jack staring after her. He was thinking of the girl on the cliff edge last night. The one in the silver coat. Could it have been Charlotte Harrison? There was something in the way she carried herself, the way she'd turned and walked off just now. But he wasn't sure.

Leaving Underwood to secure the crime scene and wait for more officers to show up, Jack started walking back across the field, unable to shake the image of the dead girl. She must have been there for some time, judging from the state of her flesh and what the birds had done to her – and the flies. It was obvious from the way the maize had been cleared that the killing had been planned. Someone had gone to a lot of trouble to ensure the body was never found.

Had anyone missed her? The first thing he'd do when he got back was check their database of missing persons. That woman – Charlotte – was a strange one. Intelligent, he guessed. And incredibly self-confident. It took some chutzpah to go into the maize, alone, to check out what the birds had been circling above, but then it was unheard of for such a violent crime to happen in these parts, let alone two of them. It seemed like too much of a coincidence.

He walked faster, wanting to get back to the office and read the file Abbie had given him earlier. All kinds of bells were ringing in his head. But it was more than that, he realized. It was a long time since he'd had a case to get his teeth into, one that would challenge even his years of experience. He was fired up in a way he hadn't been in a long time.

Sara was still behind the desk when he got back. 'Do you know who the girl was?'

Jack shook his head. 'Would you know if anyone's been reported missing?'

'I don't think so . . .' Sara looked blank. 'I'll check our records.'

But Jack wasn't hanging around. Who knew how long it would take Sara to get round to it. It would be quicker if he did it himself. Judging from the state of the body, the girl had been missing for more than a few days. There was no doubt about that. But not all missing persons got reported. It was incredible what some people turned a blind eye to, just because it was easier.

As he sat down, he glanced at Abbie's file. It would have to wait for now. He switched on his laptop, logged in to the station website and looked for the missing persons list.

It was a long list. Some of the names had been there for years, which he always found desperately sad. There was always a story – invariably a tragic one – behind someone who decided to abandon their life and their family, to just disappear. It was bad enough losing someone when you knew what had happened. He didn't know how you coped with that – not knowing where a loved one was.

The majority of the list was taken up by adults or older teenagers – many of them mature enough to make their own decisions. The police had to respect that not everyone wanted to be found. But missing children were rare. They made the national press and television news programmes. A missing child was every parent's worst nightmare – or so you'd think.

An entry caught his eye. A twelve-year-old girl with red hair. He frowned. The girl whose body they'd found looked too tall to be just twelve. He read on. Her name was Tamsyn Morgan. She'd been reported missing a week ago, not by her parents but by one of her teachers.

He read the notes. Apparently, Tamsyn had disappeared

before, several times – for as long as two or three weeks at a time, usually in the summer, when she'd lived rough or camped out in a farmer's barn, according to local sources. She was quite well known for such disappearances. The mother didn't care enough to stop her – she just let her run wild. But since the term started, Tamsyn hadn't been to school. That wasn't her usual pattern, hence the teacher had reported it to the police after a couple of weeks.

He studied the photo, taking in her bright eyes and the pale skin that often went with red hair – it was the hair that was her most distinguishing feature, and as far as he could tell, it was similar in colour to that of the dead girl he'd seen earlier. She was described as tall, independent and spirited. Getting out his phone, he found the photos he'd taken in the field, comparing them with the one on file, then sat back. There wasn't any question it was her.

He took Sara with him to break the news to Tamsyn's parents, ignoring her idle chatter as they drove towards Wadebridge, turning off down one of the typically twisty narrow lanes with steep, stone-walled sides, then down a bumpy farm track towards a pair of shabby cottages.

All the time, thoughts of Josh filled his head. He knew what he was about to tell Tamsyn's parents was the beginning of the most brutal transition anyone could go through. Life as you knew it ended in that moment you were told your child was dead.

Parking in a layby outside the cottages, they got out of the car.

'We want number two,' he told Sara, who was already walking towards a wooden gate hanging off its hinges.

'This says number one,' she called back to him.

Jack turned to the other cottage. There was a dim light in one of the windows and a curl of smoke coming from the chimney. Shutting off how this was making him feel, he started walking towards the front door.

The woman who opened it had a lined face and small, hard eyes.

'DCI Jack Bentley, Truro police. This is Constable Sara Evans. May we come in?'

'What's she done this time?' the woman said abruptly, stepping aside to let them in.

'Is anyone else home?' Sara asked, walking through into the small front room. It looked unused. It was cold in there; the curl of smoke Jack had seen clearly came from another room.

'Just me. What's going on?'

'It's about Tamsyn, Mrs Morgan.' Jack paused. 'I'm afraid there's been an accident.'

'For God's sake, that child's always in trouble.'

'When did you last see her?' Jack hadn't planned to ask the question, but this woman was anything but a caring mother.

'Tamsyn?' The woman laughed. 'I don't know. Could be a fortnight ago. Could be longer. Why?'

Even Sara looked shocked. 'And you don't know where she's been in that time?'

'Haven't a clue, love. I gave up years ago. Tamsyn does what she wants.'

'Isn't she a little young to run wild like that? How old is she – twelve?'

'You police are all the same. You don't know what it's like having a child like that,' the woman sneered. 'A law unto her bloody self, that one. More trouble than she's worth.'

'Well, you won't have to worry any longer, Mrs Morgan.' Jack couldn't help himself. 'We found your daughter earlier today.' He paused. It was that moment. 'I'm afraid she's dead.'

'That was a bit brutal,' Sara said, as they drove away.

'Yeah. I know.' But Jack was angry. No one had to have a child these days. He hated how reluctant parents like Tamsyn's mother could be so uncaring about their children, when there were so many couples who were desperate for a child to lavish love on. But there were too many people like Tamsyn's mother. Life didn't make sense. If it did, Josh would still be alive.

15

By the time Jack was back at the station, it was late afternoon. Abbie's file lay on his desk, where she'd left it earlier. Rather than stay another hour, he decided to take it with him. He'd read it when he got home, or maybe save it for tomorrow – he'd planned to work from home rather than face another day at the station. Beamer would be grateful. Since Louise had left, the dog had become his closest companion.

Sure enough, when he opened the back door, he was greeted by Beamer's grin and wagging tail. Jack didn't like leaving him so long, but he had one or two friends who would call by and let him out for a while. Their help made the situation manageable – and when he could, Jack worked from home.

'Here, boy.' He whistled to Beamer. 'Walk?'

The Labrador's eyes lit up with hope, then he trotted off and came back carrying his lead, a trick Josh had taught him. Jack stood there a moment. There were still times, like now, when the fact that his son was dead seemed unreal. It felt like yesterday that he'd still been here. Part of him still expected to hear Josh's voice echoing through the house, or his feet thundering down the stairs. Would that ever change? He missed his son more than his wife, that much he was certain of. But he and Louise had become a habit. He missed the sound of her in the house, the trivial words they exchanged. But that was what their marriage had been reduced to – familiarity and history. It wasn't about love.

He sighed. He was still working through it all in his head. Shutting the door behind him, he set off across the garden with Beamer, heading towards the woods, where the air would smell of damp earth and fallen leaves and where, in the solitude, he knew his sadness would lift slightly. He half smiled to himself. He needed to remember that, in so many ways, he was lucky.

As usual, even after an hour of walking he hadn't seen a soul. Occasionally he'd hear someone through the trees – voices, or maybe footsteps on dry twigs. He called his dog, waiting until Beamer came crashing through the bushes towards him, then turned and headed for home.

He had to think of the pluses of living alone. The fact that he could play classical music, which used to drive Louise insane. He could eat what he wanted to, as well. Tonight, after being in Spain, the fridge was empty. He'd completely forgotten to go shopping. Oh well. In the larder were a few tins of beans and the bottle of duty-free whisky he'd bought on the way home. As he grimaced at the thought of them together, he heard a car pull up outside.

Seconds later there was a knock at the door. Bemused, he went to answer it. He was less bemused when he saw who was there.

'I brought you supper.' It was Lucy, from the village shop,

holding out a casserole. 'Seeing as you'd been away and that.'
Pretty, with smiling eyes and full lips, she spoke with a thick
Cornish accent.

'Thanks.' Jack was taken aback, more so as he realized how
much make-up she was wearing and as more than a hint of
perfume reached him. Oh God, he liked Lucy, but with her
blonde hair and pink lipstick, she wasn't his type. He hoped
he hadn't said anything to encourage her.

'It's chicken.' She stood there expectantly.

Was she waiting for him to invite her in? 'It's really kind
of you,' he said at last. 'Especially as I have to work tonight,
and . . . OK, I have no food in the house, as you probably
guessed!'

Giggling, Lucy winked at him. There was no subtlety about
her.

'Honestly,' he said, more firmly. 'I'd invite you in, but I
really do have to work tonight. But thank you.'

At last she got the message. 'Oh, go on, you. I'll leave you
to it. But don't forget, all work and no play makes Jack a dull
boy . . .'

She giggled again as, inwardly, Jack cringed. Was he now to
be the recipient of casseroles from the single women in the
village? He sincerely hoped not.

'I'll drop the dish back tomorrow. Thanks, Lucy.'

As she turned and walked away, still giggling, she tripped.
Had she been drinking? Sod it, he was off duty – and he wasn't
going to add Lucy to his list of problems. She didn't have far
to drive, and she was old enough to look after herself.

The casserole was good. So was the Scotch. Reinvigorated,
Jack fetched Abbie's file, and ate as he read.

On the morning of 25 September, two runners discovered a

woman's body lying on an unofficial footpath across a field of maize on Lower Farm. Jack frowned. The second body had been found on land belonging to Lower Farm, too, according to one of the drivers. He'd check. *The woman had severe injuries, mainly to her head, and was unconscious. After being airlifted to the Royal Cornwall Hospital in Truro, she remained unconscious for two days. When she came round on 27 September, it was clear her memory was affected. She remembered her name, Evie, and that of her three-year-old daughter, Angel. Evie's ex-partner, Nick Abraham, was traced but told the police he didn't know he had a daughter. No one meeting Evie's description has been reported missing and, with the exception of one woman, no one has recognized her. The name of the woman, who knew Evie at school, is Charlotte Harrison.*

Jack stopped reading. The same Charlotte Harrison he'd met earlier, the woman who discovered Tamsyn's body – the woman with attitude. He carried on.

Evie's recollections are at best unreliable. The situation is further complicated; since she and Mr Abraham separated, it appears she changed her name. Her birth name is Jen Russell. After leaving Mr Abraham, it's believed she moved to Jessamine Cottage, a house that used to belong to her aunt, now deceased.

Jen Russell . . . The name rang a bell, but for the life of him, Jack couldn't remember where he'd heard it before.

Forensic investigation has so far failed to find any proof that a child lives in Jessamine Cottage. There is no record of an Angel Sherman at local doctors' surgeries or preschools. It's possible that Evie/Jen was living elsewhere, but clothes and food as well as forensic evidence found there would appear to suggest it is her home.

Clipped to the next page were a couple of photos. One was of a girl in her late teens, which judging from the style of her fair hair, looked as though it had been taken several years ago.

The other was more recent. A typical police mugshot of someone looking less than their best, but then, the woman was recovering from a brutal attack.

Her hair was lank and her eyes were lifeless. Something about her was familiar, though. When he compared the two photos, it was hard to believe they were of the same person, until you saw the cheekbones, the shape of her mouth. Forgetting his supper, Jack scrutinized them, then leaned back in his chair, deep in thought. Suddenly he remembered where he knew her from. It was the Danning case. Jen Russell had been the teenager who'd been looking after Leah Danning, he was sure of it.

As he read on, the last page of the summary confirmed it.

When a background check was carried out on Jen Russell, it was found that she'd been involved in the disappearance of another young girl. Three-year-old Leah Danning was in Jen's care when she went missing from her home on 18th June 2001.

Jack remembered the case clearly. Leah's disappearance had shocked him – Josh had been only a couple of years older. Louise had become paranoid, keeping the doors and windows locked, watching everyone with suspicious eyes, terrified to let Josh out of her sight.

So, Jen Russell was the woman who'd been attacked. In a twist of fate, her daughter was missing. And now Tamsyn was dead. But was any of this connected to Leah Danning?

It was only as he lay in bed that night, his brain sifting through everything that had happened that day, that a memory flashed into his head, then it was gone. He sat up, no longer tired. The person in the photos – Jen. He'd seen her far more recently than fifteen years ago. He'd seen her right here, walking in the same woods where he walked. He must have seen her half a dozen times over the past year, always at a distance, but after the second or third time, close enough to see her face, her eyes meeting his, briefly, startlingly, before she turned away from him. She always turned away . . . But he couldn't recall seeing a child.

16

'I found this yesterday. It may have come from the body,' Jack said to Abbie the next morning. He placed the pendant on her desk. It was now in a plastic bag ready for Forensics, but not before he'd carefully photographed it. Now he'd thought about it, it seemed small, childish, probably one that Tamsyn had had for years.

'Right.' Looking closely at it, Abbie frowned. 'Have you had time to read the file?'

'I read it last night. Actually, I've seen her a few times, recently,' Jack told her. 'Walking. We've never spoken. Is she Evie or Jen?'

'She calls herself Evie.' Abbie reached across to the shelf behind her. 'Here.' She opened a map on her desk. 'I'll show you where Jessamine Cottage is.' She pointed to an area on the edge of Bodmin.

'I live slightly further north.' Jack pointed to where his house was.

'Bit of a trek for you, isn't it, Jack? Truro? I never realized you lived so far out.'

'I try not to do it too often.' It was true. Whenever he could, Jack worked from home. Coming to the station on two consecutive days, like the past two, was almost unheard of.

'Did you ever talk to her?'

Jack shook his head. 'No. All I can tell you is she was always alone. There was never a child with her. She had this way of turning away, as if she didn't want to be seen.'

Abbie frowned. 'She couldn't have left a three-year-old alone – to walk that far. Surely?'

'You'd think not.' *But people did the most unlikely things*, Jack was thinking. *Even loving mothers.* 'Maybe I just didn't see the child.' He shrugged. 'There were trees. I never got that close.'

Abbie looked thoughtful. 'Sara told me you saw Tamsyn's mother?'

'Yes.' He could feel himself getting angry just thinking about her. 'She didn't say much.'

'You can't always tell how people are feeling, Jack,' Abbie said pointedly.

He knew that. He wondered if Sara had told her what he'd said. But Tamsyn's mother had been remorseless about the way she neglected her daughter. She hadn't cared.

'We had a call yesterday from a Tina Wells, who runs a farm shop not far from Wadebridge. She says Evie used to supply her with vegetables and eggs.'

Jack nodded. 'I'll go and talk to her.'

'Thank you. I can't – I'm due back at the hospital. Here's the address.' Abbie handed him the piece of paper. 'We've posted the photo of Tamsyn on our Facebook page, too. We'll see what comes of it.'

★

Back in his office, Jack was deep in thought. If for no other reason than curiosity, he needed to go back over the Danning case.

Having located the file, he made a coffee and then closed the office door before he started reading. First he read about the Danning family – Michael and Sally and their two daughters, Casey and Leah. He remembered where their house was. He wondered if any of them still lived there. He made a note to himself to check it out. He remembered going there as a young detective sergeant.

The senior investigating officer had been Detective Chief Inspector Rhodes, an imposing man, whose procedure had seemed chaotic to Jack at the time, but they'd been dealing with two overwrought teenaged girls; Casey – the missing girl's sister – and of course Jen, who'd been babysitting. The mother had been the first to come home – she'd been understandably distraught, while the father had been angry – or so it had seemed to Jack.

Rhodes had seen it all, Jack had thought at the time. He'd been working under him on the case. He'd hung on to every pearl of wisdom his boss had uttered. One in particular came to mind. *Feral children know where to hide.* By feral, he'd meant wild, free, instinctive. It also meant not abiding by parental rules, such as they were. Instantly, he thought of Tamsyn. From everything he'd heard, she was the epitome of feral. Had she known where to hide? And was it there that her killer had found her?

He turned his attention back to the Danning file. There was a whole lot more he'd read later – interviews with the teenagers, references to other cases. They'd launched a huge search and got dogs in, but no trace of Leah was ever found.

★

The farm shop was easy to find. Like many farms, it had diversified in an attempt to catch more of the tourist trade. Just selling locally produced meat and vegetables wasn't enough any more. There was a kids' playground and, beyond, a number of small accessible pens containing animals. Farming was tough. You did what you had to in order to survive.

As he walked inside, Jack couldn't help but be impressed by what the shop sold. As well as locally grown fruit and vegetables, there was a range of meats and cheeses. Then, round the corner, a display of work by local craftsmen. But he wasn't here to browse. He walked over to the desk.

'Is Tina Wells here?'

The girl behind the desk blushed slightly. She looked about seventeen. 'I'll just get her.'

Jack hovered around the desk. The shop was deserted, though he'd bet in summer it was a different matter. If Jen had brought her vegetables to sell here, surely someone must have seen her daughter?

'Hello? Are you looking for me?'

Jack turned round to find an older woman standing there. Her wavy fair hair was loosely pinned back and she was wearing an apron covered in flour. After dusting off a hand, she held it out to him. 'I'm Tina Wells. Sorry. We're making Christmas cakes.'

'DCI Jack Bentley, Truro police.' Jack regarded her with amusement for a moment. 'I'm here to talk to you about Evie Sherman.'

'Yes. Poor Evie.' She paused for a moment. 'I couldn't believe it when I heard what had happened to her. Shall we sit down? Would you like a coffee?'

'Yes, thank you.' Good coffee was a luxury when Jack was working in the office. At the police station, it was dire.

'Over here?' Tina nodded towards a group of tables that Jack hadn't noticed. 'How do you like it?'

'Black.' He followed her over. 'I like your shop.'

'Thank you. We like to support local growers and farmers. It's quiet just now, but the summer months more than make up for it.'

'Evie was one of your suppliers?'

Tina nodded. 'I met her early this year. It was still winter. I remember thinking how small and cold she looked, as though she needed a square meal or two. She told me she had a huge vegetable garden and some hens . . . Was I interested in buying what she didn't need? At first, I wasn't sure. We're quite selective here. People don't mind paying a premium but they expect good quality. But she was persistent – so I gave her a chance. She didn't let me down, either. I was wondering why we hadn't had a delivery from her.' Tina frowned. 'I suppose that with the shop quieter, I didn't give it much thought.'

'How well did you know her?'

Tina shook her head. 'I really didn't. After she delivered her first boxes of vegetables, she always used to come here early and leave them stacked on the shelves outside. You may have seen them when you came in? It's what a number of our suppliers do. It's easier that way.'

'So how did you pay her?'

'Cash. I have a book of all the payments made. I can show it to you if you like?'

But Jack shook his head. 'There's no need. When did she pick the money up?'

'The night after she delivered, I'd leave her boxes outside for her, with the money in an envelope. That way she could pick it up when it suited her.'

Jack nodded. It sounded overly trusting but it didn't surprise him. This was Cornwall after all. People were considered honest, until proven otherwise.

'So far, there's never been a problem. The arrangement works both ways.' Tina paused. 'How is she?'

'Her memory is slowly coming back.' Jack looked at her. 'Her injuries were serious – she was unconscious when she was found. But at the moment, our greatest concern is for her daughter.'

'Of course.' Tina looked anxious. 'Where is she?'

'We've no idea. I was wondering if you'd seen her any of the times Evie had been here?'

But Tina shook her head. 'To be honest, until I read the police Facebook post, I didn't even know she had a daughter.'

It was another wild goose chase, the kind that police investigations were full of. But you always had to try; had to believe that someone, somewhere, knew something. Evie must have shopped for food sometimes, no matter how secluded her life. The trouble was, round here there were so many remote village shops, and such a high turnover of tourists, that an unfamiliar face didn't stand out. It was the familiar ones that did.

On impulse, Jack took a different way home, wanting to take a look at the house where Jen lived, Jessamine Cottage. It was late, dusk seeming to fall early under the grey, overcast sky. The track to the house was rough and unmade, mostly through woodland, and after half a mile he was starting to think he'd taken a wrong turn, but round the next corner, a roof came into view.

As he pulled over, he noted that no cars were parked beside the overgrown hedge that bordered the garden. As he got out of his car, he was aware of the silence. It had the same quality as his own home. Raw and untouched; pure.

The gate was open and Jack was irritated that whichever officer was here last hadn't bothered to close it properly. Probably PC Miller. He'd spent a lot of time going over the cottage with the Forensics team. Then Jack saw that the latch was broken. He carried on round the side of the house, where the garden opened out. It was quite something, the stretch of open grass edged by towering oak trees. The path took him across the grass and through a gap in a more neatly maintained beech hedge, on the other side of which was the vegetable garden.

No wonder Jen was selling to the farm shop. It was a vast garden, far too prolific for even several people. He could hear chickens, and as he walked further a large run came into view. About a dozen birds came running over. Unsure who was feeding them, he found a bin of corn in a shed and fed them some, then topped up the empty container in the corner of the run, hoping it would last a while. There were no kids' toys in any of the outbuildings.

It had started to drizzle. Walking over to the back door of the cottage, he felt on the ledge above the frame, hoping for a key, and was amazed to find there was one. After letting himself in, he took his shoes off then started looking around. The house was sparsely furnished and uncluttered – no photos, either, unless Forensics had taken them. Upstairs, he checked the three bedrooms, but it was exactly as Abbie had said. There was no sign whatsoever that a child had lived here.

*

It was dark by the time Jack drove back down the track towards the road. The drizzle that had started while he was in the garden had turned into a steady downpour. The house was out of sight behind him and he was still some distance from the main road when something in the woods caught his eye. It was an intermittent beam, possibly from a single flashlight. Slowing down, he switched off his headlights and watched as it was joined by another, then another, then several made their way towards each other.

After everything that had happened round here, he didn't like it. Pulling over, he switched off the engine and got out.

As his eyes adjusted to the darkness, he started to make his way towards the lights, moving from tree to tree as quietly as he could, lucky that by now the rain was heavy enough to drown out any sound his feet made. As he got closer to where the torches had gathered, trepidation filled him. It was unlikely anything serious was going on, but he had to check, that was all. It was probably just kids, he told himself – only it wouldn't be kids, would it? Not in this rain, and not when there were any number of deserted barns around.

After Tamsyn's murder, then the attack on Jen, he wondered, irrationally, if whatever was going on in the woods ahead of him was related. An uneasy feeling filled him, as he felt in his pocket and turned his phone to silent. Something suddenly came to mind. It was something else his old boss, Rhodes, had said – the same man who'd talked about feral children had told him not to underestimate the presence of modern day Satanism. Jack had listened, disbelieving, as Rhodes told him that every year, a number of the so-called missing persons that appeared on their books around Halloween would actually have been kidnapped and held for human sacrifice.

His imagination was getting the better of him. There was probably some perfectly reasonable explanation for a group of people with torches gathering in the woods in the rain. Even so, he stayed hidden. Halloween was only a couple of weeks away.

Through the darkness, he watched the torches cluster together – about a dozen of them by now, too close for him to think about getting away and too many for him to think about a confrontation without backup. His only choice was to stay out of sight – and wait.

Minutes passed while nothing happened. Then in the distance, he heard someone else coming – more than one person. Two more torches were approaching the group, but instead of their steady beam, they moved erratically, as though they were struggling with something.

Through the rain, Jack heard a man's laugh. Loud, cruel, full of evil; a sound that chilled him to the core. There was another cry, a pure, high-pitched one, filled with fear, followed by more laughter. Then silence.

He had a sick feeling in his stomach. Presumably whoever was out there had done what they'd come here to do. Soon they'd leave, then he'd give them a few minutes and get out of there.

But just seconds later, he knew he was wrong. The high-pitched cry he'd heard was just the prelude to the piercing scream that now filled the air – terrified, filled with pain, going on and on before faltering, then fading into silence.

In reality, it could only have lasted seconds, but Jack was in no doubt he'd just heard a drawn-out and painful death. He reached for his phone. He needed to call for backup, then silently cursed when he saw there was no signal. Fighting the urge to throw up, he knew he had to find out what they'd done. Trying to convince himself that the victim was probably an animal, he knew also that it could be a child.

Edging closer, he tried not to think about it, slowly feeling his way, each footstep as calculated as it could be in the dark, until, despite his best efforts, he stepped on something.

At the familiar cry of a pheasant startled into flight, all the torches swung round in Jack's direction. Crouched behind a dense patch of brambles, he froze, his heart hammering in his chest.

Danger was all around him. Jack trusted his instincts. Then, from the opposite direction, came a crashing sound which saved him. As he watched, the torches swung all over the place. Straining in the darkness, Jack tried to pick out faces, catching only glimpses of eyes, mouths, hands; not recognizing them but scoring them into his mind, nonetheless.

The crashing continued. He'd no idea if it was human or animal, but the group with the torches disappeared as quickly as they'd arrived, blending into the trees, until silence fell. Holding his breath, Jack waited, slowly filled with relief. Then apprehension. Something had happened and he needed to know what.

He waited five more minutes until he was sure the men weren't coming back, before reaching into his pocket for his torch and very slowly getting to his feet, edging closer to where he'd last seen them. Directly ahead, a loud noise startled him.

As Jack shone his torch in the direction the noise had come from, he picked up first the glint of an eye, then the head of a stag. It was a large animal, standing motionless, watching him distrustfully as he moved the beam of his torch along its body and down its legs, then onto the ground between them. To his horror, Jack saw blood.

Stepping closer, he reached down and felt the warm stickiness. Suddenly, without warning, the stag ran off into the darkness. Then, as he stood up, Jack felt a hand grasp his shoulder.

17

A light was shone in his face, and for a split second, he confronted his own mortality.

'Jack? What the hell are you doing out here?'

Through his shock, he recognized PC Miller's voice. 'Dan?' Jack was overwhelmed with relief. 'What are you doing here?'

'I left my coat in the Sherman house earlier. I saw your car, then on the way back, I saw some lights. What was going on?'

'I've no idea. I started walking towards them and heard an animal crashing about.'

'It's a bit close to the Sherman house, isn't it? Did you see anything?' Suddenly Miller's voice was more serious.

'Just the same torches you saw. Probably poachers. But they've long gone.' Jack wasn't sure why, but he didn't mention the awful cry or the blood he'd seen. Maybe it was fear that they were being observed, that the group had crept back while he and Miller were talking, blending into the trees and watching them. They'd just killed. Jack was in no doubt about that. That blood he'd seen was fresh. There was nothing to stop them from doing it again.

There was the stag, too. The way it had come crashing in, distracting the group; how it just stood there, watching Jack. He didn't talk to other people about it, but since Josh had died, from time to time, he'd sensed his presence. The thought had come into his head, out of nowhere. But he knew. Somehow, Josh had sent that stag to save him.

By the time he got home, Jack was chilled through. Letting a disapproving Beamer into the garden, he had a hot shower and poured himself a large Scotch. For the second day running, he'd forgotten to go shopping. He thought gratefully of the remains of Lucy's casserole from the night before. At least he had that.

As he ate, he couldn't shake the memory of what his old boss had said, about missing persons around Halloween. Rhodes had believed that some of them were held by Satanists for ritual sacrifice. Personally, he'd never noticed a pattern – not that he'd actually looked. Going back a few years, a local boy was rumoured to be involved with some kind of Satanic group, but Jack was pretty sure that's all it was – rumours.

Jack lay wide awake in bed that night, unable to wind his mind down enough to sleep. An owl hooted outside. Too much was uncertain right now, as it was for Jen. He couldn't understand, either, how there was no evidence of a child at Jessamine Cottage.

In Jack's experience, a complete clean-up of a house was next to impossible. He'd have expected Forensics to find something, however small. But there had been at least three days before the place was identified as Evie's home. Three days in which to strip the place, if someone had wanted to. Unlikely, he knew, but it was something to think about.

One thing he did know – he wanted to talk to Abbie, and then to Evie. Maybe she'd recognize him from walking in the woods. It might even help. God knows what it was like to be in her situation; to trust yourself so little that you couldn't even believe your own thoughts.

The need to talk to her came from his gut. If she recognized him, maybe she'd trust him. He also needed to talk to some-one about what he'd seen in the woods. Again, probably Abbie. He'd no idea why he hadn't told Dan Miller about the blood he'd found – or the horrible scream that still haunted him. The way the man had appeared out of nowhere had unnerved Jack. He needed to sleep. It was amazing how sleep could clarify even the most confused thoughts.

Closing his eyes, he tried to blot out the thoughts racing through his head, telling himself that he'd known Miller for years, that he was a decent man. But it was hopeless trying to sleep. It had been the same after Josh had died, when Jack had been unable to stop his mind from overthinking, from going round in circles as he went over every detail, tormenting himself with 'what ifs' and 'if onlys'. In the end, he got up and went downstairs, putting the kettle on, as thoughts of Jen Russell and Leah Danning filled his head. With a hot cup of tea, he sat down and turned his laptop on, typing into the search bar. Occult, Satanism, ritual sacrifice – generalized, benign descriptions, but as he searched deeper, he stumbled upon something much darker.

One of the websites had published an occult calendar, list-ing dates on which sacrifices were required, whether human or animal, the age of the victim, the nature of sexual deprav-ity to take place. The second half of October was a period of abduction, holding and ceremonial preparation for human sacrifice, according to what was in front of him. Suddenly he felt cold. It was his gut again.

He'd forgotten about sleep. His mind was fully alert as he carried on reading pages that became progressively more graphic. It was common enough knowledge that many missing people were never found, but less commonly acknowledged where some of them may have ended up.

He'd talk to Abbie. She knew him well enough not to think he'd lost the plot. Right now, he was beginning to wonder. Anyway, he trusted her – and she wouldn't gossip. He was less sure about Dan Miller. Maybe that was why he hadn't mentioned the awful cry he'd heard – that and the blood.

Deep in thought, he typed into the search bar again. *Leah Danning.* Scrolling down the pages, he saw links to news items and press releases. He'd forgotten how huge the case had been. As he read, he remembered how it had seemed the whole country had been on tenterhooks, waiting for Leah to be found. That a small child could disappear without a trace had left every mother fearful for her own child's safety. He couldn't believe how long ago it was.

Jack carried on reading. So far, there was nothing to link the attack on Jen Russell and her daughter's disappearance to what happened to Leah. But this was rural Cornwall, known for its solitude and peacefulness. It was his gut again – not the cold, hard evidence the police needed – but it seemed too much of a coincidence.

Sitting back in his chair, Jack must have dozed off, awaking with a start. Beamer was barking; not the muffled kind of noise he made when he was dreaming, but a full-on alert bark, which meant he'd heard something.

'Hey, what is it?' But Beamer ignored him, barking agitatedly.

'Come on, Beamer. Quiet.'

There was no stopping him. Getting up, Jack went to unlock the back door, Beamer following, still barking. As he opened it, the dog barged past before disappearing into the darkness. Out of sight, Jack could hear him whining as he followed the trail of something. Probably a rabbit or a fox. He only hoped there wasn't a person hanging around out there.

Then the night went completely silent.

'Beamer? Here! Good boy!' Jack called, but there was no reply. Cursing the dog, he pulled on his boots, then reached for a jacket from one of the hooks beside the door, feeling for the torch in one of the pockets.

'Beamer?' Outside, he switched it on, shining the beam around the garden, but there was no sign of the dog. 'Beamer!' Jack raised his voice. There were no neighbours to worry about disturbing. The nearest house was at least a mile away.

Out there in the darkness, there was nothing. No birds, no muffled footsteps of rabbits, not even a breeze. Above him, the moon was obscured by clouds. Everything was black, silent.

He called again, then at last heard Beamer coming through the bushes – at least Jack hoped it was him – and a sense of relief filled him when the bushes moved and the dog's head came into view. He was wearing that slightly apologetic look he had when he knew he'd done something wrong. Then as Jack shone the torch at him, he saw he was carrying something.

Beamer followed him to the back door, where Jack reached for his collar, but the dog pushed past him, carrying his trophy inside. The last thing Jack wanted in the house was a dead rabbit, which no doubt Beamer would mangle on the floor for him to clean up later. Hurrying after him, he found him lying in the kitchen, the rabbit held between his paws.

Only when he switched the kitchen light on, Jack saw it wasn't a rabbit. Looking at him, Beamer whimpered and then he got up and walked away. Jack took a closer look. What he'd thought was a rabbit was in fact a bundle of fabric, maybe clothing. Picking it up, under the dirt engrained on it, he could make out a floral pattern. Then he quickly put it down, looking at his fingers, which were coated with blood.

18

Abbie's door was open. She looked up as Jack walked in. 'Glad I caught you. Do you have a minute?' he asked.

'Of course. What's up?'

He went in, closing the door behind him, then sat on the chair opposite her desk, placing the bag he was carrying on the floor. It contained the blood-stained fabric Beamer had found. 'Last night, I stopped by Jessamine Cottage to look at the place. I suppose I wanted to get a sense of where Evie lived. As I was driving away, I noticed some lights in the woods. They seemed to be hanging around. I thought I'd better take a look.'

'Go on.' He had her full attention.

'At first, there were a couple of flashlights. Then they were joined by more. Eventually there were about ten of them. I got as close as I could without letting them know I was there. I wasn't sure what to make of what happened next.' He glanced at her, but she was still listening intently. 'Two more torches appeared. I think they were carrying something between them. The beams were flashing around all over the place, as if someone was struggling with something. I heard this cry – I assumed it came from them.'

'What kind of cry?' she said sharply.

'High-pitched. Like an animal. I think . . . In all honesty, it could have been a child.' He glanced at her again. 'I thought they'd killed whatever it was, but they'd barely started. I heard someone laugh – it sounded evil – then there was another cry, more of a scream this time, which went on and on.' Jack could still hear its echo in his head. 'I tried to get close enough to see what was going on. Then I trod on a pheasant.'

He relived the moment the torches had spun round towards him. 'I honestly thought they were going to come after me. Lucky for me, a stag picked that moment to go crashing through the woods in the other direction. It completely distracted them. They scattered.'

'Did you see anything else?'

'After they'd gone, I went over to where I'd seen the torches. There was blood on the ground. Not just drops. Quite a lot of blood.' He didn't tell her about the stag, standing there watching him. 'I bent down, to see if it was fresh. Then as I got up, there was someone behind me.'

Abbie looked startled.

'Frightened the life out of me. Fortunately, I knew who it was.'

Abbie leaned forward. 'Who?'

'Miller. He was on his way back from Evie's when he saw the torches too.'

'He hasn't mentioned it to me.' Abbie was frowning.

Jack shrugged. 'He probably knew I would. Anyway, I don't think he's in yet.'

'No. Not if he was on duty at Evie's last night.' Abbie was quiet. 'What do you think was going on?'

Jack shook his head. 'It was probably poachers.'

'It doesn't sound like poachers . . .' Abbie looked at him.

Jack sighed. 'If you really want to know, last night I remembered something my old boss told me. Do you remember Rhodes?' he added. Abbie looked at him blankly for a moment, before recognition dawned on her face. 'He used to say that in the run-up to Halloween, the number of missing persons always increased. I don't know where he got his figures, but he said that in the weeks leading up to it, a number of the missing persons on our books were being held by Satanists.'

'God.' Abbie sounded horrified. 'Surely nothing suggests that's the case here.' She didn't scoff; she was acknowledging that this was something very real they were looking at.

'We're in October.' Jack paused. 'I was looking online last night. According to the calendar I found, right now it's a time of abduction, holding and preparation for human sacrifice to take place at Halloween.'

He could see Abbie thinking the same as he was. 'Which means there are people being held who have days to live.'

He nodded. Neither of them spoke. The idea of anyone being held somewhere, for the purpose of ritual sacrifice, was sickening.

'What was the website you were looking at?' Her fingers were already typing on the keyboard on her desk.

'Here.' He reached into his pocket for his phone, where he'd noted it, and read it out to her.

In seconds, she had it. 'Is this what you were looking at?'

She turned the screen so that he could see the by now familiar layout of the Satanic calendar.

He nodded.

'The attack on Evie, Tamsyn's death and Angel's disappearance . . . According to this, they all tie in with the Autumn Equinox.' Abbie looked at him. 'I'm guessing about Tamsyn and Forensics will confirm when she died, but it can't be far out.'

'I know.' Jack nodded, relieved she'd come to the same conclusion. He frowned. 'I was thinking about the Leah Danning case. It happened not long after I started here. At the time, no one talked about anything else. Last night, I was thinking that the same thing's happened again. Historically, there are no other cases. I've checked.' He looked at Abbie.

'What are you suggesting?' Abbie frowned.

'There was something about the way Leah vanished that doesn't add up. Dogs were brought in straight away. The countryside was searched and searched again. No sign of her was ever found. It's the same with Angel. The fact that there's no trace of her is the common denominator in the two cases. Doesn't that strike you as odd?'

Abbie was silent. 'And?'

'I don't know. Either we have someone incredibly methodical who's completely covered their tracks, or someone's hiding something.'

'You're not suggesting someone on the inside?' Abbie looked horrified.

Jack shook his head. 'I was thinking more of someone deliberately concealing evidence to throw us off track.' Seeing Abbie's face, he shrugged. 'Just thoughts.'

Abbie turned to the screen in front of her, deep in thought. 'Do you by any chance know Xander Pascoe?'

He shook his head. 'I haven't met him. He was a suspect for

a while when Leah Danning disappeared. But I know his mother. Janna Pascoe.' She was a formidable woman. A true matriarch, was how Jack thought of her. 'She was walking through Truro when she was hit by a car. It must have been a good ten years ago. The driver was being chased by the police. He got away, and she was rushed to hospital. She recovered but she lost the use of her legs.'

'What do you know about her?'

Jack shrugged. 'She's a tough lady. Her husband died way back and she's been running the farm ever since. After she was hit by the car, she sued the police and lost, but she has money. The house is full of antiques. And art.' He remembered it all well; the mess of the farmyard and what looked like a run-down Cornish farmhouse on the outside. Inside, it was like a museum. 'That's all I know – apart from the fact that she hates the police.'

'Right.' Abbie was frowning.

'I think that's about all I can tell you.'

'Xander Pascoe was interviewed when Leah Danning went missing. He's a strange one. Surrounded by a wall of silence is how it seems. No one had a bad word to say about him. The police were never able to prove anything, but somewhere in the notes from the investigation, it mentions that when they searched the Pascoes' home, they found a kind of shrine in Xander's room that they thought was linked to the occult. They didn't take it further because Xander had an alibi.' She paused, looking thoughtful. 'Interesting, isn't it?'

It certainly was. Then Jack remembered. 'Last night, my dog heard something outside. I let him out and he ran off. When he came back, he was carrying this.' He picked up the plastic bag containing the bloodstained fabric. 'The blood was wet when he brought it in. I'll send it to Forensics.'

Abbie hesitated, then seemed to make a decision. 'Are you busy? Or do you have time to show me where you saw the torches last night?'

Jack thought about what awaited him. This was far more important. 'There's nothing that can't wait.'

'Maybe we should go and take a look.'

Jack pulled up close to where he'd parked the previous night, Abbie just behind him. As they walked through the woods by daylight, there was none of the sense of menace he'd felt in the dark. Apart from the occasional cry of a bird, it was completely quiet.

'We need to go this way.' He pointed to a narrow path that sloped downhill. It had taken him a while to get his bearings, but now he knew exactly where he was.

'This is where I hid, watching them.' They'd reached the patch of brambles he'd crouched behind. 'The torches seemed to come from over there.' He pointed to where the trees thinned slightly.

Abbie slowly started walking in the direction he'd pointed, studying the ground as she went. As Jack followed behind, he was trying to work out where he'd seen the last two torches coming from.

'Where did you see the blood?' She stopped in the middle of the path.

'Somewhere here.' Jack gestured to an area that he thought was reasonably accurate. Slowly, methodically, both of them scrutinized the ground, but there was nothing. Then Abbie stooped down to pick up a handful of leaves, letting them flutter to the ground.

'There's nothing here.'

Jack didn't reply. He was looking at the leaves she'd just picked up, at where they'd settled on other leaves. He frowned. 'If you wanted to cover your tracks, you'd do exactly what you've just done.'

'Excuse me?'

He walked over to where she was standing, then bending down and scooping up more of the leaves, did the same. 'It would be the easiest way to hide blood on the leaves. Pile on more leaves. Unless they really looked, no one would ever be the wiser.'

After crouching down, he started to carefully remove the top layer of leaves, then the next, until it was clear he'd reached leaves that had been there a long time. Then he moved slightly to one side and repeated the process, again and again. Behind him, Abbie was doing the same.

'Jack?' he heard her say. 'You better come here.'

He walked over to where she stood and looked at the leaves she'd uncovered; the blood from last night was clearly visible, no longer fresh but congealed and dried.

She reached for her phone.

Casey, 2000

My sister was given a pretty name, Leah. With her white-blonde hair and fair skin, there was proof, indisputable, right in front of you, that I was the plain child with the plain name. Dull where Leah sparkled; emotionless while Leah's default beaming smile lit up rooms and seemed to touch people's actual hearts. It wasn't fair, Leah having that hair, that smile and skin that was soft as a peach.

I got used to it. You can get used to anything. Now, as soon as I saw Anthony's face, a haze would come over me, and his voice would seem to fade into the distance, as though I wasn't there any more. He could do whatever he liked but he couldn't hurt me.

The last time, his friend, Barney, had been there. I'd been really scared at the thought of two of them. And the shitface had seen my fear, because as he glanced across at Barney, I'd thought of a snake watching its prey, its eyes lit up, its tongue flickering across his lips.

I didn't know what had changed that time. I'd wanted to go to that faraway place in my mind, but I couldn't. Instead, I'd felt the most putrefying, stinking emotions rage through me, like sewage in my veins. I was frightened, revolted, reviled. Then suddenly, as I looked at him, at my hand obediently doing what he wanted it to, anger rose in me. Anger that was like bile, choking me, until I forgot about my fear.

As I thought about everything he'd done to me, what he was going to let his friend do, I screamed as loudly as I could. In that moment, I saw an evil in his eyes I hadn't seen before. I struggled free from him, then as I backed away, found myself cornered. A new fear had come over me. I wasn't sure what he was going to do to me. I tried to scream again but I was paralysed, then as he closed in on me, I threw up.

He jumped back, but not before the stream of vomit hit him full on. In his hurry he caught a lamp on his bookcase, sending it crashing onto the floor. Sweet relief as I heard Auntie Maureen coming. As her footsteps drew closer, Anthony begged me not to tell her.

'Why?' I stared at him, wondering how he'd explain the vomit down the front of him; liking the power I suddenly had. Why shouldn't I tell her what kind of a monster her son was? What was in it for me if I kept silent?

'She'll fucking kill me, I know she will.'

I didn't care what she did to him. I glanced around the room, latching on to the first thing I saw that interested me. 'Give me your radio.'

'Take it,' he whined, as I snatched it up.

'If you ever touch me again, I'll tell her everything,' I spat at him, just as we heard her voice outside.

I took my trophy home with me. Even though I looked at it and thought of Anthony, it represented a personal kind of victory over a world that seemed against me. I knew Anthony would never be able to look at me. And I was nearly fourteen. Old enough to be left alone. Not to have to go to Auntie Maureen's ever again.

Life breaks you down into tiny, dirty pieces. If you're one of the lucky ones, it builds you up again. When your safety is threatened, when you're forced to confront fear, they say you grow stronger. But not all of us. Some of us stay broken.

But you always learn. Not to trust people. That evil comes in many forms. That every bully has an Achilles heel. That silence always has a price.

As Leah got older, I waited for her charm to fade, for things to get easier, but they didn't. I had parents who were blinkered in their own small world and I didn't fit.

I still had that same freaking wallpaper. My father had refused to spend good money on something I'd destroy. That's how he put it. I'd already proved I wasn't trustworthy. But neither was he.

I wasn't shocked when I found out about his affair. Wrapped up in my perfect, pretty little sister, my mother pretended not to notice, but I could tell. All those excuses about staying to work late, or having important out-of-the-blue meetings, coming home with booze on his breath and someone's lipstick not quite wiped away.

It didn't change anything. I already hated him. I had a mother who only cared about my sister, and a father who only cared about himself. I'd been born into a fragmented family, where children weren't born equal, where everyone only cared about themselves.

Being alone was better, even in my dark, shabby bedroom that was the inverse of Leah's pretty, light room. Lying on my bed, I'd pick at more wallpaper, unfairness eating away under my skin, into my very soul. One entire wall had been revealed, pocked with the stubborn bits of glue that refused to budge, and I'd started on another, loosening the edge of the paper with a short fingernail, freeing enough that I could grasp it between my fingers and slowly tear it.

I perfected the art of keeping the pieces as long and thin as possible; when I finished one, I discarded it onto the floor where it joined others, not noticing the untidiness. It didn't matter. Not to my parents, not to me. They'd made it clear to me a long time ago that I wasn't deserving of better.

There was something comforting about the air of decay in there. Maybe because it was the only corner of the bland, suburban home where I felt I belonged, my frustration gouged into the windowsill in a legacy of deep scratches. On the naked wall, black-Sharpie scrawls of anger. Screw you, fuckers. It didn't actually say that in bold letters, but it may as well have.

It was the only place I could be alone. With the door closed, I could allow my mind to go wherever it pleased. Not to stupid dream worlds with handsome princes and happily-ever-afters. I wasn't naive. There were other places that were safer, where illusions didn't exist, that were more real, where the pretence that life should be happy was dropped; places of darkness.

Everything was clear in the dark. There were no distractions. Your senses – your intuition – were sharper, louder. There was no escape from what you thought, felt, or saw. And my mind wandered. I couldn't stop it, any more than I could stop seeing the images that floated past me, opaque, unsettling, whispering in the darkness, playing their stories out against my peeling walls.

In there, it was my world. I was in control, writing the script of the macabre theatre scenes, manipulating the characters as I pleased. But projected onto my wall, they were no strangers. There was my father, for instance, in his golf clothes. On Sundays, he always played golf – code for picking up bored married women he wanted to shag. He'd taken me with him, but only once, because he realized I saw too much.

The scene in my room: my father stands above a bunker, only instead of pristine white sand, it's a writhing, black pit. The word *arrogant* hangs over his head, uneven heavy letters suspended in the air for the world to see, because that's what he was. Arrogant and superior and overbearing, with a sense of self-worth I utterly detested. The caring father, successful businessman, loving husband, all stripped away; those images showed him as he was.

I enjoyed those pictures. With practise, I could make anything happen. Time and time again I'd replay them, watching as someone emerged from the shadows, beside him, or behind him, raising the gun, firing. The gunshot was real. So were the birds, their song deafening, as the breeze ruffled my hair and the red mark appeared on his forehead. As he stopped talking for the last time, as his legs crumpled. His body prostrate, unmoving, lifeless.

I killed my father many times. Sometimes the killer was another golfer, biding his time, his rifle hidden in his bag of golf clubs. Once it was a woman, her hair the same colour as mine, her eyes blank as she fired, walking slowly away after dropping the gun. And always birds that would swoop down as I reached my arms out, their sound soothing me, my hair fanned across my face by the beating of their wings.

After it was over, I'd make another mark in the windowsill, gouging through the aging gloss paint, thinking of my father's hateful face, feeling the anger build inside me because he was still alive. Needing a thousand deaths to assuage the gaping, hollow emptiness in me, because it wasn't enough.

I needed more, to make the pain, the hurt, go away. Only one thing helped. Rolling up my sleeve, I reached for the razor blade I kept hidden for such times; pressing it against my skin, carefully, with just the right amount of pressure, feeling the cool metal, starting to cut.

When the gun became too quick, too painless a death for my father, I reached into my head for something worse. Suffocation: he knew what was happening to him, was fully conscious as he realized he was going to die. A knife: straight through his heart, satisfying for its brutal imagery. I eased the razor blade into my own pale skin, seeing instead a serrated knife across my father's throat.

It made sense that a death should reflect a life; that someone guilty of inflicting years of suffering should themselves suffer. It was a thought that obsessed me as I made the punishment fit the crime, the justice lasting as long as the relief when I cut.

My mother didn't deserve an ugly death. She wasn't a bad person, just a weak, obsessive, small-minded one. When it came to her, I had the perfect murderer, a kind of ironic one. My mother was to die at the hand of the person she lived for. Leah. It was Leah who'd wind the narrow pink scarf round her neck, then pull until our mother's eyes bulged, too weak to fight as her oxygen supply was cut off.

I could watch over and over, unemotionally, dispassionately, the same, oddly quiet scene every time. The snow starting to fall, my mother collapsing to her knees. Her acquiescence as Leah slowly choked the life out of her, because Leah could do no wrong. The snow turning to glitter, so that in death, my mother's body was far more beautiful than it had been in life.

Killed so prettily, with a pink scarf, snow and glitter. For my mother, that was enough.

Of course, it was logical that after she'd killed my mother, Leah had to die too. If you asked me why, I couldn't explain. And when it came to her, I didn't have to do a thing.

We'd gone to a nearby lake, a place my mother had taken me to, just once. Leah was standing on the bank, gazing at the giant lily pads that grew there, the buds unfurling in a wave of soft pink across the water.

As I watched, she stepped out onto a pad, a tiny figure sur-rounded by flowers, jumping onto the next giant leaf, then the next.

I could have called to stop her any time. Instead, I stood and watched.

As she reached the third leaf, she turned back to look at me, starting to sink, so slowly you couldn't be sure it was happening. Silently, even with the water at waist height, all the while her eyes staring into mine.

I sat on the bank tearing the petals off a daisy, until the flowers closed over her head. Then I got up and walked away.

I didn't want to think these things. And they weren't real, but I couldn't stop myself. It was my life that had made them happen. I'd become a reflection of the light and shadow, love and hate, inside my family and out.

As more time passed, I couldn't stop thinking what it would be like without them. We had genes in common, but that was all. By now, I rarely spoke to them. Why would you talk to someone who only ever told you off or put you down? Who took obvious pleasure in pointing out how you were a failure? Who, with every word, reminded you how worthless you were? Words which could so easily have comforted or cared, that were instead chosen to destroy you.

While I was a nothing, Xander Pascoe was all things to all people. He sometimes reminded me of Anthony. It was his arrogance, the sense of the world owing him a favour. The leer that brought bile rushing to my throat. Yet underneath was steely control. He was only a little older than me, but people did what he said. It was on one of my darkest, most desperate days, that he said, 'Tell me.'

And I did.

He was the one person who listened. I told him how my parents didn't trust me. How I wasn't reliable. *Look at the state of my room,* they pointed out. *I couldn't look after myself, let alone my sister.*

No faith, no belief, no trust, because you're unworthy, Casey. Can't do anything right. No matter how hard you try, you're not good enough. Lucky for us, we have Jen.

Jen, with her sparkling eyes and her naive, trusting face. Jen, who was the same age as I was, but who was from a world a million miles away from the one I lived in, where dreams came true and no one was ever nasty. The light to my shadow.

At school, she haunted me, flitting in and out of my classes with her shiny hair and her A grades, always there, everywhere I went. Do you know how that felt, Jen? To be the shadow? To have the name teachers didn't remember, to be the girl no one wanted to be friends with? You were the lead in the school play, captain of the sports teams. Prefect, future head girl, constantly adding to the list of your achievements. But you didn't know, did you, that no one has it all; that ultimately, at some point, unfairness is redressed, light fades. That there is always balance.

For me, there was no escaping you. No shielding myself from your brightness. Not at school, when friends flocked around you. You were in my home, too. I remember how it felt, watching as they paid you to replace me – trustworthy, reliable Jen, so much better at everything than I was.

They were pretty, Jen and Leah. I used to watch them from upstairs, talking and laughing, but it wasn't until the second time she came I realized what had happened; how cheap I was. For the price of a few pounds on a Saturday morning, so quickly replaced.

I let familiar hurt stab me inside, fought the desire to cut myself, lost the battle, grateful when numbness set in. All this as I watched Leah and Jen, the pretty new sister my parents had bought her, spinning round in the garden, the sound of their laughter filling my ears, while another way came to me for how Leah could die. It wasn't my fault, was it, that I had to watch her with Jen? Or that terrible pictures filled my head, one after another, when all I wanted was for them to go away.

They were so perfect, Leah and Jen, so liked, so likeable. Jen, who was actually just another freaking teenager. The same as I was, but not the same. She lacked the cloud of reality that hung over me. So lovely, so reliable, so loved by Leah, words that crawled up the stairs and under my bedroom door, every Saturday without fail. Only on reaching me, the letters had been rearranged, so that all I heard was how unreliable I was. How ugly, how hateful.

Cutting no longer helped. I had a disconnected feeling I couldn't shake; a life that felt like someone else's. When I caught my reflection in the mirror, it was someone else who looked back at me. Someone I didn't know, with white skin and glittering eyes, from whom a power radiated out. I'd no idea what was happening to me.

A few times, the next step presented itself, dangled in front of me, daring me to be brave.

Take the step, Casey . . . How close you are. How little it would take to cut harder, deeper, until you hit an artery. Orchestrate your own death . . .

Staring at my reflection, I watched the thought reflected in those glittering eyes, wondering how it would feel; whether the draining of blood from my body would bring the relief I craved, how long it would take for my life to ebb away. For me to die.

I floated the thought around in my head. And then something happened that changed the game completely. It was as I stood there, contemplating my end, staring at the face in the mirror, that it smiled back at me, then turned away.

19

Charlotte

I stay away from the hospital for a few days, until Abbie Rose calls me.

'Evie's going home. I'd hoped her mother would be able to stay, but she's had to fly back – she lives in Italy. I wanted to ask you if you'd be able to spend some time with her. I understand if you're too busy, but it's a big step and, understandably, she's anxious.'

But also, there isn't anyone else. She doesn't have to say it, I'm all too aware. Jesus, it's as if I'm an unpaid police volunteer, or something. 'Of course, Detective Inspector.' But I'm not doing it for her. 'When's she going?'

'The plan is tomorrow afternoon. We're arranging a police guard round the clock, and I'll be with her a lot of the time. It's just . . .' She makes no mention of the body I found in the field. *Does she even know?* I wonder.

'You want someone there she trusts.'

Abbie Rose hesitates, but she doesn't take the bait. 'I suppose you could put it like that.' She pauses again. 'I was thinking more along the lines of her needing a friend.'

★

The next morning, I oversleep. I'm hungover after too much wine, trying to blot out the memory of the girl's body. It crosses my mind to cancel – but I've nothing else planned and I'm curious, wondering what it will be like for Jen, being home. Since the attack, her life has consisted of that hospital bed in that bare white room, with vile food, fussing nurses and Abbie Rose probing into her life.

I leave it till mid-afternoon. Knowing hospitals, I can't imagine her being discharged any earlier than that. Then, as I drive over to Helen Osterman's cottage, I'm reminded of the times we camped there. In truth, being outside Jen's immediate circle, I wasn't often invited. About twice, I think, during a year we had a mutual friend, Sophie. Her name comes to me. I haven't given Sophie a thought in over a decade.

I overshoot the track to Jen's house the first time. Then, as I slam on the brakes to reverse into a gateway, someone almost drives up the back of me. Resisting the temptation to shout four-letter words as they hoot then accelerate past, I breathe deeply. Saving my energy. The world is full of arseholes.

I drive slowly up the track that leads to the house, picking my way round the potholes, until I see a BMW parked up ahead, which I guess must belong to Abbie Rose. I like her choice in cars. I pull up behind it then get out, standing there for a moment, looking around, trying to remember where our teenage campsite used to be.

Round the corner, I notice the battered Peugot Abbie Rose mentioned. Then I shiver as the past comes suddenly back. Ghosts of us all, the friendships, the closed circles; the cruel exclusions caused by teenage politics. I used to be in the background of it all until I made a friend who felt the same way I did. After that, there was no stopping me.

This place isn't as it used to be. Not just because the trees need cutting back – they've grown too tall, so that they overhang the track, blocking out the light and leaving the house in shade – the hedge, too, is unkempt and wild-looking, heavy with overripe blackberries, the narrow gate in it hung unevenly.

As I walk up the path, I notice the air of neglect. The paint on the window frames is peeling and there are tiles missing from the roof. Even so, it's an interesting house. Mostly old – seventeenth century I'd guess – and not big, even with the usual tacked-on additions that have come much later, but it isn't friendly. In fact, the energy I pick up is anything but.

The front door is open, and I knock, then without waiting for an answer, go in, curious to see inside. The interior looks as though it's stuck in a time warp, with a tiny sixties fireplace that needs ripping out and a threadbare patterned carpet, under which, I don't mind guessing, are huge, uneven slabs of Cornish slate. The walls are wonderfully uneven and the furniture decades old. The odd piece is tasteful, though most of it's not. And the curtains . . . I'm still trying to find the words to describe them when I hear footsteps.

'Hello . . .' I call out. 'It's Charlotte. Harrison.'

Further inside, a door opens and Abbie Rose stands there. 'Hi, Charlotte.'

'I'm so sorry, I should have been here an hour ago. I had something urgent to attend to.' I apologize, thinking of my hangover – which has mercifully dissipated after a couple of ibuprofen and several cups of strong coffee drunk in the bracing air before I left.

'Don't worry. I was beginning to think you'd got lost. A quick word—'

'What?' *Has something else happened?*

'I understand it was you who found the girl's body – in the field.'

I nod. 'The police grapevine is as good as the surfers'.'

'I wanted to ask you not to mention it to Evie. If we think it necessary, of course we'll tell her. But right now, when she's already on a knife-edge, I think it would be better to leave it a day or two. Does that make sense?'

'Whatever you say.' I raise my eyebrows. More bloody sub-terfuge and deception at every turn, despite the fact that there's a child missing. 'But if I were her, I'd want to know.'

'I'm sure . . .' She breaks off. 'But under the circumstances, I'd prefer it if you'd let me handle this.'

'Sure,' I say offhandedly. Maybe dishonesty is the best policy. And I don't want to be the one to add another load of shit to Jen's already back-breaking burden.

'Thank you. Come through. Jen – Evie – is in the kitchen.'

I follow her along a wood-panelled passageway, through the door at the end, to where a small, hunched figure is sitting at the table with her back to us.

'Evie?' Abbie moves forward, then gently touches her arm. 'Charlotte's here. Remember I told you she was coming?'

Having seen her in the hospital, I don't know why I'm shocked, but somehow here, her appearance is incongruous, the cosiness of her surroundings only accentuating how frail she looks.

'Hi.' I have a sudden feeling I shouldn't be here. If I were her, I'd want to be alone. 'How are you?'

'OK.' She barely moves, just whispers it.

'Evie?' I have to stop myself calling her Jen. 'Do you

remember when your aunt lived here and we all camped in the woods one summer?'

Jen looks blankly at me, but then I see something flicker in her eyes.

'One of your friends – Sophie – invited me along. I only remembered her as I was driving here. I used to help her with her French homework.' It was the only reason she'd invited me. When she dropped French, she dropped me not long after. 'If I'm honest, we weren't exactly close friends. But I was always so pleased to be included.'

Then Jen turns her head towards me. I can't fathom the look in her eyes, almost as though she knows something I don't. 'I do remember. Charley and Casey. You were friends.'

'You're right.' I attempt a smile, even though I'm uneasy. The friendship had been volatile. Maybe in some ways we were too alike, both of us ungrounded, insecure, vulnerable. 'We were, for a while. But it didn't last. Funny, isn't it, looking back? How short-lived teenage friendships can be?'

She nods vaguely, as I remind myself that old friendships are the last thing on her mind. All she can think about is her daughter.

'Coming back here has been quite a shock,' Abbie Rose says quietly. 'The house isn't as Evie remembers it.'

Jen turns to look at her, then at me. 'It's all wrong,' she says, her eyes suddenly darting around, filled with anxiety. 'It's Angel's room . . .'

I frown. 'What do you mean exactly?'

'Angel's things aren't there,' Abbie Rose answers for her. 'Evie remembers her bedroom being pink, with her toys and books—'

'Someone's taken them,' Jen says tearfully. Then she stares

at Abbie Rose. 'You don't believe me. I can tell from your voice.' She says it accusingly, adding in a different, more desperate voice, 'Charlotte, please, come and see . . .'

Then she's on her feet. Her weakness is obvious as she makes her way to the door, then into the hallway and up the stairs. I walk behind her, worried she's going to miss her footing. When I glance back, Abbie Rose is standing at the bottom, watching us.

'In here.' She stumbles forward, towards the door at the top of the stairs, pushing it open, switching on the light. From the doorway, I watch her. She shakes her head, tears coursing down her cheeks, taking in the plain furniture and old fashioned bedcovers, the dusty rug on worn floorboards.

'Her bed is pink.' Her arms are clutched round herself, as if she's holding herself together. 'There should be a picture.' She points to a bare section of wall. 'Oh God, where are her things?' Suddenly she's shaking, then, without warning, she slumps to the floor.

20

Between us, Abbie Rose and I help Jen along to what appears to be her bedroom. She seems incoherent, but then I realize she's on something to numb the pain and ease the transition of coming back here.

Abbie Rose glances at me. 'I've told Evie we're looking for an explanation. But in the meantime, she needs to concentrate on resting and getting stronger.'

'Can I do anything to help?' I offer.

'Actually, I was going out to buy Evie some food – if you don't mind staying a while? I'll be an hour or so, that's all.'

'OK.' I shrug. It's probably better for Jen to have me for company rather than Abbie Rose, and she's in no fit state to be left alone.

'What about tonight?' I ask suddenly. I can't imagine Jen being alone in this house, tormenting herself with the worst kind of possibilities.

'I know.' Abbie Rose is clearly thinking the same thing. 'I hadn't planned to, but I think I might sleep here tonight.'

'Wouldn't she be better off back in the hospital?'

'*No . . .*' Jen murmurs, then tries to sit up. 'I'm not going there.'

Abbie Rose looks worried. 'She seemed so much better this morning, but being here has really set her back.'

'If you're stuck, I could stay a couple of nights.' The moment I've said it, I want to take it back. Jesus, I'm the last person to be looking after someone in Jen's state, when my own life is enough of a mess.

Abbie Rose looks taken aback. 'Really?' She glances at Jen. 'I'll cover tonight. Can I let you know tomorrow?'

God, I'm thinking, watching from the upstairs window as Abbie Rose walks down the path and disappears through the gate, *why did I offer?* I'll have to invent some excuse as to why I can't. Just being in this house makes me uneasy.

'Would you like a drink?' I ask Jen at last. 'Tea? Coffee?'

She shakes her head, then tries to sit up again. 'I need to look for Angel.' She sits there a moment. 'Can you help me?'

Slowly, I help her down the stairs. She disappears through the kitchen and into a small boot room, and comes out wearing wellingtons and a jacket that swamps her.

Abbie Rose won't be happy about this, but she's not here and I am. And this is Jen's decision, no one else's. As we step outside, she stands there, looking around, taking everything in.

'Do you remember it?' I ask.

She hesitates. 'Some things. The chickens. That tree.' She points to an apple tree, its leaves shades of yellow, its crop of apples fallen on the grass beneath. She carries on walking, stopping in front of me, staring ahead as if she's thinking of something. 'Do you have a garden, Charlotte?'

'Yes. It overlooks the sea,' I tell her. 'You can hear the waves.'

'You hear the wind here. And the birds.' She doesn't turn round. 'Angel feeds the birds.' Her voice wobbles. Then I watch as she squares her shoulders and keeps walking.

I follow her down the garden silently. Already the sun is sinking behind the trees, and in their shadow the air is cool. Jen's right about the birds. Their chatter surrounds us, otherwise it's quiet. As we walk, I'm constantly looking for anything that might indicate a child's presence here.

But there's nothing.

As we walk through a gap in a beech hedge, a large vegetable plot comes into view.

'Look at it.' Jen sounds dismayed.

I follow her gaze. She's right, it looks neglected, with too much going to seed that should have been pulled up. And there are weeds that need ripping out. But then she's walking on; it's not important right now.

At the far end of the garden there's a chicken run. Most of the chickens come rushing over. Do they recognize her? Through the wire, they regard us curiously, as Jen instinctively goes to the shed next to the run and comes back with a scoop full of food; her eyes constantly glance around, no doubt, as mine are, always searching for something of Angel's.

'Angel used to feed them.' She lets herself into the run and empties the corn onto the ground, then just stands there, holding the empty scoop as though she's going to drop it.

Then she's distracted by one of the chickens, which is hunched and unmoving, away from the others. Even when she crouches down and picks it up, it doesn't react. It looks smaller than the others, its feathers fluffed out, its eyes half closed, dull with impending death.

'Where are you going?'

She doesn't answer as I close the run behind her, then follow her as she carries the bird away to a screened-off corner out of sight of the others, acting automatically, doing what it looks like she's done many times before.

After dispatching the sick chicken, she says nothing, just carries its body to the hedge and drops it over the other side.

I'm not squeamish, but it's the unexpectedness – the almost callousness – with which she carries out the act that shocks me.

'It was dying,' she says, matter-of-factly. When you live in the country, you're more aware of how death's an everyday part of life. The hornets that destroy bees' nests. The dead birds a cat leaves by the back door; the mice and voles it torments until they're weak enough for an easy kill; the foxes that slaughter en masse, the carnage they leave behind – heads, whole bodies – that seems so wasteful, so pointless.

Nature's not intentionally cruel. It's about survival and instinct, not revenge or winning wars or hostage-taking. It's not calculating, doesn't inflict pain for the sake of it; for fun, even. That's part of the human domain, which doesn't make sense, because so is love.

It doesn't make sense, either, why someone would take a small child.

21

Overnight, the first storm hits. I'm woken in the early hours by rain battering the windows and the howl of the wind. Later in the morning, through the sheeting rain, I can make out the froth of breaking waves, thrown high by the storm-induced swell.

It's too wild for surfers. I imagine Rick holed up in a cottage somewhere with some of his mates, waiting for the storm to subside just enough for them to paddle out beyond the shore-break. Who knows, maybe it will bring him home.

Unwillingly, I pack an overnight bag, hoping it won't be needed, then throw it in my car and set off for Jen's. As I drive, I feel the power of the wind as I pick my way round fallen branches brought down by last night's storm.

The roads are covered in leaves. Until now, it's been a benign autumn, but the combination of the sudden drop in temperature and storm-force winds have brought a season's worth of leaves down overnight.

The track to Jen's house is awash with mud, and the trees sway in the wind as I pull up behind Abbie Rose's BMW, which is also covered in leaves. Grabbing my bag and pulling my coat up round my neck, I run for the back door. Finding it locked, I hammer on it to be let in.

Abbie Rose opens it. 'Sorry, Charlotte. I wasn't expecting you so early. Come in.'

'Thanks. I brought some things – I wasn't sure if you wanted me to stay.' I say it casually, hoping she's going to tell me it won't be necessary; feeling my heart sinking when she doesn't.

'Help yourself to tea or coffee.' She points in the direction of the larder. 'The doctor was supposed to be calling on Evie, just for a check-up, but with the weather as it is, she's put it off until tomorrow.'

'Cool.' Then I'm silent, looking in the larder at the mountain of tinned food and packets of pulses, the long-life milk. I forget for a moment that she's a detective inspector. 'God. You'd think she was expecting a siege.' Then I add, 'Sorry. It's just weird, don't you think?'

'I think it tells us how worried Evie was about being seen, that she had to stockpile so much food when she did go out.' Abbie Rose pauses.

'How is she today?' I ask.

'More rested. If you're staying, you should know she's on a low dose of Diazepam, to take the edge off her anxiety. She's remembered to take it today, but it might be worth asking her, if you're not sure.'

'OK.'

Abbie Rose stops what she's doing. 'I'm glad you'll be here to keep an eye on her. I think you're good for her.'

'Really?' Her comment surprises me.

'You're the same age, but also, you have the past in

common. I think she appreciates that. After what she's been through, she needs a friend.'

'If you say so.' I've no idea why Abbie Rose trusts me, but in Jen's uncertain world, I suppose I'm the only friend she has.

Jen sleeps most of the morning, through the continuous heavy rain, through the conversation Abbie Rose clearly has in mind to start with me.

'Can you fill me in a bit more on the Danning family? I still don't really understand why they felt the need to ask Evie to babysit when Casey was the same age.'

'Like I said, I didn't really know them at the time. It was obvious Casey and her parents didn't get on. By the time we were friends, it was probably a year or so after Leah had disappeared . . .' I pause, remembering our escapades, our combined recklessness, which came from both of us running from our parents, the rules, the system. We were less intent on the past, more concerned with what the future held. 'I suppose if something happens to your sister, that's when you most need a friend. People weren't kind to her. They didn't understand her.'

Abbie Rose frowns. 'Why was that?'

'I'm not sure.' I try to think how to explain it to her. 'Everyone had decided she was strange, even before Leah's disappearance. She used to dye her hair jet black and she wore it so it hung across her face. Her skin was pale – like alabaster. She was beautiful, unconventionally so, but she'd convinced herself she was ugly. It was as though she deliberately set out to sabotage her looks. I don't know why. Everything seemed to cave in on her. I think she felt the world was against her. She used to cut herself . . .' Poor tortured Casey, her pain carved into her skin. 'It definitely got worse after Leah disappeared. She seemed to self-destruct. She missed a load of school. I think she was in therapy for a while. It was after that, when she came back and we started in the sixth form, that we started hanging out together.'

Then I pause, not sure why I'm holding back. 'Like I said, we weren't friends for long. There was this guy we both liked. There's always a guy, isn't there, Detective Inspector? Anyway, he liked me more than Casey. She couldn't take it. She completely lost it. Never spoke to me again.'

All the time I've been talking, I haven't noticed that Jen has come into the kitchen. Her voice startles me.

'You took her boyfriend.' She says it accusingly. I find myself frowning, because it wasn't like that. We were teenagers, for Christ's sake. A time of selfishness and impermanence. It wasn't like I stole her husband.

'She hated that you were Leah's babysitter, Jen. I'm sorry, Evie . . .' I glance at Abbie Rose. 'She told me how she used to watch you from her bedroom window. You can imagine how she felt. It wasn't personal, though. It was her parents' fault. She'd have felt the same about anyone. She just resented the fact that her mother didn't trust her to look after her own sister. Then after what happened to Leah, she was racked with guilt.'

'Casey wasn't reliable.' The hostility in Jen's voice makes my skin prickle. 'She let people down.'

Suddenly it's like we're back at school, as always, Jen the superior one. I find myself smarting on Casey's behalf. 'I felt quite sorry for her. She never had a chance to prove herself. That was the trouble. She always said that her mother was obsessed with Leah. It was Leah this, Leah that . . . No one paid any attention to Casey.'

'She was crazy. Everyone knew that.' Jen's staring at me, a look of hostility in her eyes.

'You know, I actually don't think she was. Not really,' I say carefully, wanting Jen to see it from Casey's point of view. 'Just very sad and lonely and unloved. As well as emotionally neglected by her selfish, fucked-up parents.' I pause for a moment. 'She had moments she used to go off by herself, but it was hardly surprising. She was a loner. After we left school, she seemed to disappear. Then I moved away.' I shrug.

All the time I'm speaking, I notice Abbie Rose listening intently. I wonder just how many crimes she's trying to solve here, because there are several.

'Did you know she drowned, Evie? The police were never sure if she intended to take her own life,' Abbie says. 'She didn't have a driving licence, but she borrowed a car and drove herself to Porthleven, where she went surfing during a violent storm. This was about a year ago.'

Abbie Rose has been doing her homework. When I think back to our teenage years, it seems like one more typical Casey gesture. A finger up at a world she didn't feel a part of, before she took the matter into her own hands and left it for good – without a thought for anyone else. But she'd always told me people didn't think about her, so why should she have cared?

'Rick's told me about Porthleven – it can be dangerous. Particularly after a storm.'

Abbie Rose nods, then goes on. 'Her board turned up a few days later, smashed to pieces on the rocks. Her body was never found, but given the waves at the time, it was hardly surprising. She'd left a letter in the car. Not exactly a suicide note but enough to make it clear that she'd given up . . .'

She breaks off, reaching a hand out towards Jen, who's sitting at the table, tears streaming down her face, her body racked with silent sobs; maybe guilt, too. But when a child goes missing, they're not the only victim. There are many.

22

I can't help thinking that Abbie Rose seems too preoccupied with what happened to Leah and the Danning family, when she should be more focused on finding Angel. I have the feeling there's something she isn't saying. Something she's discovered, linking Leah's disappearance to Angel's?

Or maybe it's part of a strategy. Jen's starting to remember disjointed fragments of the past that she's trying to piece together. Far from convinced I'm helping Jen, I worry that all I've done is bring up memories that would be better forgotten. I'm thinking about her savage assessment of Casey, too. There's no denying that she was the archetypal bad-ass teenager who hated her parents and flunked her exams, but she had her own take on the world, a world she felt she didn't belong in. No one got her. No one made allowances for how she was, just told her she should snap out of her self-indulgent shit and get over it like everyone else had to.

She'd gone through an emo phase, with that jet-black hair worn draped across her face. So far removed from Jen's girly cliques – all shiny fair hair and pink lip gloss, laughing at anyone who wasn't just like them. They had no idea about the pain that came in waves in Casey's head, or how her heart had been sliced open. Jen's crowd was only skin deep. None of them even thought about what happened on the inside.

There was always a darkness in Casey, a bleakness in her soul, which no one understood. No one ever got in there with her and said *It's OK, babe, I understand* . . . Except for fleeting, brief interludes where she let me in, she was alone.

After our first conversation, she'd shut me out for several weeks, before apologizing.

'I'm really sorry. It's just that something happens and I can't stop myself. It's been freaking me out . . .' Her voice wavered, her black-rimmed eyes were red from crying.

'Tell me,' I'd clutched her arm. 'I'm your friend.' Then I'd hesitated, unsure if declaring my friendship out loud was a step too far, but she threw her arms tightly, awkwardly round me.

'OK.' Pulling away, she swallowed. 'Only if you swear not to tell anyone.'

'I swear.' Who would I tell?

She'd sat there, hunched, not moving for a moment. I wondered what could be so terrible that she didn't want to tell me. Then, as she slowly slid the sleeve up her left arm, I saw.

The more she kept herself from other people, the more irritated everyone was with her. An argument we had comes back to me, where she ended up screaming at me, calling me a selfish fucking bitch who didn't care about anyone. All over a boy, whose name I can't even remember and who made it clear he preferred me to Casey. She was wearing her trademark shapeless, over-sized black clothes, which hid the fact that underneath, she'd lost weight. But they didn't hide her hollow cheeks and tiny, scarred wrists. There was a madness in her eyes that seemed to come from somewhere deep inside her; she was troubled. Most of the time she was on something, too. Drugs and alcohol were the only way to smooth her passage through life.

Whatever. I'd walked away from her. The last thing I needed was a psycho yelling shit at me. Anyone who behaved like that wasn't a friend. I'd had enough of her.

As the afternoon wears on, Jen becomes restless, clearly wanting to go outside. She stands at the window, watching the rain. Abbie Rose goes off to another room to make some phone calls. She shows no sign of leaving and I'm beginning to wonder why she even wants me here.

'It's foul out there,' I say to Jen. 'You wouldn't believe how much water is on the roads.'

She's silent for a moment, then without turning round, she says, 'I wish it would stop.'

I know she's thinking of Angel, wondering if she's safe somewhere, dry, looked after. Or, after Nick denied all knowledge of her and after she found the child's bedroom she pictured wasn't there, can she be thinking the unthinkable? That Angel doesn't exist?

'I know she's out there.' She says it fiercely, as if reading my mind. 'Abbie might not believe me, but I know.' The *I know* is spoken with a quiet ferociousness. Then she turns round and looks at me. 'When this stops –' she means the rain – 'will you help me, Charlotte? Look for her?'

'Of course I will.' I hesitate for a moment, not wanting to tell her that if the police and the extensive search parties haven't found Angel, I'm not sure there's much point. 'Everyone's looking for Angel,' I tell her gently. 'The police have searched the woods and fields for miles around. They were knocking on doors, at one point.' Then I stop, before I make it sound as though there is no hope of ever finding her.

Jen looks exhausted as she sits down on one of the chairs. Painfully thin under the oversized clothes she's wearing, she starts to shiver.

'You're shaking. I'll find you a blanket.'

Upstairs on one of the beds, there's a blue checked throw. I bring it down to the kitchen and wrap it round her shoulders. 'You must try not to worry.' I'm hoping to reassure her, but I can see how impossible that is.

'How can I not?' Her jaw is clenched and she shakes her head bitterly. 'If it wasn't for these bloody pills, I'd be climbing the walls. Do you know how wrong it feels, taking pills to blunt the pain, when I deserve to feel the worst a person can feel?'

'But you don't,' I try to calm her. 'You really don't.'

'I do.' Her eyes are wide as she stares at me. 'Don't you see, Charlotte? I'm all she has and I've let her down.' She pauses, then when she continues, her voice is distant. 'When you're a parent, you're charged with one thing. You keep your child safe. And I've failed.'

I try to distract her. 'Why don't I run you a bath? It's probably good you're resting today. Hopefully the rain will stop and tomorrow we'll be able to start looking.'

It seems to make sense to her. She gets up.

'And then I'll make some supper?'

Jen looks at me doubtfully. 'I'm just going to feed the chickens.'

'I can do it,' I offer. I've no desire to go outside and wade through chicken shit just to feed a bunch of birds, but she looks so small I can imagine the wind blowing her away.

'No,' she says sharply. 'For Christ's sake, I need to get out of this house, just for two minutes.' Her voice rises with every word, as she snatches back the little control she has right now.

'OK.' I hold my hands up, backing off. 'Just trying to help, that's all. Please yourself.' There was no need for her to bite my head off. I remember what Nick said. *I'd stay away from her, if I were you. She's bad news.* I'm beginning to see what he was driving at.

I busy myself hunting in the fridge and the larder, to see what I can cobble together for a meal. I don't notice Abbie Rose come back in.

'Where's Evie?'

'Gone to feed the chickens.' I'm going through the mountain of tins in the larder, trying to see what else is in here.

'I'll go and look for her.' When I turn, Abbie Rose is already walking towards the door. 'I'm not sure we should leave her alone right now. She's not thinking straight.'

'Oh.' I frown, not sure what she's getting at.

The wind catches the door, slamming it behind her as she disappears into the rain. But only seconds later, she's running back towards the house.

'Charlotte?' Abbie Rose stands in the open doorway, rain dripping off her. 'Get your coat. She's gone.'

Jesus. Bloody rain and bloody Jen. I follow her out into the storm. Why the fuck couldn't Jen wait for it to stop? Every so often, Abbie Rose shouts her name.

'*Evie . . .*'

Each time, it's muffled by the rain and the wind through the trees. In no time, my coat is soaked. I wasn't expecting to be tearing through the woods in this. I've no idea where to look. The woods stretch in every direction.

'You go on.' Abbie Rose points towards a path that's covered in fallen leaves. 'I'll go that way. Shout if you find her.' She breaks into a jog and suddenly her urgency is contagious. It'll be dark soon. Jen's frail. A night out here will have her back in the hospital.

I walk faster, and Abbie Rose's shouts grow fainter as she calls 'Evie' again and again. Suddenly, above the rain, I hear another voice, faint, but clear enough.

'Angel . . .'

It's Jen. I listen, trying to gauge which direction it's coming from, running towards it, hesitating for a split second, because if I were her, I wouldn't want anyone to stop me from looking. Then, as she comes into sight, I hear someone behind me. Abbie Rose has heard her too.

She pushes past me. 'Evie . . . We've been worried sick about you. You're soaked. Come on, we need to get you home.'

But Jen wrenches her arm away from Abbie Rose. 'No,' she cries. 'You don't understand. I need to find her . . .'

'It's getting dark.' Abbie Rose turns towards me. 'Charlotte, for heaven's sake, help me.'

I hurry to join them. 'She's right, Evie. We can't do any more tonight. Let's leave it till tomorrow. Like I said, I'll go with you.'

Something seems to get through to her; very reluctantly she turns for home.

'Have a bath,' I say, trying to persuade her when we get back to the house. 'It'll warm you up.'

But after taking her coat off, she just stands there, shaking violently. 'I can't, Charlotte. I can't walk. Help me.'

The day has sapped her strength. She's too weak to make it upstairs. With Abbie Rose and me on either side of her, she makes it through to the sitting room. It takes immense effort to reach the sofa, where we leave her while I go upstairs for some dry clothes. But by the time I come back down, her eyes have closed.

'What were you thinking?' Abbie Rose is quietly furious.

'What do you mean?'

'When I found you, you were standing in the woods, watching her. Were you seriously considering leaving her there?' Her tone is accusing.

I stare at her. 'You know what? I was actually thinking that if I were in her shoes, the last thing I'd want is a pair of interfering busybodies trying to stop me from looking for my daughter.'

There's an icy silence. 'I'm sorry, I overreacted.' Abbie Rose sounds weary. 'I'm worried about leaving her. To be honest, the state she's in, I'm not sure how much more she can take.'

'I'll watch her.'

Abbie Rose sighs. 'It's quite a responsibility to leave you with. If she's no better tomorrow, she may be better off in the hospital. There'll be a police officer outside the house tonight – I'm not sure who, yet. But they'll knock on the door and let you know when they're here.'

She's worrying unnecessarily. 'We'll be fine.'

23

Without disturbing her, I cover Jen with the blanket. When PC Miller arrives for the night shift, she's still sleeping on the sofa.

'She hasn't eaten,' I tell him. Whatever I said to Abbie Rose, she's right about it being a responsibility. I'm concerned that after being outside in the rain, searching for her daughter, along with the enduring stress she's under and going without food and drink, Jen's going to set herself back.

'Probably best to let her sleep,' Miller says. 'I'll be outside if you need me.'

She's still on the sofa the next morning when I go downstairs. It's nearly eight and it doesn't look as though Jen's moved all night. When I check my phone, there's a message from Abbie Rose saying that she'll be here by ten and that a doctor will be calling, but probably not until later on.

'Charlotte?' Jen's voice comes from behind me. Drowsy, she sounds surprised to see me.

I half open the curtains to let some light in. 'How are you?'

She blinks, taking in the blanket covering her. 'I must have fallen asleep . . .'

'You were exhausted. It was walking in the woods.' I watch as the events of yesterday come back to her.

'What time is it?' She starts to get up. I can see from her face the effort it takes.

'It's only just gone eight.'

She's still unsteady on her feet. I can imagine what she's thinking – that she needs to be outside searching for her daughter.

'Has it stopped raining?'

The blanket slips to the floor. I pick it up. 'Just about. Don't you think you need to take it easy today? You could barely walk last night. You don't want to end up back in the hospital.'

'I'm . . . fine.' She tries to walk, then sits down again, looking at me helplessly. 'I have to go out.'

'Evie –' I speak firmly – 'you need to wait for Abbie to get here. She said a doctor's calling in at some point, just to check you over.'

'I don't want to see the doctor.' That she's angry is probably healthy, but it doesn't change the fact that she's verging on extreme exhaustion. 'Can I have a cup of tea?' She's being so brave, but as I look at her, there are tears in her eyes.

'Talk to Abbie when she gets here. Would you like me to help you to the bathroom?' When she doesn't protest, I move closer and take her arm.

After she's washed, she joins me in the kitchen, her weakness clearly showing in each step she takes.

'Here.' As she sits, I place a mug of tea on the table in front of her, then sit down opposite. 'I've made you a bacon sandwich. I hope that's all right?'

She nods, but her hand is shaking as she picks up her mug and tea slops on the table. She puts it down. 'I don't need to see a doctor,' she says, obstinately.

'It won't do any harm. But like I said, talk to Abbie Rose about it.' It's not my place to argue with her. 'You've only just come out of hospital. If the doctor tells you it's fine to go off for hours across the countryside, the police can't stop you, can they?'

The policewoman arrives earlier than expected and I leave her alone with Evie, but from the room next door, I hear them talking about the latest forensic findings PC Miller has brought. They don't seem to amount to much – there was little in the way of fingerprints or personal possessions in the house, and none which appeared to belong to a child.

When I hear one of them moving around the kitchen, I go back in. 'I told Evie I'd walk in the woods with her today.' I look uncertainly at Abbie Rose just as the doorbell rings. 'Do you want me to get that?'

'It could be the doctor.' Abbie Rose glances at Jen, who looks pissed off. 'Thank you, Charlotte.'

Abbie Rose is right. Dr Ghyllen has clear eyes and shoulder-length, greying hair. 'Hi. I'm Charlotte, a friend. Come on through – Evie's in the kitchen.'

Closing the door, I lead her through.

'Hello, I'm Dr Ghyllen. I understand you're having a difficult time.' Her voice is full of compassion. 'It's not surprising that DI Rose was worried about you.'

'There's really no need.' But Jen's voice lacks conviction.

I leave them to it and go upstairs to the room I slept in, listening to snippets of conversation as they filter up through

the floor. After ten minutes have passed, imagining Jen meta-
phorically cornered, I go downstairs and knock on the kitchen
door before entering.

'Sorry to barge in.' I'm right. As they all look at me, Jen's
face looks strained. 'I just wanted to say that I'm happy to
spend time here with Evie, if it means she can stay at home.
I can't move in . . .' I flounder. 'But surely it's better for her to
be here than back in the hospital.'

Abbie Rose looks disapproving. 'The doctor was just saying
that maybe a few more days being looked after and resting is
what Evie needs.'

I shrug. 'There's no reason why she can't have that here. Is
there?' I gaze directly at the doctor. 'As long as she does rest?'

'I can't force Evie to do anything,' the doctor says. 'But you
will rest, won't you?' she continues, addressing her patient.

Gratitude flickers across Jen's face, as the doctor looks at
me, then at Abbie. 'Believe me. I do understand,' she says
finally. 'And I'll agree, but only if you really look after yourself.
Leave the searching to the police. I understand they have a
huge operation going on. If you think of somewhere they
should look, you can tell DI Rose. Isn't that right?'

Catching Jen's eye, I nod.

'OK,' she says quietly.

'Your body needs to rest,' Dr Ghyllen goes on. 'And the
sooner you recover, the sooner you can get back out there.
You can't help your daughter if you don't look after yourself.
I'm going to prescribe you some pills. The same as you had
before, but a slightly higher dose. I think they'll help get you
through the next few days.'

She writes out a prescription, then hands it to Abbie Rose.
Abbie Rose hesitates. 'I don't suppose you could leave it

with the chemist in Truro? I could get one of our officers to pick it up later, on their way here?'

'Of course.' Dr Ghyllen stands up. 'Evie, I'll see you in a few days.'

After she's left, Jen curls up on the sofa again, the blanket pulled over her.

'Evie?' I'm unsure if she's asleep, but as I say her name, her eyelids flicker involuntarily. 'I'm going home for a while. Abbie's here.' I pause. 'Can I get you anything before I leave? Or get anything while I'm out?'

'No. Thank you.' She whispers it, blinking at me, then her eyes close.

Leaving her to rest, I go through to the kitchen, where Abbie Rose is sitting at the table going through what look like more Forensics reports, but the sound of sobbing makes me hurry back to the sitting room. On the sofa, Jen's in agony, crying as though her heart's breaking. Sitting down next to her, I rest my hand on her shoulder. 'Oh, Evie . . . I know how hard this is for you.'

But I don't. I can only guess. Unless you've lost a child, you can't know how it feels. All I can do is offer comfort, letting her cry until she stops.

'I'm starting to remember,' she manages at last, when her sobbing subsides. 'Yesterday, I found a place in the woods . . . We'd made a den. I could even show you.'

'You will show me,' I tell her. 'As soon as you're up to going out again.'

She looks at me. 'It's all there, Charlotte. In my head . . .' Choking on her words. 'In pictures I can't share with you.' Her eyes are filled with pain.

'Tell me,' I urge, watching more tears roll down her cheeks. Then, more gently, I add, 'Tell me what you remember.'

'Her smile . . .' Jen falters. 'Her laugh . . .' Her eyes are haunted as she looks at me. 'How her hair is always tangled from the wind. How she likes to feed the birds.' Her voice cracks. 'She loves pink. Her bed is pink.' A frown flickers across her brow as she thinks of the bed she remembers, that should be upstairs and isn't. 'Every night I used to read to her . . .' Her desperation shows on her face as she looks at me. 'I can't bear it.' Her voice wavers, then she starts to shake uncontrollably.

Casey, 2001

The moment everything changed. When before became after; when a child became an empty space. Life, fucked.

The police came, with dogs and pointless questions. My mother rushing back from work. She thought it was my fault. I could tell from the way she looked at me. But ugly people are to blame for all the evils in the world.

It wasn't Jen's fault, was it? How could it be? She had shiny, fair hair and sparkling blue eyes. Everyone liked her. She couldn't possibly have anything to do with a missing child. Innocence and carelessness weren't deadly. So unfortunate the tragedy happened when Jen happened to be looking after her. Oh, the deluded shit people tell themselves.

Even after, everyone wanted to talk to her. What was it like? What did the police do? What do they think? How do you feel? Blue eyes and pretty hair made everyone rally round you. Poor Jen, who was so trustworthy. How could this have happened? It would be understandable if the sister had been looking after her. That ugly girl who no one likes. What did you say her name was? Their whispers: 'You know what they say about her;' 'It was probably one of her druggie friends.'

I learned so much about people. What they're really like. How shallow, fickle, cruel. So easily swayed by prettiness and money. People like Jen knew the rules. It's how the world works. Play along or suffer, Casey. Dye your hair and smile at the right time; and whatever you do, don't tell anyone how you feel. Bury it away, where no one can force it out of you.

I chose to suffer.

It's a law of nature, of the universe, that there is balance. Leah's disappearance tarnished the fairness of Jen's hair, dulled her eyes. I knew that when she was less pretty, her friends would drift away, leaving her alone. Then, we'd be equal. That was when it was supposed to happen, when the same balance was supposed to lift me up, make my hair shine and skin glow, bring light to my world. It didn't. Jen had taken that away, too.

I wanted to miss my sister. To feel heartbroken and desolate and fractured. Was it wrong that I didn't? Life had taught me to bury my emotions, somewhere where they couldn't hurt me. Now, with my sister gone, how was I supposed to feel? The numbness was supposed to thaw, the feeling return to my fingers, my mind, then my heart, at first smarting, stinging; a prelude to the onslaught of agony.

But apart from hatred of Jen, I felt nothing.

24

Charlotte

When I return to the cottage later that afternoon, the house is silent. Abbie Rose is in the kitchen. There's no sign of Jen.

'Is she OK?'

'She's better than she was.' Abbie Rose switches off her iPad. 'She had soup for lunch, but apart from that, she hasn't moved.'

'I brought a chicken pie. Assuming she eats chicken.' I think of the birds in the garden, wondering if Jen's one of those sentimental nutters who gives them names and thinks of them like people. Then I remember the way she dispatched the sick bird. She definitely isn't.

It's a day during which Jen remains wrapped in confusion, in grief. That's what this immeasurable sense of loss she's feeling is. Grief. For her daughter, their life, their future. No easier because there's the frailest hope Angel may be alive. And if she is, if Jen never sees her again, if she never finds out what's happened, it will be a million times worse.

When PC Miller returns for the night, I give Jen the pills

he's picked up from the chemist, hoping they offer her some respite from the emotions battering her.

The following morning, there's no sign of her on the sofa. Quietly pushing her bedroom door ajar, I see she's in bed, still sleeping. I take it as a positive sign that she got herself up there.

The weather has blown through, leaving a lovely morning, the sun glistening through the trees, the birds in full song. Downstairs, as I draw the curtains and open one or two windows, I hear the sound of someone moving around.

When I go back upstairs, Jen's door is more ajar. 'Hi? Evie?' I knock, then push it open.

'Charlotte?' She's standing by the open window, wearing a jumper over her pyjamas. It hangs off her gaunt frame, drawing attention to how thin she is.

'Hi. I thought I heard you. I wondered if you'd like some help.'

She turns away from the window. 'I was about to come downstairs.'

There's a silent understanding between us as I say, 'I'll help you.'

I get her sitting at the kitchen table, then make her some breakfast, but she doesn't eat much, just nibbles at some toast.

'Thank you for staying with me,' she says at last. 'I mean it. I thought they were going to insist I go back to the hospital.'

'So did I.' I sit down opposite. 'But they can't force you, Evie. Not if you don't want to go.'

'I don't know what the police are thinking.' Suddenly her face is stricken with anxiety. 'I don't understand. Why hasn't anyone seen us?'

Yet again, I'm trying to imagine how it is to have all these disconnected strands of thought, none of which make sense. 'It looks as though you were hiding.' I pause. 'Has anything come back to you?'

She looks blank. 'No.'

'Do you think it's strange that there aren't any medical records?' I ask.

She shrugs. 'I've been thinking about that. But if Angel hadn't been ill since we moved here, I wouldn't have taken her to the doctor, would I?'

It's the only logical explanation. 'It's possible . . .' I hesitate. 'But most mothers of young children like to know they've registered somewhere – just in case.'

'Maybe I was going to . . . I just hadn't got round to it.' Jen looks away.

Outside, I see Abbie Rose walking towards the back door. There's a rush of cold air as she opens it.

'Morning. How are you today?'

Jen nods. 'I'm OK.'

Abbie Rose pulls off her gloves and jacket, then sits down at the table with us. 'Someone else has recognized you from the photo on our Facebook page. A Tina Wells. Apparently she buys your vegetables and eggs for her farm shop.' She looks at Jen expectantly. 'Do you remember her? Her shop is on the outskirts of Wadebridge.'

Jen's frowning. 'I'm not sure.' But as has happened before, the name seems to set a process in motion, as Jen searches for something to link it to.

'Don't worry for now. It may well come back to you later on.' Abbie Rose pauses, a more serious look on her face. 'Evie? There's something else I need to talk to you about.'

There's one of her strategic pauses. 'I'm afraid there's been another attack.'

About bloody time someone told her, I'm thinking, wondering what else Abbie Rose is keeping to herself.

Jen looks ashen. 'Who? When?'

'About a week ago, a girl was found in a field that's part of the same farm where you were attacked.'

'Found?' Jen stares at her. 'Is she dead?' Then more fearfully, 'Why didn't you tell me sooner?'

Abbie Rose pauses, then nods towards me. 'It was actually Charlotte who found her.'

Here, in Jen's kitchen, it seems surreal to hear Abbie Rose talking about the body I found. Jen's reaction makes it plain why the DI's waited so long to tell her, wanting to delay another shock unless absolutely necessary.

Jen's eyes flit from one of us to the other. 'Why?' she says at last. 'Why didn't one of you tell me sooner?'

I want to tell her the truth, which is that I thought she should know, but Abbie Rose asked me not to. 'Honestly, we just thought you have enough to worry about . . .'

'How could you?' Her words are accusing, her eyes glittering with anger. 'Both of you. How could you hide it?'

I glance at Abbie Rose for help. 'Charlotte's right, Evie. You haven't been well.'

'I'm not a fucking child.' Her voice is high-pitched. 'It's linked. It's obvious, isn't it?' She seems to shrink in her chair as she stares untrustingly at both of us.

'There's no proof as yet, but yes, we're considering the possibility. Two attacks at around the same time and the same place, seems quite a coincidence.' Abbie Rose speaks quietly.

'How did you find her?' Jen's eyes bore into me.

'I was walking – along the coast path. I saw these birds circling. It seemed odd, so I went to look.' The image comes back to me, of the mutilated flesh, the dried blood. I try to block it out.

'Do you know who she is?'

'We think so.' Abbie Rose pauses. 'She was a local girl – only twelve years old. She was reported missing by her teacher two weeks ago. Apparently, she was always going off on her own, so to start with, no one thought much of her disappearance.'

'Not even her mother?' Jen's incredulous.

I can imagine what Jen's thinking, because I'm thinking the same. How can a mother let her child go off, for days on end, without even knowing where she's gone?

Abbie Rose sighs. 'According to everyone we've talked to, Tamsyn did what she liked when she liked . . .'

A look of shock crosses Jen's face. 'What did you say her name was?'

'Tamsyn.' Abbie Rose frowns at her. 'Why? Do you know—'

But Jen interrupts. 'What does she look like?'

'Tall for her age. And lanky. With red hair and freckles.' Abbie reaches for her phone, scrolling through emails until she finds what she's looking for. 'Here.'

As she passes it to Jen, her hand goes to her mouth and her eyes widen with horror as she recognizes the girl. Looking across, even on the small screen, there's an attitude in the set of the girl's chin, the look of defiance in her eyes.

Suddenly tears are pouring down Jen's face.

'You know her, don't you?' After Jen's lack of clarity about almost everything, it seems like a breakthrough. Abbie Rose looks at her sharply. 'Do you have any idea how? Or where you might have seen her?'

But her hopes are short-lived, as Jen shakes her head. 'All I remember is her face.'

'It's strange you know her.' She looks at Jen more closely. 'When you think no one round here seems to know you, and no one's looking for you. With the exception of Nick and Charlotte and Tina Wells from the farm shop, she's the only person so far who's familiar to you. I have to call the station and let them know. When you think of her, does anything else come to mind?'

'No . . .' Jen shakes her head. 'Just her laughing. Loudly. She was outside. She wasn't with anyone. That's all I can remember.'

'OK . . .'

When Jen falls silent, I can't help wondering if this will trigger her to remember more.

I go outside to feed the chickens. By the time I come back, unbelievably after Abbie Rose's revelations, Jen's curled up on the sofa, asleep.

'It's probably a good thing,' Abbie Rose says quietly. 'She needs to rest in order to heal.'

Gathering my things together, I'm about to go back home for the day when I hear Jen calling out.

I follow Abbie Rose to the sitting room, where Jen's sitting with an expression on her face I haven't seen before.

'I had this dream. When I woke up, I could remember things – about the past and Nick and where we lived. In detail. It's happening. My memory's coming back.'

25

'I don't remember before or after,' she says urgently, as Abbie Rose sits in the armchair with her notebook, while I hover on the edge of the sofa. 'It's like looking at a single chapter of my life – in isolation. Nick's in it. We're not in this house, though.'

'This is good, Evie.' Abbie Rose gets out her phone. 'Do you mind if I record you? That way, you can just talk, freely. It's probably better than stopping and starting while I write.'

'OK.' Jen waits for her to set her phone to record.

'It's on. You can start.'

Jen begins. 'We'd been looking for a family home. Not too far for Nick's commute. But we needed space, Nick said. Air that didn't reek of traffic fumes. Somewhere quiet enough so that when you sat outside, you strained your ears to hear anything. It was Nick who found it. The first time we went there, I remember just staring at the rambling house in front of me. I wasn't in love with it. I wanted to be, if only to share how Nick was feeling, but it was too big. Too dark; an L-shape of grey-brown stone and clapboard the colour of tree bark.

'Nick was ecstatic, striding around the outside, enthusing

madly about everything. His eyes were bright with excitement, with his dreams. I could tell from his face it wouldn't matter what I said. He'd already moved us in.' She pauses. 'Nick was a dreamer. I knew all his boxes, too, and this ticked every one of them. He'd found his house, with room to host parties and big, noisy family Christmases. The family house he wanted us to grow old in. I remember I was gazing at it, when he came up behind me and grabbed me, holding me still, not moving. Whispering. "This is what silence sounds like."

'I listened, hearing nothing, not a voice, nor a single car; and a feeling of fear came from nowhere. Fields separated us from our nearest neighbours. After city life, it was quiet, with too many twisted pines and oaks that were knotted with age. It looked as though someone had reached in, parted the canopy of branches and placed the house beneath.

'As I'd stepped inside through the front door that first time, I remember I shivered. It sounds weird, but the house felt hostile, almost as though it didn't want us there.

'It needed too much work. It was far from perfect. We'd talked all weekend about it, until Nick persuaded me that we should make a silly offer and leave it in the lap of the gods. Convinced we didn't have a chance, I let him, but I was wrong.

'We'd already had an offer on our own house and I'd never got round to telling him that I couldn't shake my sense of unease, that I just felt my life spiralling out of control. After that, it had all happened so fast, so effortlessly. We moved in on the hottest day of the year. I remember being in one of the bedrooms, pausing, leaning on the windowsill, looking down at the parched lawn, at the flowers bravely holding up in the heat, then across the garden towards the woods.

'I wasn't sure about the woods. After living in a town, they were too dark, stretched for too many miles. Anyone could be out there and you wouldn't see them. I always felt someone could have been watching me and I wouldn't have known. It was his dream. Not mine.'

I'm flabbergasted by the detail with which she recalls what happened. Then uncertainty flickers on her face.

'Are you OK?'

She nods. 'It's just . . .' She breaks off. 'How can I be sure that what I've remembered is real? It doesn't seem like I'm talking about my life. I don't feel anything. It's as though I'm talking about someone else's.'

I'm not sure, either. It doesn't sound like the Nick I met.

'Take your time, Evie. It's OK.' Abbie Rose tries to reassure her.

'I don't *think* I didn't want to move there.' She goes on. 'I *know* I didn't. The house was too big. And just now, talking to you, I've remembered how unhappy I felt.'

'What happened between you and Nick?' Abbie Rose sounds curious.

She's silent; thinking. 'It feels like that house changed something – or something happened while we lived there. It must have.'

'And this was before Angel was born?'

Jen nods. 'I can't remember exactly when we moved there, but that would make it at least four years ago. What I told you just now . . . I remember it's how he was. Always pushing me, to want what he wanted. Frustrating me, because he never listened.'

'You don't remember how long ago you split up?' I can see what Abbie Rose is doing, trying to fill in the gaps in Jen's fragmented narrative.

But suddenly it's as though she's said enough. 'I've told you everything I know,' she says, anxiously.

'It may seem confusing now,' Abbie Rose tries to calm her. 'Think of it like jigsaw pieces. On its own, each piece doesn't tell you much, but the more of them you put together, the more of a picture we can build. It's OK, Evie. At some point, all of this will make sense. I'm sure of it.'

Her reassurance seems to work, but Jen's frown returns. 'It's Tamsyn.' She's clearly anxious. 'What if her disappearance is connected with Angel's in some way? Could she have seen someone take her? Could it be the same person who went after me?'

I'm silent. But maybe somewhere in the depths of her damaged mind, it's Jen who has the answers.

I can't get out of there fast enough. Jen's fear, anxiety, uncertainty; they're a miasma, filtering through from room to room, until the entire house is infected. In my car, with my music turned up earsplittingly loud, a sense of normality returns.

But as I drive home, too late I remember my promise to Jen that I'd go walking in the woods with her. Not that she's up to it yet. I can imagine Abbie Rose voicing her disapproval. But I know, also, that my escape is no more than a brief respite. Later this afternoon, I'll be compelled to drive all the way back, a fly in a spider's web – needing answers as much as Jen does. Trapped.

*

Living where Jen does, someone could have watched her house for weeks. She would never have known. As I drive back there a few hours later, I imagine a child abductor surveying their next victim – victims, because Jen's one too. I wonder about the thoughts that must torment Jen; was she lured away and beaten almost to death before they came back here for Angel? Or did they somehow get in and take Angel first? Did Jen go upstairs, tiptoeing across the bedroom, bending down to kiss that little pink cheek, her heart stopping as she found an empty bed, her child gone? Pitched into every parent's worst nightmare as she ran outside, through the woods and across fields, screaming her daughter's name. Maybe Jen had heard her scream, and followed her voice like a seagull's cry on the wind across the dark landscape, desperate to find her daughter, her Angel.

26

As I turn off the main road, Abbie Rose's car drives down the track towards me, heading away from Jessamine Cottage. I pull over to let her pass, but she slows down and lowers her car window. 'I'm glad you're here, I have to get back to the police station. Evie's distracted. She wanted to go walking in the woods; I managed to persuade her to stay at the house, but tomorrow I think it might be more difficult.'

I nod. 'OK. I'll talk to her. I was going to stay overnight again.'

'Thank you, Charlotte. I'll see you tomorrow.'

When I park alongside the hedge outside Jen's house, I get a sense of what she must be feeling, of how she must always be wondering if she's being watched by an unknown presence; never sure. There are no neighbours here, no one to call out to. I'm aware of fear, too – Jen's fear surrounds me, so tangible I can almost touch it.

When I get inside, she's rummaging through one of the large kitchen cupboards.

'What are you doing?'

'I can't find it.' Her voice is agitated. She opens another cupboard, pulling out the contents.

'What are you looking for?'

'My gun.'

I'm taken aback. 'What kind of gun?'

'An air rifle. It's usually in the cupboard under the stairs. I only remembered it this morning. I went to get it but it's not there.'

Another memory unlocked or her imagination? I go along with what's she's saying. Isn't that what you're supposed to do? 'Are you sure it was there? Perhaps you moved it.'

'I've checked all the cupboards. Do you think Forensics have taken it?'

'Why don't you ask? Why do you need it?' Why is she worried about her gun, now of all times? Maybe there's another reason. Maybe she's frightened and having her gun to hand makes her feel safer.

'I don't.' Then she stops looking and turns to face me. 'It's just that it should be there, but it's not.'

'When did you last see it?'

A noise comes from her – exasperation, tinged with impatience. 'I can't remember. I probably used it to shoot a rabbit.'

'You shoot?' The picture I have of Jen doesn't fit with the image of a woman who kills for sport.

'I learned. Have you seen the rabbits, Charlotte? Crawling around disfigured and blind, with myxomatosis? They're the walking dead. It's kinder to shoot them.' She's matter-of-fact, and I'm reminded again of the way she killed the sick chicken.

Her eyes are expressionless. 'I wanted Angel to understand how a quick death from a gun is kinder than a long, drawn-out one from disease. I wanted her to see –' her voice wobbles – 'that death can be a release.'

It seems a lot for a small child to take in. As she speaks, it's not hard to see it isn't rabbits she's thinking about, it's her daughter. I try to distract her. 'Is there anywhere else we should look?'

'I've looked everywhere.' Her eyes are filled with panic. 'It's gone.'

'Come on. I'll help you tidy up.'

She doesn't protest. When everything's put away, I put the kettle on and she goes through to the sitting room. After another day where the police seem no closer to finding Angel, she's exhausted.

The rain starts. I can hear it on the windows, light at first, steadily growing heavier. It's obvious we won't be going out in the woods now, and I say so. As it grows darker, Jen starts pacing from room to room like a caged animal. I realize then that she's teetering on a cliff edge. Waiting for the worst to happen. Waiting to fall.

'You need to remember there's a huge investigation going on,' I tell her. 'You do realize, don't you? Officers have been drafted in from neighbouring stations, and the public are help-ing with the searches. Photos are being circulated. Everything's being done that can be done.'

She nods, her face devoid of colour. 'Outside . . . When the police first came here, there would have been footprints. Mine, Angel's, the person who took her . . .' She seems dis-tracted. 'Would Forensics have checked?'

I nod. 'I'm sure they would have. Talk to Abbie about it. She'll be able to tell you exactly what they've done.'

'She would have told me, wouldn't she – if they'd found anything.' Her voice is dull.

I'm silent. I suppose she would have.

She goes on. 'After she didn't tell me about Tamsyn, I'm not sure what to think. What else do you think she's hiding?'

I shake my head. 'She hasn't said anything to me. Look, about Tamsyn, I wanted to tell you, Evie. I really did. Abbie Rose asked me not to.'

Jen's silent for a moment. When she looks up, her voice is ferocious. 'If there's anything else, will you tell me? Charlotte? Will you promise?'

Jesus. I promise, just to keep her quiet, even though it's a promise I may not keep. 'If I were in your shoes, I'd want to know too.'

Too early, it's half dark outside, the sky heavy with more rain that's been swept in off the Atlantic, battering against the side of the house.

Jen brings her tray through to the kitchen. She's barely eaten anything. As I wash up, she just stands there, not saying anything. After the frenzied restlessness of earlier, there's something disturbing about her blankness.

I turn round suddenly. 'Are you taking the pills the doctor prescribed?'

She nods. A strange look comes over her face, as though she can hear something I can't. Then she whispers, 'He left me.'

I look up sharply. 'You mean Nick? Are you sure?'

She's nodding. 'It's what happens,' she whispers. 'People leave me.' Then her eyes start to close.

I take her arm and lead her towards the table. After what Nick told me, what Jen herself has remembered, it makes no sense. 'Tell me.'

Very slowly, she pulls out one of the chairs and sits down, a look of confusion on her face. 'After Nick had gone, I remember staring blankly at the windows as the daylight faded, as the trees turned into silhouettes, until all I could see was myself reflected in the glass. I had this thought.' She breaks off, then shakes her head. 'It was like I was on the outside staring in. Why do I remember that?' She falls silent. 'There's something else I remember, too. This picture, of Nick, laughing, taking my hand, pulling me outside, where the rain has stopped and the sun's so bright it's blinding me. I can hear giggling – it's Angel, wearing a pink tutu over her jeans, dancing across the grass towards me, her small, plump hand reaching for mine.'

Outside, a crack of thunder makes us both jump. I get up and close the window. 'That's some storm out there.'

But she doesn't reply, instead leans forward, holding her head in her hands. Then she looks up again. 'I can remember Nick and Angel, the three of us together.' I watch the blood drain from her face. 'It doesn't make sense,' she whispers.

She's right. It's completely impossible. Then another explanation occurs to me – *unless Nick was lying*. But why would he do that?

'Me and Nick with Angel.' She's whispering again. 'That's the memory – our happy little family. Except we weren't, were we? He didn't know about her.'

I watch her. She's torn between the few facts she has and

the drift of ghostly images from her past. 'What I remember didn't happen. It couldn't have . . .' She whispers it again, clearly terrified. Then she's sobbing. 'I feel like I'm going mad . . . What's happening to me?'

27

'Evie . . .' I try to calm her. 'You mustn't worry – it's your mind playing tricks. I don't understand why, but it's like it's connecting the wrong things together.'

'But I saw us, Charlotte.' She's still sobbing. 'Me and Nick and Angel . . .'

'You couldn't have,' I tell her firmly. 'Nick said he didn't know about Angel. Maybe it was your dream, what you wished for, when you had your miscarriage.'

'You think so?' She raises tear-filled eyes to meet mine. 'Can you imagine what it's like? Having all these memories that aren't real?'

'No,' I say truthfully. I'm way out of my depth with all this. 'But listen – when Abbie Rose gets here tomorrow, she needs to get that doctor to come back, or refer you, or something. This must happen all the time, after head injuries. Or maybe you just need more rest – and time. But whatever, you need someone to reassure you.'

'You think?' She desperately wants to believe me.

'It's OK,' I tell her quietly. 'It'll all be OK.'

It seems to calm her. She stares blankly ahead. 'That memory, of the three of us, it seemed so real.'

'I know. But you know how dreams can be so vivid that when you wake up, you're sure they're real? Maybe it's like that?'

It seems to satisfy her – for now. She gets up, her arms tightly wrapped round herself, as if otherwise she'd fall apart, then walks over to the window, staring outside, unseeing.

That she's trying to make sense of things – and failing – is knocking what little confidence she has. Even the weather seems to reflect the turmoil she's feeling. There's another crash of thunder and the intensity of the rain picks up, hammering on the window, for a moment drowning everything else out. If I were Evie, alone in this house, after everything that's happened, I'd be terrified.

I go upstairs to draw the curtains, then head into the bathroom, where the rain is blowing through an open window, soaking the curtains. I close it, leaving the curtains dripping on the windowsill. When I go downstairs again, Jen's gone.

As I start checking all the rooms on the ground floor, the lights go out. It's the storm. After feeling my way into the kitchen, I fumble around and find my phone, looking for the torch on it as a flash of lightning briefly illuminates the room.

'Evie?' There's no reply. I try to think if I've seen a fuse box anywhere. Using my torch, I finish searching the rooms, aware that the front door has been blown open in the wind. I slam it shut and try the lights again, but they're dead.

My heart is thumping. 'Evie?' There's still no reply. Going

through to the hallway, I call upstairs. 'Evie? It's Charlotte. Are you there?'

There's no sign of her. Were we being watched? Did someone open the front door or has Evie gone outside?

My hands are shaking as I fumble with my phone to call Abbie Rose, but there's no signal. I can tell from the wind howling through the house that the front door has blown open again. This time, when I go to close it, I see a light outside. There's someone out there, coming up the path. In the dark, in the heart of this storm, I'm completely terrified as the figure walks up the steps and stands in the doorway.

A light is shone in my face, and I realize with relief who it is.

'Jeez, you gave me a fright. What's going on here?' PC Miller closes the door behind him.

'I'm worried about Evie. I can't find her anywhere.'

'I'll see if I can get the lights on.' He walks down the hall, shining his torch around. 'Do you know where the fuse box is?'

'No. I'll search the bedrooms.'

I leave him looking as I head up the stairs. Halfway up, a flash of lightning illuminates the staircase and I call out again. 'Evie? Are you there?'

Finding the first two bedrooms empty, I hurry to the third. Then I hear a whimper just as the lights come on. She's crouched in the corner, a look of terror on her face. I wonder if hearing the door fly open, and people walking around, has brought back the memory of being attacked.

Very slowly, I go over and sit down beside her, then take her hand.

When we go downstairs, PC Miller's still there. 'Up to you,

but if you'd like me to, I could sit down here tonight – rather than in my car. Only if you don't mind? Just till this storm has passed.'

Jen's relief is palpable. 'Thank you.'

28

The storm leaves a blue sky and a still landscape of rain-washed grey stubble fields. Beyond the hills, the smallest sliver of sea – the colours clearer, brighter, after last night's deluge.

The ground is still damp when I go outside to feed Jen's chickens. That so much rain has fallen is a nightmare for the police. Any remaining evidence will have been washed away. As I go back in, I see Abbie Rose walking up the path, and I wait.

'She's not great,' I tell her. 'Last night, when I got here, she was looking for her air rifle. She said she used to shoot rabbits with myxomatosis.' I look at Abbie Rose. 'She couldn't find the gun. Later, she had all these memories that didn't make sense. It really upset her. Then there was the storm and the lights went out . . . Nightmare.'

'Forensics found an air rifle.' Abbie Rose is frowning. 'What did she remember?'

'In a nutshell?' I pause. 'Her and Nick and Angel, the happy little family – her words, by the way. Of course, she knows they weren't. Her mind had created an image that felt completely real to her – she'll tell you about it. Right now, I'm not sure she trusts herself.'

Abbie Rose shakes her head. 'You're sure that's what she said?'

I nod. 'She described it vividly. But at the same time, she knows it couldn't have happened. I wondered if it could have been a kind of wish fulfilment thing after her miscarriage. Of course, the other explanation is that Nick's lying.' But I don't think he was. He was too emotional. Liars are cold and calculating. Nor am I sure he's smart enough to tell a convincing lie, and certainly not twice, to both me and the police.

Abbie Rose shakes her head. 'He didn't lie. He has an alibi – at least for the night that the attack took place. We're interviewing his mother, so hopefully that will shed more light on their relationship.'

I shrug. 'Do you think Evie should see someone? A shrink? It's hard to tell if anything she's saying is real.'

'I know. I'll talk to the doctor. Thanks, Charlotte. Have you checked on her this morning?'

'I thought I'd leave her to sleep. After last night, I didn't want to disturb her.'

Maybe it's because she knows Abbie Rose is here, but as we go into the kitchen, there's the sound of someone moving around upstairs. Then a few minutes later Jen appears in the kitchen doorway.

'Evie. How are you? Charlotte was just telling me about the storm and the lights going out. Did you manage to sleep?'

Jen looks tired. She nods, then she looks at the photos Abbie Rose places on the table.

'You've seen them before. They're the ones from school.' They're the photos of a group of girls in sports kit, wielding hockey sticks. 'I thought we should look at them again – later. Why don't you have some breakfast?'

It's another attempt to remove one of the layers of doubt that have settled over Jen's life. But after last night, I wonder if she's up to it. I watch as she looks at the photos, homing in on the girl with fair hair and laughing eyes, which so clearly is her.

Spreading the photos on the table, she studies the faces of the other girls, saying nothing. It's the same in all of them; a teenaged Jen stands out from the others.

For ages, she stares at the table. 'I wish I could remember,' she says at last. Even though Abbie Rose is trying to help her, it's as though she's creating an identity Jen doesn't relate to. Suddenly tearful, she pushes the photos across the table. 'I've still been attacked, my child is still missing . . . Nothing else matters, don't you see?'

When I get home, I'm astonished to find Rick's Jeep parked outside. When I go in, he's sprawled on the sofa, his large feet hanging over the end of it, the silence of the empty house punctuated by his snores. I go through to the kitchen, putting on the kettle and opening the fridge to look for some breakfast, then change my mind. Rick's presence has unsettled me. After days without any communication, I've no way of knowing if he's still angry with me.

Maybe it's the remains of last night's hangover – I drank a bottle of wine once Jen had gone to bed. But now I'm home, the house that usually fills me with a sense of security suddenly feels claustrophobic. In the boot room, I pull on my running shoes.

The early morning chill has long gone, giving way to a

glorious autumn day as I walk across the grass towards the coast path, then turn west towards the distant outline of the Rumps, trying to tune out the noise in my head; breathing in the pure sea air, then exhaling, feeling the pressure of everything that's going on, needing life to be simplified.

I get back an hour later, closing the door quietly so as not to disturb Rick. It doesn't work. His body twitches, then his eyes open and he yawns. 'Hey, babe. You just got back?'

'For the second time,' I tell him unnecessarily, hoping the 'babe' means he's in a better mood than when I last saw him. But my head is still full of what's happening to Jen. 'Where've you been, Rick?' I perch on the edge of the armchair opposite.

He pulls himself up so he's sitting on the sofa. 'Sennen,' he says briefly. 'How about you?' He looks at me suspiciously. 'Where've you been?'

'For a walk.'

He stares at me for a moment, then he laughs, but not a friendly laugh. 'Yeah, right, Charlotte. I got back last night. I waited up. Where were you?'

'With a friend.' Then I clam up, because I don't like his tone of voice.

'Yeah. Like you have friends.' He says it softly, folding his arms, watching me.

'If you must know, I was at Jen's. I'm doing something useful, Rick, like you're always nagging at me to do. She can't manage on her own, so I'm helping her – just until she's better.'

'Nice try,' he says sarcastically.

But I can't be bothered to explain further. 'You know what, Rick? It's none of your fucking business.' Turning round, I storm upstairs.

'You always do that, don't you?' I hear him shout after me. 'Yeah, Charlotte. Run away. Like it solves everything.'

Much later that afternoon, after Rick's gone out again, my mobile buzzes. It's Abbie Rose.

'Hello?' I walk across to the window, where the signal is stronger.

'Charlotte? It's DI Abbie Rose. Are you at home?'

'Yes.' Too late, I'm wishing I'd said no. I see enough of her at Jen's. I don't really want her coming here.

'I'm on my way home. I wasn't sure if you were going back to Evie's tonight?'

I hesitate, thinking of Rick. 'I'm not sure. Do you think she'll be OK on her own?'

'I wondered if I could call in briefly. We could talk about it then. It won't take long.'

I give in to what seems inevitable. 'All right, Detective Inspector. I'll be here.'

When she arrives five minutes later, my heart sinks further. What I'd really like to be doing is uncorking one of the bottles in the fridge, then drinking it by the open window, watching the sea, forgetting about Jen and Rick; letting today wash away into a distant memory.

Abbie Rose clearly has other ideas.

'Come in, Detective Inspector.' I stand back to let her in, then close the door and walk over to the sofa. 'Would you like to sit down?'

'Thank you. I've arranged for PC Sara Evans to stay with Evie tonight. I thought you could do with a night off.'

Resentment rises in me. I'd been dreading the idea of going back to Jessamine Cottage again, but I don't like people making decisions for me. 'Whatever.' Then I add, 'As long as she's OK.'

'She'll be fine.' Abbie Rose frowns. 'Actually, I wanted to talk to you about Tamsyn.' I raise my eyebrows. 'I didn't ask you earlier. Did you know her?'

'No, I didn't.' I pause. 'I've never heard of her. I told the police who came to the field where she was found everything I know.'

Abbie Rose looks thoughtful. 'We've been looking back into the Leah Danning case. Does the name Xander Pascoe mean anything to you?'

As she speaks, bile rises in my throat and, with it, a whole chunk of the past that I thought I'd buried for good.

'He went to my school,' I say evasively, intentionally keeping my voice cool. 'He wasn't really my kind of guy.' It isn't a lie. For a while I thought he was, but he proved otherwise.

'Can you tell me anything about him?'

I wonder if she notices my hesitation. I shake my head. 'I'm not sure I can.'

Abbie Rose frowns slightly. 'You said he was at your school. Can you remember who he used to hang out with? Or anything at all about him?'

'I didn't really know him.' What's she expecting me to say? Even when you spend a lot of time with someone, how well do you ever know them? 'My friends were mostly in the same year as me. He was older. You know what it's like at that age.'

Maybe my answer is too fast. Even without looking at her, I can feel Abbie Rose's eyes fixed on me. I wait for the next question. She's thinking – taking her time.

'You see . . .' She pauses again. When she looks at me, it's clear she doesn't believe me. 'You were friends with Casey Danning, weren't you?'

'Yes.' Uneasily, I wonder where she's going with this.

'Casey and Xander were an item for a while. It's been confirmed by several people who knew them at the time. I would have thought, being her friend, you would have known that, too.'

'Of course I knew.' I try to shrug it off. 'But I didn't have anything to do with Xander. He was Casey's boyfriend, not mine. We'd fallen out by the time she hooked up with him. You asked me if I could tell you anything about him. I can't.' It's all true. I watch her lips tighten as she thinks.

'Let me reword my question,' she says at last, looking directly at me. 'How about this, Charlotte. What exactly do you know about Xander Pascoe?'

I feel my breath taken away as I stare at her.

Do you have any idea, Abbie Rose, what you're asking?

29

Why did she have to come here? I thought this was about Jen. Not Leah Danning and Xander Pascoe and Tamsyn. Can't she see none of them have anything to do with this?

Should I lie? Is this one of those instances where it's better for everyone if the truth doesn't come out? Abbie Rose is still watching me. She knows I'm holding back. And I haven't lied to her. Not yet. But now, I have to. I have no choice.

'If you want to know, Xander Pascoe was bad news for anyone and everyone he got involved with. He had his own Cornish mafia, for want of a better way of describing it. Everyone knew that if you wanted something done, Xander could take care of it for you – as long as you had money, of course. If you crossed him, you had to watch your back. The teachers hated him. He was a perfect example of how you didn't need exam results if you had a sharp brain and an eye for business.'

'So why the secrecy?'

'I don't think you'll find many people who are prepared to spill the beans on Xander Pascoe,' I say cautiously. 'People were frightened of him. It was years ago, I know, but I'd still be wary about crossing him. But also, I suppose, I feel a loyalty to Casey.' I shrug. 'Xander treated her really badly. She got dragged into everything he was involved in. And she'd already been through so much.'

'So why are you protecting him?'

'I'm really not.' My voice is unintentionally heated at her comment. Then I get a grip of myself. 'You can't talk about Xander at that time without Casey being involved in some way too, just by association. It's how it was. It's difficult to tell you anything about Xander without making Casey look bad. In all honesty, there's nothing good to say about him. He screwed everyone over. And I don't really want to dredge up the past.'

Abbie Rose doesn't say anything. What I've told her is true. There's no reason why she shouldn't believe me, but for some reason, I know this wasn't the answer she was looking for.

'When did you last see Xander?' she asks eventually.

I shrug. 'Years ago. I couldn't say how many.'

'Would you have any idea if Jen knew him? Assuming you'd tell me?'

There it is. On the table between us. Her suspicion of my lack of honesty and my reticence to tell her what I know.

'Honestly? I don't think she did. Pretty little rich girls with expensive clothes and long, flowing hair really weren't Xander's type.' Again, it's the truth – and I don't mean to sound bitter but it's out before I can stop myself.

Abbie Rose looks interested. 'Oh? What was Xander's type, exactly?'

I shrug. 'Casey was . . . She and Jen couldn't have been more different. They knew each other only because they were in the same year at school, not because they were friends. Then Casey's mother asked Jen to babysit. You can imagine how that made Casey feel. I'm mean, her own mother, for Christ's sake . . . Sorry, Detective Inspector. Like I said, I can't really tell you any more than that.'

It seems to satisfy her, but only for now. I know she'll have more questions. It's a kind of dance, her questions and my answers, both of us tiptoeing around each other. It can't go on. I glance pointedly at my watch, hoping she'll take the hint. She does.

As soon as I close the front door behind her, I walk through to the kitchen. Knowing I don't have to drive this evening, I fetch a glass and the bottle of white rioja from the fridge, then take them outside, pulling a fur throw from the back of one of the armchairs as I pass.

It's dusk. My mind is elsewhere as I make for the wooden table at the far side of the garden, where I sit looking out over the bay. Wrapping the throw round me, I pour the wine, drinking the first glass quickly, then the second more slowly as I go over the day's events: Rick coming home, clearly still unhappy with me; the mention of Xander Pascoe; the memories of the past dredged up.

Abbie Rose is good, but even so, this is challenging her. She's not like other police officers I've come into contact with. She's intuitive; seems to know instinctively what to ask.

I wonder if she's asked Jen the same questions. Even if she has, there's a fundamental problem with everything Jen says right now. Poor Jen, with her memory shattered into a million pieces, most of them scattered out of reach. Last night proved that her answers, however convincing they seem, are meaningless. She's unreliable. Without proof, no one can believe a word she says.

By the time I've drunk most of the bottle, it's almost dark. There's still no sign of Rick. He's probably drinking beer somewhere, reliving the day's waves with some of his mates. I'm glad. Today's events have unsettled me. I've always thought Rick and I are uncomplicated; about drinking and sex, which is fine by me. I've no desire to share anything more with him, yet there's something he's not happy about. I'm sure of it.

Pulling the throw closer round me, I shiver, but I'm not ready to go inside. It's too beautiful out here, the last of the sunlight fading into the horizon as the first of the stars become visible overhead. It takes a bottle of wine and all of this, the vastness of the dark sky, the sound of waves crashing against the layers of purple-hued slate below, the sense of solitude, for my mind to at last become still.

Then I think of Casey. How she let the sea carry her away from all her troubles. How easy it would be to do that right here, in the bay below. If you picked the right time of year, a big enough storm, the right swell, it would be so easy. It's possible to reach the waves without anyone seeing you. No houses overlook the narrow footpath through the gorse bushes that leads down to the rocks below. If you were desperate enough, if you didn't want anyone to ever find you, a hair's breadth separates you from the might of the elements, the fragile boundary between life and death.

My thoughts are interrupted by the sound of a car swinging round, too fast, on the gravel drive. *Rick*, I'm thinking irritably, *the stupid fucker*, before realizing it's too powerful to be his car, which means he's probably drunk and some of his friends have brought him back.

Reluctantly getting up, I'm wishing they hadn't and had just left him to sleep it off in one of their camper vans. Then as I start walking back across the grass towards the house, I hear the crunch of footsteps, before a figure comes into sight. It's silhouetted against the light from inside the house. Sudden panic flickers inside me. It's taller, broader than Rick – just for once, I dearly wish it was him. As I watch, from his stance, the way he's walking towards me, I know exactly who he is.

Casey, 2001

It was the start of a time I remember little of. And when it was over, nothing would ever be the same.

Life had lessons for me – things only cruelty can teach you. That, or loss. I learned how simple it was. How you gave people what they wanted. You didn't confront them, didn't challenge them. That way they left you alone.

'She's upset about Leah,' my mother kept saying.

'You mustn't be surprised if you have feelings of anger,' the doctor told me. 'When something like this happens, it's usual to feel angry and upset. And, however illogical, guilty, too.'

I hung my head; nodded now and then, enough so they knew I was listening.

I even said, 'But I do. Feel so guilty.' It was true. Guilt hung over me, its heaviness clogging up my lungs, suffocating me, just not for the reasons they imagined, but I couldn't tell them about the scenes I'd given life to on my bedroom wall. Giving them what I knew was an acceptable response. Glancing at my mother, my lip wobbling.

'If you ever need someone to talk to,' the doctor was saying, 'we can arrange it for you.'

I nodded, but my sight had blurred and I was trying to focus. The doctor seemed to have two faces. The friendly, understanding one, but there was another, too; more menacing, that snarled over the desk at me in the silences.

Did everyone have two faces? The one they liked you to see, and one that came out when they dropped their guard and showed what they were really like? As the friendly face looked at me again, I shrank in my chair. I knew the menacing, snarling part of her was there, it was just hiding.

Your best face, I thought distractedly, as I sat there, hunched forward slightly, clasping my hands. Was it the kindest, nicest part of you, or the most honest? Because honest was sometimes the worst thing a person could be. If right now I told that doctor how empty I felt, how for years I'd thought about my family dying grisly, pain-filled deaths, how close I'd come to killing myself, they'd take me away.

It was too hot in there. Behind the doctor, I could see a window, clamped shut. Without thinking, I rolled up my sleeves.

After, they said I'd done it on purpose. A subconscious cry for help, was what everyone called it. All those fucking shrinks and that was the best they came up with. I hadn't concealed it all this time to let some crummy two-faced doctor find out.

'Why?' I'd always remember my mother's cry, a wail of resentment that made me wince, that said, *How can you do this to me? After everything with Leah? Me, me, me.* Not, why have you suffered? Why didn't you tell me? Tell someone? Anyone?

Even the doctor couldn't explain. Another worse than useless adult letting me down, when I craved an explanation for the cavernous darkness in me, that only pain could fill.

'It can be a way of coping with intense emotions or relationship problems. Has this started since you lost your sister?'

I nodded, the bullshit answer, because it fitted. Simpler for my mother, the doctor – I'd lost the plot when I lost my sister. Nice and tidy and logical, to keep everyone happy. Stop them from digging deeper.

'I'll arrange for you to talk to someone. It might be good if you all went. As a family. But you can discuss that.' The doctor looked at me, both of her faces blurring into one momentarily, before the snarling face lunged towards me again, snake-like, spitting venom at me.

Stupid little cunt. Waste of space. The wrong sister died, didn't she? It should have been you, but you know that, don't you . . .

I shrank back in my chair. Even the doctor could see how worthless I was. It was the night I came closest. Came just a whisper from that last, deeper slice of the blade. It seemed the only way. To cut harder, drawing more blood, so that it spewed onto my bed, taking my life force with it. Only my mother knocking on my bedroom door stopped me.

2002

I learned a lot in therapy. About people's expectations and how there's only room in society for normal people. No one mentioned that there were any number of recipes for fruitcake. What I didn't learn about, was myself; why I wasn't happy and why dark thoughts plagued me. But I hadn't expected to. And by now, it was part of who I was.

Just as I'd learned to keep everyone off my back, I learned too that a long spell in therapy gave you special dispensation to behave however the fuck you wanted to.

'It wasn't my fault. Charley Harrison made me do it.' That's what I told my mother, when she was called in to talk to the head teacher at my sixth form college.

I was in trouble again, but I really didn't care. My mother didn't say anything, not straight away, but it was written all over her face. It wouldn't have mattered what I said. She didn't believe her own goddamned daughter. Just because Charley was an A-star student who, in the eyes of teachers and parents, could do no wrong; it was always someone else's fault. I loved that about Charley, how brilliance somehow made her irreproachable.

And I wasn't lying. It *was* Charley Harrison's idea to write the dumb poem on the dumb whiteboard. Only at the last minute she chickened out and someone had to save the moment. Who gave a fuck about school, anyway? She and I knew where we were headed in life. Up, up and out of there.

It was Charley who told me that life doesn't just happen. You had to grab it by the balls. After years of rain, Charley was the first ray of sun in my world.

'If you want to see science in action,' she whispered to me, during a biology class, 'look at all the losers who'll get dull jobs and die early, of boredom. Natural selection!' She winked. 'If you settle for mediocrity, you get what you deserve.'

Right from the start, I liked her philosophy, her optimism, trying it on for size, enjoying how invincible it made me feel. We were different, she told me. Her eyes gleamed and as I listened to her, I could believe every word. Like me, she saw the world differently, but unlike me, she'd played it smarter.

When you've faced death and come out the other side, there's nothing left to fear. I became a rebel rather than a victim. It was what I most loved about Charley – her wild streak even when we were at our most reckless.

'Chasing happiness,' Charley called it. 'It's already here, Casey . . . You just have to take what's waiting for you.'

Charley's happiness wasn't butterflies and summer days and the little pink iced cakes my mother used to make that I detested. It was about pushing limits, skipping class and catching a bus out of town, leaping off in the middle of nowhere, running faster, harder, longer; until our legs gave way and we fell on the grass, our hearts bursting.

It slowly grew into a restless need for always wanting more. Illicit smoking and flirting with Davey Watts, who was older and drove a little red sports car; the drinks she'd take from her parents' fridge, which we'd consume in the park under a tree. Cold beer, wine, vodka.

I realized I was trusting her. And then the fear was back, choking out the light, all the more debilitating after its absence. I couldn't do it, couldn't run the risk of her letting me down, the way everyone else had. Reminding myself I wasn't like her, as the darkness closed in around me.

I avoided her at school, pretending not to hear when she called out to me. Until one day, she followed me outside and grabbed my arm.

'What the fuck is it with you?' Her eyes glinted dangerously at me. 'I thought we were supposed to be friends. You're a fucked-up selfish bitch, Casey. Don't mess with me.'

'I'm sorry.' I mumbled it, wanting to explain about how the darkness had come back, how it was like swimming through treacle just to get through each day. How conversations like this were too loud, too intense, making my head hurt. 'I can't help it. Something happens – I just have to be on my own.'

'Are we friends or not?' she demanded to know. 'If not, I'll leave you alone.'

'Yes,' I said suddenly, meaning it, not wanting to lose her, feeling the darkness lighten a shade.

She forgave me and we got over it – that time, at least. She hadn't written me off. Not yet.

'Have you ever done it with a boy?' she asked me. It was a Tuesday afternoon and we'd bunked-off last lesson to go to the park, rolling down our socks and hitching up our skirts under the sun's itchy heat.

'No.' My heart in my mouth, telling myself it wasn't a lie. The only way I could deal with what Anthony had done to me was shut it off. For good.

'I have.' She fell back on the grass. 'Twice.' Then when I still said nothing, she added, 'Aren't you going to ask me what it's like?'

'So?' I fell back next to her, trying to ignore the churning in my stomach, both of us gazing at the sky.

'It's OK. Don't know what the fuss is about. The second time was better.'

'Who?' I was consumed with curiosity. 'Oh no, Charley. Please don't tell me it was—'

'Yes!' she giggled. 'Davey Watts! In his car! I'm such a whore!'

Suddenly, Anthony was in my head. Summoning all my strength, I forcibly pushed him out, then I found myself giggling. I couldn't remember the last time I'd done that. Suddenly I couldn't stop, and the laughter ripped out of me, Charley joining in, as if it was the funniest thing in the world. It was only after, when we stopped, I noticed the tears streaming down my cheeks.

Together, we were invincible. In a shifting, transitory world I didn't trust, Charley was my only constant. I had no doubts that we'd do everything we'd set our hearts on, and much more. We were already saving money to travel. Travelling was the first part of the plan – Paris, Monaco, Rome, Athens, Charley said. Once we were eighteen, no one could stop us.

I was counting down. Watching weeks fall away. This time next year, our exams behind us, we'd be out of here for good. A year was a long time, but to me, it was tantalizingly within reach. It was going to happen, Charley kept telling me. It filled my head every waking minute – up until the moment I fell in love.

It had come out of nowhere, the most unexpectedly delirious feeling that first shocked me, then flowed into the emptiness, soothing the ache deep inside me. Stuart felt the same – I could tell from the way he held my hand, from the first time he kissed me. Everything was falling into place. I'd seen it in other people. Now I'd found the start of my very own. Happiness.

It was like nothing I'd ever known. I stopped cutting; began to trust more than just Charley. I stopped picturing my family dying, too, as thoughts of Stuart filled my head. How even with scars on my arms, he loved me. He loved the broken person I was inside.

It made it real, didn't it? I believed that, I told Charley. Trusting her with my heart as I'd slowly learned to trust her with everything.

'Be careful, Case.' Her eyes were guarded. 'Don't love too much.'

'I won't! Have some of my happiness!' I called blithely, not thinking to ask her why she'd said that as I ran to meet him.

She didn't ever ask me if we'd 'done it'. Truth was, just the thought left me fighting for air. There were too many memories of Anthony resurfacing, trying to drown me. Stuart had sensed something wasn't right and he hadn't pushed me, but at some point, I knew I had to get over it.

I liked the feel of his skin on mine; being wanted by someone who said he loved me. But I couldn't look. Not that first time. The spectre of Anthony's ugly, leering face hung over me, ruining it. More than ever I wanted to escape him, but even now, it was impossible.

It was the ultimate injustice. Here, Casey – this is what love feels like. Feel how it softly wraps itself round you, how safe it makes you feel . . . But don't get too used to it. It won't last. But then nothing does.

Just when I'd started to believe I was like other people, I was reminded that I wasn't. Love was for everyone else, not me. I tried to talk to Charley, but I sensed a change. Stuart avoided my eyes, making excuses; stopped telling me he loved my scars, stopped talking to me altogether. And all the time, in the background, I hadn't seen Charley, watching my heart break with sharp eyes, waiting for her moment. And when I wasn't looking, she stole him.

When your best friend, the only person in the world you trust, commits the ultimate betrayal, you have no one. She took away my breath, my hopes, my dreams. After the pain subsided, I locked my feelings away for good. It was another lesson not to need people. Another reminder not to trust.

I tried not to watch her and Stuart together, her remorseless flaunting of how much better than me she was. Reminding me when I'd forgotten that I wasn't enough.

Relationships were about using people, I could see that now. My parents knew that, so did Charley. I'd been stupid to imagine otherwise. They served a purpose, for however long, were inter-changeable and, ultimately, disposable. Families were no less fickle; as I saw it, childbirth and the gene pool no guarantee that you'd be noticed, that people would care.

Yet Leah's loss was like acid on the fabric of my family, so that slowly it was falling apart, thread by thread, until the day came when there was nothing holding us together.

It was the summer when I was seventeen. I was over Charley Harrison and hanging out with Xander Pascoe again, against my mother's weakly verbalized protests. Everyone knew that Xander and his mates got their kicks out of shoplifting and smoking weed. 'You can't, mustn't . . .' 'Don't you dare,' 'You're better than them . . .' Deluding herself with the latter, because I knew she didn't really think so. And she was right. I wasn't.

Xander didn't care about anyone, but he didn't frighten me. Rules were for fools, he was always telling me, his lips curved in a cynical smile. You had to make your own, he told me. Or better still, manage without them.

I was a willing sponge for his philosophy, desperate to make it my own. To be as invincible as he was, objecting loudly and angrily when my parents booked a holiday for the three of us. I was furious. I had my own plans that summer. I didn't want to spend it with them. What little was left of our family was held together with fraying threads.

'Just for once, couldn't you do this,' my mother asked, wearily. As I looked at her, I saw my own feelings mirrored back at me; grief still clouding her sad, grey eyes, along with the knowledge that my father didn't love her. It was the only time I felt the smallest shred of solidarity – my father had betrayed her just as Charley Harrison had betrayed me. It was enough to do what she asked.

But I instantly regretted it. Worse was to come when I told Xander. I knew from the look of scorn on his face how weak he thought I was. I'd no idea what I'd be missing, he told me, but too bad if I wasn't going to be around.

The hotel was low-rise; cool and white-painted, just a few steps above the sun-baked sand and a flat, turquoise sea. Even in my antagonistic mood, I couldn't help noticing the colours, the scents of herbs and pine, intensified in the sun's heat.

None of it could hide the truth. Under their holiday best, which made them look like everyone else, my parents' marriage was rotting. The new clothes and forced smiles didn't fool anyone. We were three unhappy people, bound only by name, keeping up appearances. I knew that more than they did. They shared breakfast and side-by-side sunbeds under thatched umbrellas, while I found a place in the shade; my father ordering iced drinks for all of us, his air of bonhomie forced against a backdrop of stony silence.

At first, I'd brazened the horrified stares of other holidaymakers; imagining their hushed, judgemental comments to each other made me flaunt the scars on my arms all the more, while I watched their shock from behind my sunglasses. I didn't care what they thought. It was no different here from at home.

It was as the sun set on the third night that I felt resentment set in. I hated the bar, filled with the clinking of glasses and the murmur of happy people, all of them better at pretending than my parents were, their mood elevating with the number of drinks they consumed. So contrived it was killing me.

I fantasized about leaving, taking a taxi to the airport, flying home alone. More than ever I didn't want to be there. As I sipped my second glass of wine, looking around, there wasn't anyone I wanted to talk to. Charley's betrayal meant I wasn't thinking straight. If it wasn't for her, I wouldn't have come. There was nothing here for me at all.

Anywhere else, at any other time, it wouldn't have happened. The man's name was Alistair. He was like my father, only more so, in every sense. Younger, taller, louder. He and my father sat at the bar together, the same smug, misguided arrogance leaching from both of them as they talked over each other, neither interested in anyone but themselves.

I knew there was a woman with him. I didn't need to hear her tell my mother to know she was bored with him. They had that much in common, my mother and the woman – both of them here with men they'd be better off without.

Once you started looking, sex was everywhere in this place; in the sun's heat, the lethargic stillness; later fuelled by cocktails into a different, restless kind of heat. Occasionally, I'd see a touch or a look that reminded me of Stuart, feel a yearning to have that again, before quashing it. If you wore your heart on your sleeve, it was only a matter of time before someone came along and tore it in half. As I knew already, you could trust no one.

That evening, the same restlessness was getting to me, too. Avoiding the gaze of a couple of boys my own age, I watched the woman take my mother's arm and lead her outside.

I was left at the table alone. It was square, wicker, glass-topped. I swung my feet, then turned away from the bar, wondering how long I could bear to sit there, hearing my father's loud guffaw at something Alistair had said.

Suddenly, I got why the woman was bored. People were so fucking selfish, weren't they? Left a trail of damage without so much as a glance behind them. Look at Charley Harrison, who'd destroyed our friendship for the sake of a quick shag with my boyfriend. Look at my parents, practically ignoring their own daughter, instead deep in conversation with strangers they'd never see again, who meant nothing to them. My mother and that woman, no doubt bitching about their partners. My father and Alistair, drinking too much, finding everything suddenly so funny. They were pathetic, all of them.

I should have seen it as my cue to get out of there. They wouldn't have missed me. But I didn't. Instead, hitching my skirt up slightly, I shifted my legs, glancing briefly at Alistair. He'd noticed; I could tell from his eyes, darting from my father's face back to me. I crossed my legs, knowing I was giving him an eyeful, tossing my hair over my shoulders. God, he was so predictable.

By then I really was bored. Getting up, I walked down to the beach, where the sea lapped quietly on the pebble shore, the moon's reflection sparkling on its glassy surface. It was beautiful – and empty – but I didn't mind that. People ruined everything.

People like Alistair. It didn't take him long to find me.

'Fancy a walk?'

I heard him before I saw him. Turning round, I met his eyes. 'Not really,' I said, coolly.

'I saw you in the bar. You knew exactly what you were doing.' His audacity breathtaking, in the worst possible way.

'You seem to have forgotten you're with someone.' I turned away from him and gazed out across the sea.

He stepped closer. 'Is it about money?' he asked presumptuously, his eyes glistening in the moonlight. 'How much do you want?'

As I stared at him, I thought about it. Sex was power, I already knew that from Charley – boys, men, would do anything for it. Nothing could be worse than Anthony. And money bought choices.

I glanced back towards the terrace. I could dimly make out the figures of my parents, both now with Alistair's lady friend. They hadn't even noticed I'd gone.

'Two hundred.'

He opened his mouth to protest, but I didn't care one way or the other. Cutting him short as I uttered the lie that I knew would close the deal.

'I'm sixteen. Take it or leave it.'

I didn't find him attractive, but that wasn't the point. As he pushed himself inside me, I made myself think of Anthony, then Stuart. Felt the nausea, disgust, shame, this time holding on to them. I could do this. I wasn't weak. I was strong.

He didn't hurt me and it was over quickly enough. And unlike with Anthony, this was my choice, under my control. I liked how I felt when he paid me, how easy it was when he found me the next night and every night thereafter.

It was no one else's business, least of all my father's, but on the last night, Alistair got plastered and told him.

Outraged, my father defended his daughter's honour and punched him. With some satisfaction, I watched Alistair's blood spurting from his nose. After all, he was the grown-up who'd preyed on a teenage girl young enough to be his daughter. If Alistair hadn't asked, it wouldn't have happened.

But it was my parents' fault too. I hadn't wanted to come here. My father yelled at me, calling me a slut, demanding I give back the money. I'd handed over enough notes to keep him quiet, which I never saw again. I didn't tell him about the rest and I'd come home five hundred pounds richer.

I hid the money inside my underwear drawer. No one would find it. I knew no one would care enough to even look.

The day we got home, I saw Xander and we got drunk together. The day after, I heard the rip that set my teeth on edge as my father

broke the last strands holding my family together. But I wasn't surprised. I didn't even care by that stage, because I got it. We were a
random group of people, linked by genes, who didn't belong
together. My mother had been connected to him only because of a
decision they'd made when they were younger. One he regretted.
He didn't care about me at all.

30

Jack

Nick Abraham's mother, Sheila, had turned out to be difficult. No wonder her son had such an attitude. He'd learned from the best. She'd rambled on at length about how she'd welcomed Jen like her own daughter, but Jen had deceived all of them. What she'd done to them all, especially to Sheila . . .

Jack had pressed her for information concerning the time that Jen had left Nick.

'I suppose we got off to a bad start. I tried so hard to make it up to her, but she wouldn't have anything to do with me. I gave up in the end. There's only so much you can do, isn't there? I don't know what she was thinking, but then she didn't know how easy she had it. How she could have walked out on my Nicholas I'll never know.'

It was as though she was trying to say the right thing, but her words didn't ring true. The concern didn't show on her face. There was a meanness about her, from her small, piercing eyes and thin lips. The mean-spirited and bitter were always unhappy, Jack had observed over the years. Sheila Abraham was no exception.

'How well did you know Jen, Mrs Abraham?' Jack tried to keep her focused. But Sheila Abraham clearly saw this as an opportunity to air her dirty washing in public.

'Well enough to see straight through her,' she snapped. 'Oh, she could turn the charm on, but she didn't fool me. Still, Nicholas sees that now. He's better off without her.'

'Did you know Jen was pregnant?' Jack gritted his teeth. He had endless patience, more than most, but this woman was pushing even him.

'Of course.' She sniffed. 'It would have been disastrous. She was too selfish to be a mother. Maybe it was God's way—'

God's way? Jack couldn't believe what she was saying. 'I mean her second pregnancy? Did you know about that?' He knew it was unlikely, but Jack couldn't help himself, watching with satisfaction as the vindictive Sheila Abraham was at last stunned into silence.

'I expect she made it up,' she said after a pause. 'Don't believe everything she tells you. She's a schemer.'

Jack sat back, silent. Apart from the fact that he could see where her son's less-than-charming personality came from, this was a complete waste of time. Sheila Abraham was one of those blinkered women who thought only about themselves.

It was his first formal meeting with Evie Sherman. He wasn't sure whether to call her Jen or Evie, settling for Evie because it was the name Abbie used. He wondered if she'd recognize him from when their paths had crossed, while walking.

'DCI Jack Bentley.' He held out a hand. Tentatively, she shook it. 'I think we might sometimes walk in the same part of the woods. I live a couple of miles the other side.'

She frowned at him, unsure.

'I've seen you – at a distance. I walk with my black Labrador.'

'I'm sorry.' She shook her head.

As her eyes met his, behind the fear and uncertainty, Jack saw something else. Physically she was fragile, there was no doubt about it, but inside, he sensed steel.

Then, as he watched, it was as if the fog lifted momentarily from her imploded, uncertain world, as she remembered something.

'She has a pony.' She turned agitatedly to Abbie. 'Can I borrow your iPad?'

'Of course.' Abbie went out to the kitchen and came back with it. 'Here.'

He watched as Evie fumbled. Abbie caught his eye, but Evie managed to google and somehow find what she was looking for quite easily.

'You've clearly done this before,' Abbie said quietly.

Evie ignored her. 'This is it.' Her hands were shaking slightly, her voice animated as she passed the iPad back to Abbie so that she could see the image of the soft, grey-brown toy with mournful eyes and fluffy mane. 'It's exactly like this. Except Angel's pony, called Pony, only has one ear.'

'I'll make sure it gets passed on. Also,' Abbie hesitated, 'is there any chance you might have told Nick's mother about Angel?'

'No.' The word came out instinctively. An honest, gut feeling, Jack noticed. His own experience of Sheila Abraham told him she wasn't someone anyone would confide in. Evie seemed sure. 'We didn't talk. She never liked me. After Nick and I split up, she wouldn't have wanted anything to do with me.'

'Do you know why?' Abbie was frowning.

Evie was silent for a moment. 'I wondered if she was one of those jealous, possessive mothers. You know . . .' She glanced at Abbie, then at Jack. 'The kind for whom no woman is ever good enough for their beloved son.'

It happened. Jack had come across a number of women who saw their son's lover as a threat.

As the light seemed to go out in her eyes, Evie's hands started to shake. 'How do people do this?' Tears were rolling down her cheeks as she turned to Abbie.

Jack could see Abbie swallowing as she reached for Evie's hand. 'You hold on to hope –' she looked at Jack, then back to Evie – 'really tight, because sometimes, it's all you have.'

Jack could feel the strength in her words. As she spoke, he saw the expression on Evie's face change.

'We're doing all we can.' He spoke quietly, but with as much conviction as he could muster. 'I know, right now, it's really hard.' He paused. 'You have all these memories coming back, and a lot of them don't make sense, but you mustn't let this incapacitate you. If you do, you won't be able to help Angel.'

He watched Evie blinking at him. But Jack was right, he knew he was. She had to rise above this, the desperation, the agonizing worry which didn't go away, which wanted to cripple her, and somehow find the same strength he'd managed to find when Josh was in the car crash. The human spirit had an instinct for survival, even when it seemed impossible, when the world was crumbling around you. And only when she'd summoned that strength could she think clearly. Start to make sense of what was already coming back to her; to examine every detail she remembered of the minutiae of her life, before it was too late.

Evie got up and walked over to the window, where she seemed to be engaged in a battle with herself. Then she turned round to face them.

'Oh God . . .' She looked agitated again. 'I don't know if this will make sense, but I need to talk about Nick again.' She looked at Abbie. 'This isn't like before – when I talked to Charlotte.' She spoke fiercely, her body tight, as she stood there. 'I can't explain how, but I know it's different. I need to tell you, Abbie . . . Both of you.' She glanced at Jack. 'Everything I'm remembering, right now, before I lose it again.'

They needed to let her talk. Jack could see how urgent this was for her; how frightened she was of losing it all again.

Glancing at Jack, Abbie nodded, then got up, reaching into her bag for a notebook, then getting her phone. 'Do you mind if I record this, like last time?'

Relieved, Evie nodded.

'Right. And like before, if you want to stop at any time, just say.'

Evie waited for her to set the phone to record. 'Where do I start?'

'You and Nick,' Abbie said. 'How you met, where you lived, why you parted. Other people in your lives – like family or ex-lovers; anyone who might have been jealous of you. People who wanted to break you up.'

31

'It was Nick's idea to move,' Evie started. 'We were living in Croydon at the time, which was an easy commute for him – he worked in the City. But after we got engaged, his grandfather died and left him some money. Moving to the country was something we'd talked about on and off – for the future. Not for now, when we had jobs and friends where we were.'

She thought for a moment. 'Suddenly Nick was in a hurry. He kept saying how he didn't want to be one of those people who talked about what they wanted but never did anything. He couldn't see the point in putting it off. I was less sure than he was. But he was insistent. Once he'd made his mind up, Nick was like that.' It resonated with the Nick the police had interviewed. His portrayal of Evie's reticence had been nothing short of scathing. 'We started to look at houses. None of them were right. I thought maybe he'd give up on the idea. Then I discovered I was pregnant.'

Evie shook her head sadly. 'He was elated, emotional. And impatient. I wanted to wait until after the baby was born. But he wouldn't listen.' She stared at Abbie. 'It's like a large, brilliant picture playing in my mind. I can remember expressions, emotions. Nick's face, his enthusiasm. Even my reticence. They're all part of it.' Then she frowned. 'You don't think I'm making it up, do you?'

'It's fine, Evie.' Abbie tried to reassure her. 'You're doing really well.' She glanced at Jack. 'Keep talking.'

'We saw this farmhouse. Nick fell in love with it.' Evie's voice was flat. 'I could see why. It was everything he'd wanted. It was huge – with room for a family to grow, for us to have friends over. I was less sure, because it was so much further from everything I knew. But he kept on about how villages were friendly, how I'd get to know everyone and we'd probably end up living there forever.'

She paused. 'The thing is, if we'd stayed together, it might have been like that. He's persuasive. People are drawn to him. And he's hugely sociable. We would have had parties and got to know everyone . . . But I suppose, even before we moved, I wasn't sure.'

Jack watched her. She believed every word she was saying. Had his colleagues misread Nick? Was there a charming side to him? Somehow, he doubted it. From what he understood about the man, it was more likely Nick had bullied her.

'I didn't understand why Nick was so sure about moving. I was happy with city life. And just because you live in a small village doesn't mean you're surrounded by instant friendships.'

'Were you happy there?' Abbie asked quietly.

'I wanted to be.' It came out too brightly, and then her eyes were suddenly full of tears again. 'I tried to want what he wanted, but I couldn't.'

'What happened after you moved there?'

'I lost the baby.' Pain washed across Evie's face. 'I miscarried at six months. Just one of those things. It happens – to more people than you'd think.'

She must have gone through labour knowing her baby was dead. Jack tried to imagine how that would be. 'Was that when you left?'

She shook her head. 'We'd been there nearly two years.' Evie paused, as if trying to work it out. 'I could remember, because we'd planned to celebrate with champagne in the local pub. It had been Nick's idea to mark the date. That evening, he was late getting home. He used to catch the train from Haywards Heath. I tried to call him but he didn't answer. I even checked the trains to see if the one he usually got was delayed. Everything was running on time.' She swallowed. 'It's all coming back. I don't think I've ever talked about it before.'

It was easier not to, Jack was thinking. He didn't talk, that was for sure, just buried what was painful rather than confront it head on.

'When he eventually got home, he said his train had been cancelled. There was alcohol on his breath. All that time I wasn't happy, it seemed Nick wasn't, either. Soon after that, things started to fall apart. Two months later, I left him. I went to stay with a friend.'

'And you were pregnant again.'

'Yes,' she whispered.

'What about Nick's mother? After you split up, did you see her?'

'No. There was no point. Anyway, she was poisonous. She hijacked our break-up with her lies, saying how I'd betrayed Nick, and how I wasn't good enough for him. How I'd let all of them down, including her. I couldn't believe the force of her attack. But looking back on it, I don't think she could cope with me leaving her perfect, handsome son. She said I was ungrateful. I remember her saying to me, "*Who do you think you are . . .*"' Her voice faded.

Jack was silent. People made each other so miserable sometimes. It reminded him of when he discovered Louise's affair. It was after Josh had died, when he'd naively believed things were OK between them and that they'd found some semblance of happiness. Then out of the blue, he'd discovered they weren't. *Happiness severed*, was how he remembered that time.

Abbie frowned. 'It must have been difficult for you.'

'Yes.' Evie stared at her hands, at the finger that used to wear an engagement ring.

'I mean, having to move away,' Abbie went on. 'Especially after losing your baby, when you were pregnant with your second.'

'I didn't know I was pregnant when I left. I found out soon after,' she mumbled. 'I was staying with a friend – then I found out I was pregnant again. After that, I wanted my own place.' She stared ahead of her. 'I got my old job back, but Nick came looking for me. He wanted us to try again. When I said I didn't want to, he got nasty. He called my boss and told him I'd lost my last job because I was unstable. It wasn't true. He did it out of spite, because I wouldn't do what he wanted. He has a controlling streak. I knew that if he ever found out I was pregnant, I'd never be free of him.'

'Nick wouldn't give up?'

'No.' She shook her head. 'But for all the wrong reasons. It was about pride, possession. Obsession, even. Not because he loved me. He's like his mother.'

'We've talked to Sheila Abraham,' Jack interrupted, then watched alarm register on Evie's face.

'Why?' Suspicion clouded her eyes. Right now, it was clear, Evie didn't trust anyone.

'I'm sorry, Evie. I know you didn't want her involved. But we have to talk to family members. Apparently, when you and Nick split up, she was shocked – so she says. According to her, you got off to a bad start. She said she'd tried – several times – to make things up with you, but you refused to have anything to do with her.'

Jack watched as Evie started to shake, whether with anger or fear, he couldn't tell.

'She's not the kind of person you can trust,' she said, her jaw set.

Jack glanced at Abbie. As far as he could tell, it was an accurate assessment of Sheila Abraham.

'So what happened after you moved into your own place?'

'I knew I couldn't go back. I didn't love Nick. I scraped by until Angel was born, then I moved to Cornwall. That was when I changed my name. It was a chance for a fresh start. And I had Angel. I didn't need anyone else. She was my reason to go on living.'

After a moment, Abbie turned back to her notebook. 'Do you know why you felt the need to hide?'

Evie stared straight at her. 'Is it really that strange? Plenty of people live quiet lives. And it was because of Nick. Every day I lived in fear that he'd find us.'

Abbie looked perplexed again. 'The trouble is, if he's her

father, don't you think he had a right to know he had a daughter?'

Evie looked distressed. 'Nick's best friend is a top lawyer. If he'd found me, he'd have done everything in his power to take Angel away. I know he would. Between them, they'd concoct proof that I'm an unfit mother. Nick knew about the medication. He wouldn't think twice about using it against me. I wouldn't have a chance.'

'And now he does know.' Abbie's voice was gentle.

'Yes.' She took a breath.

'And he knows he may not be her father, doesn't he?'

Jesus, what a mess, Jack was thinking. But when you were desperate, you did things you wouldn't ordinarily do. 'You do realize that he can't just take her from you?'

Evie nodded. 'He said he wants a DNA test.'

'It's reasonable.' Jack looked at her. 'And if it proves he isn't Angel's father, it will be the end of it.'

'Yes.' She nodded.

'It was brave of you. You're quite isolated out here.'

'I couldn't think what else to do. I thought I could give Angel the childhood I wanted for her, with beaches and clean air and open space. To start with, the isolation worried me. But as the months passed, and as Angel got a little older, I realized I felt safer without people around me. No one knew I was here.'

'Safe?' Abbie stopped her. 'Do you remember feeling that you were in danger?'

Evie leaned forward, burying her head in her hands. Then she looked up. 'I suppose I must have. But I don't know why.'

Abbie looked at her. 'Evie? This feeling of being unsafe, it's impossible to prove but do you think it could be related to your attack? It seems that the closer we get to it, the more fragmented your memories are. You know you were afraid, but you don't know why.' Abbie paused, letting her take the words in.

'I don't know . . .' Evie clasped her hands. 'I can remember being frightened, but when I try to remember why, there's nothing there.'

'Charlotte said you'd had this conversation and she was convinced you were hiding from Nick.'

Suddenly Evie looked up. 'What if Nick knew? He could have pretended he didn't know about Angel. What if he found me? What if he's taken her?'

32

If there was one thing Jack knew about, it was emotional pain.
The heartbreak of his wife's betrayal and subsequent departure; the grief he suffered after Josh's death. Dark, desperate
months when he'd wished he, too, had died, unable to believe
he'd get through that terrible loss. Grief was a lonely place;
only had space for one. He hadn't got over losing Josh. You
never did – not with your own child. It had changed the world
– changed him, too. He wasn't the same person he had been
before.

As for Evie, he hardly dared think how long and unbearable
each day must be. Days during which she imagined Angel
somewhere, with an unknown someone; knowing the little
girl would be missing her mother, wouldn't understand why
she hadn't come. Imagining the best outcome, which was that
she was being cared for, before glimpsing the worst, waiting
for the onslaught of pain, embracing its violence, holding on
to the only thought that kept her sane: that every day they
didn't find a body, there was still hope.

Sometimes it was all you had – hope. He'd clung to it as he

and Louise had rushed to the hospital. Even when they'd stood at Josh's bedside, watching him, wired up to drips and machines, his eyes closed, his breathing mechanical. The realization had hit Jack like a thunderbolt – though his body was still functioning, Josh had gone.

From what he knew about Nick, he wasn't sure the man could have attacked Evie – not with the level of brutality that had left her fighting for her life. He believed in listening to his gut and right now, his gut was telling him Nick hadn't done it. But from bitter experience, Jack knew that until there was proof, no one could be sure.

Having seen her face, the distant look in her eyes, the dullness of her responses, Jack knew about the uncertainty that had Evie in its grip, that verged on insanity. He knew she was on pills that numbed everything, slowing the rate at which her brain worked, blunting her thoughts, her feelings, until they were running at half speed; all there, just less so. He remembered it all too well. It made it bearable, if you could call it that – her head just above the water, so that instead of drowning, she could float.

What he also knew was that inertia killed you. When your child was in danger, if there was anything you could do, you had to do it. Evie had been stuck first in hospital, then in the house, apart from the brief episode when she'd run off and worried Abbie half to death. He had a day off today. Instead of chopping yet more firewood and sitting at home, letting the emptiness of the house get to him, suddenly he knew what to do.

'Meet Beamer.' His dog was wagging his tail with characteristic enthusiasm. 'Are you OK with dogs?'

'I like them.' Evie reached a tentative hand out for Beamer to sniff. 'I have a cat. He adopted us after we moved here.' She frowned. 'I haven't seen him for a while. Sometimes he's gone for a couple of days, but not longer than that.'

'Maybe he got shut in somewhere,' Jack suggested. Cats did their own thing. One had somehow got locked in his shed without him knowing.

Evie was silent.

'He'll turn up. It's a bit of a mess.' Jack was talking about his car. 'I thought it made sense to drive up the road a bit and walk from there.' He'd thought by driving some of the way, she could conserve what little energy she had, save it for walking.

Climbing into the car, she didn't say anything. He drove down the track carefully. 'I keep looking,' he said quietly. 'All the time. Everywhere I go. The villagers round here, they're all looking too. They want to help, did you know that?'

Through the trees, a ray of sun caught his eye. Nothing sounded right. It was good everyone was looking, but Angel hadn't been found. What else would it take?

'Is there anywhere in particular you'd like to go?' he asked.

She shook her head. He wondered how much of the countryside she recognized. He didn't like to ask. Half a mile up the road, he turned up a dirt track through the trees and, after a hundred yards or so, pulled over and parked. 'These are the same woods that your garden backs on to. Searches have combed the area closest to your house. Does this seem like a good place to start?'

The woods had many moods. On a morning like this, they were beautiful, with the low sun filtering through the branches, dazzling in his eyes. It was hard to believe they were the same woods that had seemed so hostile the night when he'd seen the stag.

It was clearly an effort for Evie, even though they walked slowly; every so often they paused for her to lean against a tree.

'Are you OK?'

'No.' The word stuck in her throat, making her cough.

Jack shook his head, exasperated with himself. 'I'm sorry. Of course you're not. How can you be?'

She dragged her gaze up, and her eyes appraised him. In their depths, he could see her sorrow. He felt a shock of compassion, as something unspoken passed between them. A knowledge that came instinctively.

Somehow she knew – something had happened to him too.

'I know how you feel.' He was compelled to reach out to her. It was impossible not to. Only when you'd been through what they both had could you know how it felt. As she looked at him again, he could see that behind her sadness, she believed him.

'I lost my son.'

Here, under the trees, the connection between them was tangible. In all the time her daughter had been missing, all the people she'd spoken to, he was the first person who understood.

As they walked, he told her about his police career, about how so much had changed when Josh was killed.

'One of his friends was driving. He'd passed his test a month earlier. Josh was sitting in the passenger seat. They were going to a party.' His voice was level, matter-of-fact, as if he was talking about a stranger.

'The friend pulled out in front of a lorry. He died instantly. Josh was seriously injured. He was in a coma for two weeks before he died.'

He saw the shock register on her face. He wasn't after sympathy. He was telling her so that she knew he understood.

'When did it happen?'

'Three years ago. My wife never got over it. Jesus, nor have I.' Jack fell silent, not wanting to burden her when she was already dealing with so much.

She hesitated. 'Was he your only child?'

'No.' The word was lost, as though he'd swallowed it. 'No,' he said again, more clearly. 'We have a daughter. Stephanie. She's twenty-two. She moved out, after. Things got difficult between us. My wife had an affair . . .' He looked at her. 'She moved out not long ago.'

Suddenly he was back in the hidden, unspoken world of parents who'd lost children, who didn't talk about what had happened to them because it was too heartbreakingly sad, or because no one wanted to listen. It overlapped with Evie's world, yet was miles apart. Jack's son would never come back, but Evie could still hope.

'I'm so sorry.' Her words were heartfelt, as the echo of his loss filtered through. She touched his arm. 'So very sorry you lost him.'

The lump in his throat prevented Jack from speaking. Instead, they continued walking, the path narrowing until their arms were touching. For the second time this morning, it was there. *Hope.* He wanted Evie to feel it, surging through her veins, rousing her from her bleakness. It wasn't always better to know the truth. It was better to have something to hold on to, for as long as you could. To believe Angel could be found, to only give up when hope had finally gone. You had to keep going.

As they walked, the trees became more densely planted and it was as though the sun had dimmed, holding the woods in a kind of half-light. Jack wasn't familiar with this area. He could see Evie glancing around for anything out of place; the effort it was taking was obvious, but she seemed driven onwards by that same flicker of hope.

After a while, the woods become sparser again, the trees thinning out, sprawling rhododendron bushes on either side of the path. Ahead of them was a patch of sunlight where the trees cleared altogether and, as they got nearer, Jack could make out a lake.

Evie stopped suddenly, her face stricken. 'Will the police have searched here?'

'As far as I know.' Jack wanted to reassure her. 'But I'll check.'

As they got closer, he could see narrow streams leading into and out of the lake, each of them lost in thick banks of reeds, and over them, a series of small, arched stone bridges.

There was something incongruous about the bridges, set in such wild surroundings. He walked over the first, Evie close behind, then round to the other side of the lake, where there was another, steeper bridge. He paused on top of it to look for a moment, into the black, inky water beneath. There were no visible signs of life, no tendrils of weed floating on the surface, no insects, no lily pads. Apart from an occasional bubble reaching the surface, there was nothing.

There was something eerie about the place; its heavy

silence, the stillness, the only visible life the towering nests crawling with giant wood ants. Avoiding them, he kept walking, round to the far side of the lake from the path they'd come out of the woods on, where there was another bridge over another, smaller stream.

The bushes were denser here, the path narrower, pushing them closer to the lake's edge. Up ahead, a small, derelict building blocked the path. An old workman's shed, Jack guessed, finding himself drawn closer. Built of wood and bricks, it was in a poor state of repair; tiles missing from the roof, the original door wrenched off and replaced by a rusty grill, held closed by a heavy chain and padlock.

Stopping in front of it, he peered inside, but there was nothing, just what looked like years of dead leaves covering the floor, pushed up at the sides in some places where the wind had caught them.

'I can see something.' Evie was beside him. 'There.' Her hand was trembling as she pointed.

Jack stared more closely, trying to focus on where she was pointing, able to make out the shape of something through the gloom.

Reaching into his pocket for the torch he always carried, he switched it on, pointing its beam through the grill, then felt himself recoil as he saw something that didn't belong there.

Beside him, he felt Evie stiffen. 'What is it?' There was a note of panic in her voice.

Holding the torch steady, in the beam they saw a severed doll's head.

Evie gasped. On its side, seeming to stare up from the floor at them, the doll's head was ghoulish, making the back of Jack's neck prickle. Evie jumped back.

'It's OK.' Jack turned. 'Just kids messing around.' Did kids really do that these days? Plant dolls' heads in strange places?

'Can we go?' The sight had clearly disturbed Evie.

Jack nodded, and she turned round, starting to retrace their footsteps, then broke into a shaky run.

'Hey, Evie. Hold on. There's no hurry.' She looked so weak, Jack was worried about her stumbling. Catching her up, he grabbed her arm. 'It's OK,' he said again. But as she turned to look at him, he could see it wasn't.

'I can't bear it.' Her voice was tinged with hysteria. 'I keep thinking I remember a man at the door. But I can't see his face. Even when I'm alone, I can't get away from this voice in my head. It tells me to trust no one.'

Jack could see she was at the end of her tether. Wherever Evie turned, there was no respite for her. How could there be?

There were cars outside Jessamine Cottage when they got back. Jack frowned. He hadn't been aware of another search so close to the house today. There was no sign of Abbie's car, he noticed, suddenly worried about leaving Evie alone. Everything was too traumatic, and she wasn't strong.

'I thought Abbie would be here.' Jack stopped the Land Rover beside the gate. 'Will you be OK?'

Evie nodded, a slight movement that was almost lost in the poor light. 'Thank you.' As she looked at him, he was surprised to see the gratitude in her eyes.

'You're welcome. I'm only sorry we didn't find anything.'

She looked away.

'You better go inside.' He nodded towards the gate.

Opening the car door, she looked at him briefly, then got out.

'You take care,' he said softly, putting the car into gear and pulling away. As he turned round, above the sound of the engine he heard her scream.

33

Pulling on the handbrake, Jack leapt out and ran towards the gate. On the other side, he could see Evie surrounded by a group of about half a dozen people.

'Tell us what happened, Evie. Who do you think's taken your daughter?'

'Go away.' Evie stood there, swaying, her hands over her ears. It was the press – the last thing she needed. Jack ran into the middle of them and took her arm. 'Leave her alone.' He was furious. 'You're on private property. Get out, all of you.'

He led her towards the house, but one of the reporters overtook them and stopped in front of Evie. Turning, Jack tried to shield her from the camera's flash. Bloody press. They were like vultures preying on the vulnerable.

'Are you all right?' he asked, as Evie fumbled with a key and unlocked the back door.

Hunched inside her jacket, she nodded. She looked far from all right as she went inside.

★

Jack hadn't wanted to leave her, even though he'd called the station and had been assured that Sara was on her way. He'd waited until Evie turned on lights and closed curtains, making her promise not to open the door to anyone other than the police. Nor had he planned to go back the next morning, but the intrusion of the press and her vulnerability had preyed on his mind overnight.

He parked a little way down the lane, and as he walked through the woods the night lingered, in the dark shapes of trees and bushes, the still-bright moon and the slight crunching underfoot from the first frost that would only last until the early sun broke through. Above, the sky was clear, a hint of palest silver in the east heralding the sunrise.

He was looking for the stag, under the canopy of branches that held the darkness in, blotting out the coming dawn. He knew the way with his eyes closed. The path that twisted through the brambles, then straightened between the rows of tall pines, the floor beneath them carpeted with needles. He breathed in the air scented with damp earth as his feet took him to a hidden place of soft grass and fallen leaves and empty chestnut cases, a place that in spring was carpeted with bluebells.

The stag was a symbol of hope. Sometimes you needed a sign that you were on the right path. That you weren't about to lose your mind. *There's a child out here*, Jack was thinking. The police investigation had got nowhere – not in any sense that meant anything. If there was any kind of balance in the world, any unifying force, he needed help, *now* . . . Jack's fists were clenched. He didn't know why he was asking, demanding, for help from an unseen, questionable source. None had been forthcoming when his son had needed it.

The sun was edging up from the horizon as he reached the place where he'd seen the stag, the first rays reaching through the branches, casting a blinding light across his face. Listening for the giveaway sounds of cloven hooves rustling through leaves and fallen twigs, he knew almost straight away that it wasn't here. Blinking, he turned away from the sunlight, then at his feet, he saw them: verdant shoots poking up through fallen leaves. It never ceased to amaze Jack how they survived the elements.

He crouched down, lifting away a few of the decaying leaves, puzzled. In spring, slender green spears like this carpeted the woods. They were bluebells, which thrived here because of the fallen leaves; they offered enough protection so that the bulbs could start to grow underneath. The trees kept the ground cooler and damper here, so that for a few short weeks, tens of thousands of tiny flowers would paint the floor hyacinth blue.

It was all connected, he suddenly realized in a way he hadn't seen before. The flowers, the trees, their roots reaching deep into the ground where they tangled with each other, their branches overhead outstretched towards each other until they touched.

But as he looked down, there was something out of place. This was autumn. The verdant shoots emerging through the soil and poking through the leaves – they were snowdrops, he was almost certain. But it was far too early for them. Carefully, he lifted away more dead leaves, and saw a single, tiny white bud. They *were* snowdrops, by some miracle flowering early.

The strangest feeling came over him. He'd come here to find the stag and, instead, he'd found a single, fragile flower.

But it didn't matter. Suddenly he could feel it again, not elusive and intangible, the way it usually felt, but flowing through him from the air in his lungs and on his skin, from the ground beneath him. The miracle that was hope.

Whistling to Beamer, Jack walked back towards Evie's house. He felt energized. He just wished she could feel that way, too. This time, there were no cars parked outside. Sara must have left early. Evie was alone.

Walking up the path, he was too busy watching the robin perched on a wheelbarrow, his head on one side, to notice Evie walking down towards him.

'It's Angel's robin. At least, that's how I always think of him.' She stepped closer to the bird. 'Have you seen her?' she asked it, her voice quiet, not wanting to scare him off.

'*You saw, didn't you? Did you see them take her things, too? What happened? Where did she go?*'

The robin glanced at her before darting away. As her voice faded, she looked up. In the trees, Jack saw the hooded shapes of crows, also watching them.

'You see all the birds? I imagine them watching us, watching what we do. I wonder if one of them knows where Angel is.' Falling silent, she dropped her gaze. 'You must think I'm mad.'

She was no more mad than he was, taking strength from the sight of a flower or imagining his dead son sending a wild stag to his rescue. 'I really don't.' He went on. 'I came to make sure you hadn't had any more trouble from the press.' It wasn't the real reason, but he didn't want to freak her out.

She shook her head. 'I suppose they'll come back.' She said it half-heartedly.

'If they do, let us know.'

She nodded. 'Would you like to come in?'

He followed her into the kitchen and leaned against the door frame as he watched her put the kettle on, then find mugs, coffee and milk. It was like watching someone whose mind was tuned out. That was a pretty accurate description, he reminded himself. A mind that was constantly numbed by a cocktail of drugs and fear.

He remembered the wretched pills. They solved nothing, just lowered a veil over your senses, a veil that slowly dissolved to reveal the full horror of what had happened all over again – until you took more pills, drew another veil. An endless cycle on repeat, until you stopped it and waited for the onslaught of pain.

There were tears rolling down Evie's cheeks again. All that suppressed emotion had to come out somewhere. Jack imagined the robin flying after Angel; having the answer that Evie so desperately needed, but unable to tell her. Probably the crows, too.

One of the mugs smashed onto the floor. Evie slumped down beside it, unable to stop herself crying, as if her heart was breaking all over again.

Jack helped her up. She put him in mind of a wild animal, constantly on edge, ready for flight. But then how could a mother rest, when her child was missing? Even as she sat at the table, the tears kept coming, silently, her face devoid of the pain locked inside.

There was nothing he could say. Jack knew, at times like this, words made no difference. The only thing that would help was if he found Angel. As he passed Evie a mug of coffee, her hands were shaking.

The police needed a break of some kind. Having looked everywhere obvious in the immediate area, when you were surrounded by miles of countryside, rolling fields, dark woods, streams, impenetrable brambles, all leading to the rugged coast path and endless miles of ocean, where did you go next?

'Why don't you try and sleep? Just for a while?' She'd hardly touched the coffee and was just sitting, staring blankly ahead of her. 'I can hang around a bit if you like – or I could go home and come back a bit later . . .' He wasn't sure which she'd prefer.

Evie nodded, then getting up, disappeared through the doorway. When she didn't come back, Jack walked after her. But glancing into the sitting room, he found her curled up on the sofa, asleep.

Quietly Jack let himself out. But he was worried about her. As he walked down the path, he called Abbie.

34

Abbie had asked him to go to Evie's the next day. When Jack got there, his colleague was in the kitchen, on her phone.

'I'll call you later on,' Abbie was saying. 'After I've spoken to her. I have to go.' She turned to Jack.

'Thanks for coming over, Jack. Evie's in the garden. I wanted to get your take on things.' She looked puzzled.

'What's the problem?' Jack pulled out a chair and sat down.

'It's about Nick. I think there's something he's not saying. The way he and his mother describe Evie doesn't ring true. Charlotte said that Evie was frightened of him – it's possible he's the one she was hiding from. But what Evie tells us hasn't been reliable, though she's far more lucid now . . .'

'Then there's the Leah Danning case.'

'Yes.' Abbie was thoughtful. 'I asked Charlotte more about that. She was cagey, but she's protective towards Casey Danning. They were friends. So far, other than Evie, there's no obvious link between Leah and Angel.'

They were interrupted as Evie opened the back door. She looked better today, Jack thought.

'Hi.' Did he imagine the flicker of pleasure across her face as she looked at him?

'Evie, I hope you don't mind that I asked Jack to come over. He has far more experience than I have – and I thought three heads are better than two. Would you like a cup of tea?'

Evie shook her head. 'What did you want to talk about? Have you heard anything? I just thought, with the papers and the news and everything . . .' Clinging to hope.

'We've had one or two leads,' Abbie said quietly. 'After a press release, there are always leads . . .' She hesitated. 'You have to sift through the time-wasters, all seeking their moment of glory. But there's been nothing of any significance. At least, not so far.'

Abbie sat at the table. 'I hope you don't mind, but Dr Ghyllen's coming to see you tomorrow.'

Evie looked annoyed. 'There's no need. I'm really all right. The only thing I need to do is stop the pills.'

And find her daughter . . . Jack said nothing. Everything was a battle, he could see that. He could remember the need to wrestle back some degree of control when Josh was in hospital.

'She did say she wanted to check you over again. She also said she'd like to refer you to someone who specializes in memory loss. She said she'd come before she starts afternoon surgery. About three, she thought. Is that OK with you?'

Evie sat down, shaking her head. 'No. Cancel her.'

Jack shook his head at Abbie. You could suggest, support, prompt, but you couldn't force. Evie was firefighting. It wasn't worth adding to her battle.

'All right. If that's what you want.' Abbie paused. 'I spoke to Nick again.'

'What about?'

'He wants to see you.'

Evie stood up. 'I don't want him here. This is my house. I don't want anyone here.' She was shaking. 'Tell him I don't want to see him.'

'I can't do that.' Abbie looked troubled. 'If we're looking for a missing child, we have to explore every possibility.'

'What do you mean, *if*? Angel's missing, Abbie. I know that. You know that.'

'Evie, it's OK. We're on your side.' Jack tried to reassure her.

'What did Nick say?' Her voice was shaking, too. 'You have to tell me, Abbie. It's my daughter who's out there, missing. What did he say?' Her voice was rising all the time.

Abbie shook her head. 'He said he doesn't think there's a baby, Evie. He said you had a breakdown after your miscarriage. It looks to him like losing the baby brought the past back – your memories of Leah – though he didn't know about her at the time.'

Evie's mouth fell open.

'I wasn't sure what to think. So I called where you used to work, when you were with Nick. The person I spoke to said they'd suggested you take some time off, until you were feeling better. Apparently, you flew at them. They had to escort you out of the building. They were quite generous with your final pay packet. It's probably how you could afford to buy your car.'

'No.' Evie was shaking her head in disbelief. 'Don't you see? Nick's set the whole thing up, just to get at me. It's exactly the kind of thing he'd do. He and his mother are in it together. I wouldn't be surprised if that's where Angel is – with them.'

233

'Sheila's moving into residential care,' Abbie said quietly. 'The police have been searching – but there are no records of an Angel Sherman or an Angel Russell. There's no birth certificate, Evie.'

'So I didn't register her. Does it even matter right now?' Evie was defensive. She looked stunned. 'God. After everything I'm going through, you don't believe me.'

Jack was uncomfortable with the direction this was going. He knew Abbie was doing her job, but when you were a parent, when your child's life was in danger, didn't she know how vulnerable that made you?

'No one's saying that,' he said, intervening. 'They're really not.'

'Not yet,' Abbie added. 'But you have to agree it's bizarre, that everything connected with Angel has vanished into thin air.'

'You don't believe me, do you?' Evie looked at them in utter horror. 'I'll find something. Proof. Give me a minute . . . *Please* . . .'

She rushed from the room. Jack heard her footsteps on the stairs, then upstairs, as she went from room to room, opening doors and drawers that had already been searched multiple times, before the house fell silent.

'It might be a good idea to put Nick off coming here.' Jack looked at Abbie.

'I was thinking the same. The problem is, there's still a child missing – we think. We need answers, Jack. Right now, Evie's the only person who has them.'

She broke off as Evie came back into the room. 'Evie . . .' Abbie paused. 'Come and sit down.'

She waited as Evie pulled out a chair.

The silence was broken when Abbie's phone buzzed. 'Yes? Now really isn't a good time.' Looking irritated, she glanced at Evie then shook her head. She sounded resigned. 'OK.'

She ended the call, but whatever it was clearly wasn't OK. She looked directly at Evie.

'I'm sorry. This isn't my doing, but it's Nick. He's on his way here.'

Jack saw that Evie's face was stricken. What was she frightened of? Was it Nick? Did he have some kind of hold over her? He was trying to work it out as Evie stood up and started pacing round the room.

'Someone's trying to get to me. Someone who's taken my child. Who knows how I've been living. The same person who attacked me.' She raised terrified eyes towards Jack. 'What if it's Nick?'

35

As Abbie glanced away, Jack could see that she too had concerns about Evie's safety. 'You don't have to talk to him,' he told Evie.

Evie stared at him. 'You don't know Nick. He'll come back. He won't take no for an answer.'

Jack glanced at Abbie. 'Then maybe it would make sense to let him in? While we're here? That way we can be here the whole time – or in the next room, if you'd prefer.'

But Abbie was frowning. 'If Nick had been to the house, don't you think you would have remembered?'

'I've told you everything I know.' Evie was desperate for Abbie to believe her.

Abbie hesitated. 'The trouble is, it's all words. Words that anyone can make up, if we're being brutally honest here. I wish we had more, Evie. I really do.' She glanced at her watch. 'And you have to believe me when I say that I'm really sorry about Nick turning up like this.' She paused. 'I suppose it was going to happen at some point. Maybe it's a good thing it's now – while we're both here.'

It was clear from Evie's face that even with the police there, she didn't want to see him. But there was the sound of a car door slamming, then, a few seconds later, a loud knock at the door. It was too late.

'You didn't tell me Helen had left you this place.' It was the first thing he said to her, slightly accusingly, as he looked around her kitchen. There was disdain in his voice, as though he couldn't see beyond the dated interior to the heart and soul of the cottage.

'I didn't know about it – before I left you.' Evie was obviously trying to keep calm. 'And when you came to the hospital, I couldn't make sense of anything. But you didn't come here to talk about the house.'

He smirked. 'Don't you mean before *I* left you? Actually, we probably do need to talk about it. What's yours is mine and all that?'

Bastard, Jack was thinking, biting back his anger. 'I suppose the same goes for the farmhouse,' Evie said shakily. 'Do you still live alone? Or has your girlfriend moved in with you?'

Jack read Nick's silence as surprise, but it was only momentary. 'You're forgetting it's my house, Jen. I bought it.'

'And Helen left this one to me. Don't be a bastard, Nick. We both know it isn't as simple as that. What do you want?'

'That accident you had . . . How did it happen? Have they found who did it yet?' Jack couldn't believe it; Nick sounded amused.

There was another silence before he carried on. 'What about your daughter, Jen? Is she mine? Or did you make her up?'

'Stop it . . .' Evie cried out. 'You don't know anything, Nick.'

'Really? After all that time we lived together? Suit yourself. But if I'm a father, why the hell didn't you bloody tell me?'

He was a piece of work. Several times, Jack wanted to intervene, but Evie was holding herself together admirably.

'Why the interest all of a sudden?' Evie's clear voice cut through Nick's bluster. 'Oh, I get it. You want to absolve yourself of any responsibility for Angel. I'm right, aren't I?'

Nick's silence spoke volumes.

'What is it, Nick? Are you getting married?'

'God, no.' Jack could hear the smile in Nick's voice. 'Actually, Maria's pregnant.'

'That's the real Nick,' Evie said bitterly after he'd left. She looked exhausted. 'His mother is the same. She'd never admit to anything that didn't make her or her son look like saints. When Nick and I met, he was engaged to Kirsten. I don't even know if this is relevant.' She glanced at Abbie, then at Jack.

'Go on,' he said quietly.

'Sheila's always been angry with me, because I took her perfect son away from fucking brilliant, beautiful Kirsten, who could do no wrong.' Jack couldn't believe the animosity in her voice. 'She made it very clear from the start that she blamed me for breaking them up. I don't think she ever got over it.'

'Can you tell us what happened?' Abbie looked expectantly at Evie.

'Soon after Nick and I met, he had a row with his mother and shortly after that he broke it off with Kirsten. He knew it would be a big deal for his parents, because they were best friends with Kirsten's parents and the wedding was booked . . . But he knew he had to.

'"I don't love her," he told me. "It's you I want to be with."
He looked triumphant, which I couldn't understand, because
love or regret would have seemed more appropriate. But over
time I understood, in a way I hadn't before, clear as day. It
wasn't about either of those things. I was simply a pawn, used
to out-manipulate his manipulative mother.

'She begged him not to call it off. Told him what a huge
mistake he was making.' Evie looked incredulous. 'Oh my
God – it all makes sense.'

'But surely,' Abbie frowned, 'over time, if her son was that
important to her, if she thought he was happy with you, she
must have accepted you.'

'That's just it. I don't think he ever loved me. He just used
me. I can't believe I've only just seen it.'

Abbie looked confused. 'I don't understand.'

'It was complicated,' Evie said, glancing away. 'Sheila and I
didn't get on, but I don't think she'd do anything to hurt me
– or Angel if she'd even known about her. And I don't think
she did.'

'Maybe not.' Abbie was thoughtful. 'But there was something else she said—'

'What?' There was a sudden flush to Evie's cheeks.

'She said you hadn't been well, Evie.' Abbie's voice was
gentle. 'She said . . . you had a breakdown. After the miscarriage.'

'It wasn't a breakdown.' Evie spoke through gritted teeth.
'It's Sheila's way of saying that I left him.'

Abbie stared at her. 'Just now, Nick clearly said he left you.'

'Just more lies.' Evie was matter-of-fact. 'Nick and I didn't
split up. I walked out while he was at work one day – without
telling him. I couldn't go through the motions of holding our

relationship together, when it was clear he was having an affair.

'I knew he'd been seeing someone. I couldn't bear to always be wondering, waiting, imagining he was late because he was with her . . . The woman's face is murky, but it's there, in my head somewhere. I knew who she was.

'It wasn't a good time. That first winter was hideous. Long dark days in that enormous house, which at their worst felt like an endless kind of night – or nightmare, as I thought of them at the time. One that I only escaped from when I slept. It was different for Nick, going back to his job and civilization every day, but I'd been stuck there, in that quiet, empty house, feeling more and more like a prisoner, my resentment building, until one day, it got the better of me.

'I packed enough clothes to last me a few weeks and left Nick a note, telling him not to come after me. I needed time to think, away from him.

'The first week I stayed with a friend, who lied for me when Nick called, then I met Richard. After that, summer in the city was a blast. Smart restaurants, theatres, art galleries . . . I fell in love, not with him, but what he represented; the buzzing city life I still craved. It was when I realized, too, that Nick had been a mistake.

'I didn't go back to my old job.' Evie shook her head. 'I'm not even sure why I said that. There's still so much that isn't clear.'

'What happened with Richard?'

'It didn't last. All the time I was putting off what I knew I had to do, which was to face Nick and tell him. I left it for ages before eventually I called him to arrange to meet. We had this awkward phone conversation and set a date, only then I'd discovered I was pregnant.

'At first I assumed it was Nick's baby, but I couldn't be sure. My periods had always been irregular. I slept with Richard two weeks after I'd left Nick – it could have belonged to either of them.

'Already the pregnancy was obvious. My body remembered.' She looked mildly embarrassed. 'Nick would have known instantly. There was no way I could face him, his scathing condemnation, the searing contempt on his face, when I told him I couldn't be sure who the father was.

'When I told Richard I was pregnant, he told me to get rid of it or it was over between us. I left his flat and went back to my friend's, and stayed there for another week while I found myself a studio flat. It was the last I saw of Richard. I'd neither cared about nor been surprised by his reaction. I soon forgot him, as I obsessively threw myself into impending motherhood, determined to do my best for my baby. It was a textbook pregnancy, ending in a short labour and that life-changing moment when I first set eyes on my daughter.

'Angel was my miracle, my new beginning. To me, she signified hope, a chance to start a new life and get it right. But when Angel was two months old, I bumped into Nick.

'I remember him staring at her and me making a flustered excuse that I was looking after her for a friend. I barely recognized him at first, but only because my blinkers had finally fallen away. Instead of the good-looking, outgoing, sociable person I thought I'd loved, I could see only self-obsession, greed, his constant calculating in the shifting of his eyes.

'My heart was fluttering as I tried to walk past him, but he'd grabbed my arm, determined to talk to me. When I tried to wrench it away, he held tighter, hurting me, until a passer-by stopped to ask if I was OK.

'I told the man that I needed to get this baby home to her mother. I couldn't meet Nick's eyes. The man nodded, waiting there as Nick let go of me. I pushed the buggy down the road, while Nick stood watching me, until I went round the corner, out of sight.

'That was when I knew that, in the bustling anonymity of the city, I wasn't safe. Amongst so many who were harmless, all it took was one person.

'I packed up my flat and a week later loaded everything I owned into the car I'd bought. As we drove away, I knew the future started right then. I knew also, my life would only change if I made it change. Finding out I'd been left Jessamine Cottage had come at exactly the right time. I saw it as a sign.

'I wondered how long it would take for Nick to give up on me and move on. He'd never liked being thwarted. That last time, when he'd grabbed hold of me, I'd felt the full force of his anger. I'd hoped time would defuse it, but I wasn't taking chances. You can't change the past. All you can do is leave it behind and look forwards.'

There was silence, then Abbie spoke. 'Are you sure that's what happened? That you've really remembered everything this time?'

'I'm sure.' Evie's voice was full of angst. 'But how is any of this going to help find Angel?'

'It's surprising how even the smallest detail can help,' Jack said. 'Go on.'

'Nick really frightened me,' Evie said. 'After that, I decided it didn't matter who Angel's father was. It was no one's business but mine. Richard ran and Nick proved himself unworthy.

It was about trust, and I couldn't trust him, least of all with a small child.

'As a mother, you have a duty to do what's best for your child.' Evie gazed towards the window. 'It isn't always easy, but it's like having another sense, or an instinct.'

Abbie folded her arms. 'Evie, I don't know what to believe any more. You've told me all these different versions of you and Nick.' She shook her head. 'Right now, I don't know what to believe. You've completely lost me.'

'They all feel real when I tell you.' Evie looked scared.

Abbie continued. 'If Angel is Nick's daughter, he should be helping you financially.'

But Evie interrupted. 'It's why he came to see me, isn't it? It was about money, not because he cared if he had a daughter. Anyway, I don't need his help.'

Abbie paused, then went on. 'Angel has family she doesn't know. You may not like them, but they are still her family. What were you going to do when she asked you about her father. Lie?'

'No.' Evie had clammed up again. 'But that's the least of my worries just now.'

'Nick wants a DNA test. Even if he's not the father, don't you think Richard should know?' Abbie was staring at her. 'Right now, I've no idea what the truth is. But let's just say that Nick had found you and Angel. That he knew she wasn't his child. Is it possible he'd do something like this to punish you?'

Evie turned pale. Jack thought of everything he knew about Nick. It wasn't beyond the realms of possibility that he could have come here, marched upstairs and taken Angel from her bed.

'Did he come here that night, Evie? Force his way in and go

upstairs to get Angel?' Abbie asked. 'Maybe you knew where he was going and you went running after them, across the fields, trying to catch up.' Evie's face was ashen with shock. 'He'd have been furious, wouldn't he? More so, because for the last three years, you'd lied – by omission, if nothing else.'

Evie gasped. 'I don't know.'

Abbie carried on. 'Maybe you threw yourself at him, to try to get Angel from him. He could have lost his temper. Do you think he could have attacked you? If he'd been angry enough?'

Evie stared back at her, horrified. 'Oh God. It must have been him.'

36

'No, Evie. That wasn't what happened.' Abbie spoke firmly. 'Nick has an alibi for that night. We know for sure that he wasn't the one who attacked you.' There was a long pause. 'I'm sorry, but I'm afraid we still can't trust your memories. Not about any of it.' She paused. 'Now I need you to listen to me, just for a moment. You know, don't you, that for the last month, we've had as many officers as possible involved in the search for Angel. But now . . .'

Jack couldn't sit still and listen to this. He got up and walked over to the window.

'You can't stop. You can't. Oh God, Abbie . . . Don't do this . . .'

Jack folded his arms, dreading what he sensed was coming. The truth was, he didn't share Abbie's uncertainty. OK, so the evidence was lacking. It wasn't conclusive. All that meant was that they had to keep looking until they found it.

'You lost a baby, Evie. You were a teenager looking after Leah Danning when she disappeared. That on its own was a major trauma. Then you were attacked, there's no question about it, and we're continuing to investigate that. But it's looking more and more likely that your head injury has affected your memory in such a way that your past is confused with the present.'

'But you're wrong!' Evie was outraged. 'What about Angel? Where does she fit into this?'

Abbie sighs. 'The truth? It's possible that in your mind, Angel's the baby you lost, Evie. The baby you miscarried. You were six months pregnant when it happened. You would have had dreams about her growing up, about the future. It was another traumatic loss for you, especially after what happened to Leah. Losing her was like losing the future you'd pinned all your hopes on. It would be understandable if, all this time, you've kept her alive in your head.'

'No.' It came out a whisper.

Jack frowned. He hadn't been as involved with this case as Abbie had, but even so, he knew that the mind could play the cruellest tricks. After Josh died, he was sure he'd seen him, several times. Abbie could be right. Angel could be the baby Evie lost years ago. Then he found himself doubting it again. If it was true, how could Evie's emotions still be so raw? But it was possible too, that the fear and the trauma had brought them back.

'I want to see Charlotte,' Evie said suddenly.

'She's at home, as far as I know. When did you last hear from her?'

'A few days ago.'

Jack made a mental note to call Charlotte Harrison. It was clear Evie needed a friend, now more than ever.

*

'That was necessary,' Abbie said briefly, as they walked down the path towards Jack's car.

He didn't reply.

'I can't help thinking,' Abbie went on, 'that in some way, the attack is linked to Leah's disappearance. Did Evie see something that day? Or during the days before? Something her mind has blocked out, because she was too traumatized. When she moved back here, she could have lived in this cottage for months without anyone seeing her. But what if, one day, completely by chance, her path crossed with whoever abducted Leah?'

Jack frowned. It sounded too far-fetched, but anything was possible. 'There's no proof.'

'Right now, there's no proof of anything. I think the intention was to kill her,' Abbie said quietly. 'On that particular path through the maize field, the time of year – no one was likely to find her for some time. The attacker took everything that might have identified Evie, covering their tracks, knowing that because of the way she lived, no one was likely to report her missing.'

'And knowing that within a couple of weeks, the maize field would have been harvested and the evidence destroyed.' Jack was thoughtful. 'You think someone was watching her?'

Abbie nodded. 'It's likely. I think they came to her house and somehow lured her outside. Maybe Tamsyn saw what happened and that's why she had to die. Whoever did this hasn't left anything to chance.' She frowned. 'What I'm not sure about is how Angel fits in – assuming she exists. Was she the reason for the attack?'

'Whoever took her must have carried her some way.'

'That's occurred to me, too. We just don't know. There's so much we don't know,' Abbie said quietly.

Jack glanced towards the house. From an upstairs window, he could see Evie watching them.

'This time last year, I found a dog.' The image was imprinted on Jack's mind. 'A black and white dog. Its throat had been cut and its eyes gouged out. It was on top of a makeshift altar, with all these other dead creatures around it. Rabbits, squirrels, birds . . .' He shook his head, trying to rid his mind of the image.

Abbie was silent for a moment, before saying, 'You think that was Satanists.'

He nodded. 'Remember I told you about what Rhodes said? It coincided with one of the days on their calendar which required them to carry out an animal sacrifice.'

He shivered. The temperature had dropped while they'd been talking.

'Halloween's ten days away.' This time, it was Abbie who shivered. 'What you said about the missing persons being held by Satanists, it doesn't bear thinking about, does it?' She was thinking about Angel. 'I don't think we should mention this to Evie.'

'No.' Jack completely agreed. She was already torturing herself. If she knew what he'd just told Abbie, it could tip her over the edge. There was something else he'd been meaning to ask her.

'Did Miller ever mention what happened that night in the woods?'

Abbie stared at him. 'The night you saw the torches? No.' She was silent. 'He definitely didn't.'

'Don't you think that's odd?'

Abbie frowned. 'Yes. Very.' She looked at Jack. 'Especially as he was on duty and you weren't.' She looked puzzled. 'Have you read about Xander Pascoe? He was interviewed when Leah Danning went missing. I only mention him because there were rumours that he was linked to a Satanic group. There was no proof, of course. And on the day Leah disappeared, he had alibis that put him nowhere near the scene of the crime. Alibis that some people believed were false . . .'

Jack nodded. 'His father was convicted of murder. He's still inside.' And his mother, Janna Pascoe, was tough as old boots.

For the next couple of days, Jack was buried in paperwork, breaking the monotony by venturing out to walk Beamer. He heard on the police grapevine how over the following week, the searches for Angel were to be cut back, then withdrawn completely. When he called Abbie, she sounded regretful, guilty, sad.

His call to Charlotte went to voicemail. He made a point of calling round to see Evie, and found the house locked up and the curtains drawn. Eventually he saw her face at an upstairs window and he waved at her. When she came down and opened the back door, he was shocked. The little strength he'd observed coming back seemed to have ebbed away.

'I came to see how you were.'

Evie shrugged. 'They're stopping the search.' She always said 'they', as though she didn't associate Jack with the police. 'They think I'm confused and inconsistent.'

'The investigation is still open,' Jack told her. 'You mustn't give up.' For a moment, he wondered if he saw a spark of something, but then she turned blank eyes towards him.

249

'Maybe they're right. My mind is shot to pieces. Maybe I just made everything up.'

But Jack knew she hadn't. However unlikely it was, however lacking the evidence, he'd seen the strength of her emotions. It had reminded him of Louise, when Josh died. It had been real. The police had done everything by the book, but the investigation had been fruitless and inconclusive. They were still investigating the assault, but the fact remained that as far as they were concerned, without paperwork or forensic evidence, there was no child.

'I have an appointment with a counsellor who specializes in memory disorders. There's a card somewhere.' She glanced behind her, into the kitchen. 'Abbie did say to call her, if I found anything new, anything conclusive. So I looked, Jack. And I did find something, something everyone else missed.'

He stared at her.

'A picture.' Her eyes filled with tears as she whispered it. 'It's a picture Angel drew for me. It had slipped behind the fridge. It must have got caught in the back of it somehow. It's the first actual proof—'

'Did you tell Abbie?'

She nodded. 'It's just a child's drawing done with coloured pencils, of a person with a triangular body and stick legs, with a round yellow sun in the top left corner. Do you know what she said?' She paused. 'She said, "It's not enough, Evie. I know what my boss will say, that anyone could have drawn it."'

Evie was sobbing, back on the knife-edge. 'God, what will it take? *Her body?*'

He knew the turmoil she was feeling, her need for some kind of closure. When you can't rely on your own mind, you're fragile, and each day is uncertain. That was how Evie's life was right now, all the time. Anything she remembered was potentially no more than a dream.

Her body was shaking with her sobs, as she grieved for the baby who had died before she could give birth to her. Jack could imagine her thinking of the baby her body had failed to sustain and that her memories of her pink-cheeked child, alive and smiling, were no more than wish-fulfilment. Images that had comforted a mind that has suffered too much.

The trouble was, Jack was thinking, he knew how grief could take you over. The counsellor had explained it to him, after Josh died. It could delete the most painful times, the heartbreak, eventually leaving you memories to hold forever, to embellish, to alter, painted crystal clear on your mind.

He knew that had happened to Evie, but he also believed in the intensity of her pain. This was a recent loss, one that time had not yet softened. He was sure of it.

'Listen. Never mind what they've said to you. You have to trust your gut, Evie. If you know you have a child, you can't give up. So you didn't register her birth. Do you know how often that happens? Maybe she was born here in Cornwall. We don't actually know, and we haven't yet been able to check all the hospital records in London. But this isn't about the police. It's about someone very clever who's made them think you've lost your mind. You can't let them get away with it.' Jack paused. This wasn't professional, but he didn't care. He wasn't here on police business. He was here as a friend.

He watched for some response from her, but Evie had frozen. Then she looked at him. Jack couldn't stop himself. He stepped forward and put his arms round her.

Casey, 2004

The world's an accessible place. A career, fame, happiness, dangled like the proverbial carrot. There for the taking. As if we're all born equal, each of us with a right to the best there is in life. Another lie. We're not all born the same.

Even without Charley, I was going to travel. After that, I wasn't sure where I was going, but that could wait. First, I knew I wanted money. If a career and happiness came with it, I wouldn't turn it away, but money was the clincher. Without it, you weren't going anywhere.

Natural talent can take you far. On the stage or in politics, for example, but thanks to my parents, I'd stumbled across my own niche market for making money. And it was easy.

You have to find your own way, and I'd found mine. I became this person who, if you looked closely, resembled me in height and eye colour and the shape of my nose, but who for as long as it took, wasn't me. Who wore a bold print dress cinched at the waist and tight black boots. Whose dewy skin wasn't natural but was squeezed out of a tube and applied with a soft brush, her eyes wide between her eyelash extensions. Her hair was her best feature, I always

252

thought – long and thick, a glossy black. Did you know that money makes your hair shine?

Her lips were painted to match the red oblique stripes on her dress, and she wore a gaze that lingered that extra second, a smile that showed even white teeth. A smile that, once she was in her car, dropped its brightness as she drove the seven miles. I always took the same route, imagining who I was going to be, half anticipating, half not wanting to arrive. Sometimes I pretended I was Charley. Someone I hated; who'd hate what I was going to do.

The man paid me, mostly just to peel off my clothes while he sat in the corner of the room and watched me. Pervy bastard, I'd thought the first time. A bigger fool than most of them, paying me, just to watch. That was all he wanted, to start with.

Being paid so a man could look at you was no big deal. It was what we'd agreed. That was why the first touch broke the rules, electric-shocked me. The next just sparked. After all, his eyes knew every inch of my body. Was touching so different? And it was worth more. I didn't even have to ask. There was more money in the envelope he gave me that time. And the time after.

Only a matter of time before he wanted sex. Thanks to Anthony, then Alistair, I didn't feel. It was a good lesson – learning to switch feelings off – one everyone should learn. And I had a good body which I was prepared to use to my advantage. At least I had something to show for letting him have me, not like the indiscriminate couplings amongst other people I knew. The drunk one-night stands which were so pointless. Or the affairs my father had, which had devastated my mother and driven my family apart. What I did affected no one. And it was no one's business. Sex was a transaction and all the more satisfying because of it; it was about money instead of gratification – or love.

Eventually, I found my own kind of love, if you could call it that.

One that temporarily assuaged the emptiness. Not the gentle, bland couplings that held some people together, woven into their lives alongside their meaningless jobs and crippling mortgages. That wasn't for me. With that kind of love came pain, I'd found that out the hard way. That was for other people – love with its meaningless words and eloquent declarations, too easily and fervently spoken one moment, only to be withdrawn the next.

You couldn't trust it. And what I sought was more carnal, brutal even. It left me with the same feeling I used to get when I cut myself. I wasn't alone. There were plenty of men who wanted the same.

While it lasted, in a hotel room or somewhere less private, it added to the thrill, I'd found – I could forget the hurt, the betrayal, the loneliness, losing myself in the brutality of the act. It had to be brutal. Then after, there'd be no sentimentality or exchange of numbers that would later be forgotten. We existed in the moment. Then we were gone.

2007

People were all the same. All using me, drawing me into ever more complicated games, wringing out of me every last drop of my blood; sapping me. Leaving me with the same emptiness.

It didn't matter that I tried. Take Ed, for example. Hadn't I loved him unconditionally? Done everything for him? I'd turned his characterless flat into a cosy home. Cooked him proper meals. Made him cut his hair, too, getting rid of those curls I hated. Short, straight hair looked so much better on a man. Yes. I was good for Ed. It was because of me that he got the promotion he wanted. I'd coached him, pushed him way further than he'd ever been able to push himself. But that was what it was about, wasn't it? Knowing what was best for someone? Even if they swore at you or called you a nagging cunt.

He'd known I was right. He'd thanked me, too, with that diamond ring that I'd been so touched by; the same one that when I came to sell it, turned out to be a cheap fake.

That had hurt then angered me. It had shown me how little he thought of me, that I wasn't worth more than that. How stupid he thought I was. I wasn't, though. I'd proved, too, that he needed me. I was an integral part of what he'd become. Just as I'd built him up, I could as easily bring him down.

It hadn't taken much. So many people are vindictive, I'd discovered. Only too willing to bad-mouth their so-called friends; always ready to believe the worst in someone. Everyone's looking for a fall guy. Too bad it had happened to be Ed's turn.

I'd almost finished with him, dismantling his life piece by piece. I'd begun with his home; giving his landlord notice, forging his signature, just as I'd forged it on a cheque made out to myself. His status had been next; a few carefully worded social media posts, untimely gossip to the right people. I'd watched his friendships start to crumble. Then I'd moved on to his career. I'd listened to him enough to know the right people to whom a few well-timed words would make the difference between repute and contempt, success and failure, and took a savage pleasure in his downfall. But then the darkness caught me up.

So many times, I'd questioned why. Why, just as I was rebuilding myself, finding strength in being alone, did I meet someone who loved me for what I was? Hadn't I learned enough, from all those past hardships – those broken hearts, the betrayals, all those fuck-ups – not to trust?

I hadn't met him like I met the others – clandestine rendezvous arranged solely for sex, in some or other cheap hotel room. Never at someone's home – just as questions were never asked, no picture could be drawn of the other's life.

From the start, it was different with him – uncontrived – our meeting sheer coincidence: my missed train and his cancelled appointment. I sat drinking my latte, aware of the irritation that festered inside me at having to wait, my eyes flitting, uninterested, my thoughts elsewhere.

I saw him come in, instantly pigeonholing him into the category of arrogant and smug, people like my father, who didn't know what it was to struggle. It was in his unlined face, the expensive shirt, the way he spoke into his mobile. But there was warmth in his eyes as he listened, smiled. He seemed happy in his own skin. It never ceased to amaze me how anyone could be like that, living a charmed life that had effortlessly fallen into place. They weren't my kind of people, though. Not people like him, which was why the flash of jealousy I felt had shocked me.

I watched him at the bar, talking to a friend, noting his easy confidence merged with a lack of self-consciousness, catching his eye as he happened to glance my way.

The two of them carried on talking, while I concocted their life stories. They were old friends, probably from school days, who both worked in the City, catching up now and then. When his friend left, after a few minutes, he made his way over to where I was sitting.

Had he felt it too?

I agreed to another latte, but already, in a few words, a meeting of eyes, it was much more than that. There was an inevitability, a sense that our meeting was more than just chance. I wasn't looking, that late September afternoon. But fate had intervened, and I found him.

From the start, he was different. The first time, in the dark quiet of the hotel room he'd booked, it was there. I felt it in my bones, the rawness of connection to him, a need for his body against mine that was so much more than sexual. I hadn't known sex could be like that. It had always been about control and pushing boundaries, doing whatever it took to break into the numbness that surrounded me, even briefly, so that I could feel. But not like this – not joining myself to another soul.

Somewhere, deep in my dark, twisted heart, I'd discovered an ache, a craving for more, and I tried to stifle it, because it frightened me. I didn't want to feel like this. When you hooked up with some-one for no-strings sex, you existed in the bubble of the moment. Love wasn't part of the deal. But this was different.

That moment, that incredible moment I'd never forget, when he held my face in his hands, the intensity of his eyes burning into mine, as he told me he'd fallen in love with me. I didn't know what to say, just had a miraculous sense, for the first time, of coming home.

My cynical self stepped in at that point and stopped me from making a complete fool of myself. I knew, didn't I, that love was for other people – those who were older, the successful, those with normal expectations of life, who wanted children, who had an ability to feel. When I was so fucked-up, it was ridiculous to imagine anyone would love me. But eventually, I let my guard down, feeling love wash over all the years of abuse I'd subjected myself to, soothing the chaos in my mind. Discovering that euphoria didn't last, but gave way to a new pain, the kind that came from being apart.

We didn't talk about other people, other lovers. It had always been one of my rules. In my world, you met for uninhibited sex, for a couple of hours, usually in the afternoon, then went back to your separate lives. I didn't know how to be in love.

It was his idea for me to move in. I'd thought about it, wondered if he'd ask, waited for it to come from him, letting surprise spread across my face, then delight. Relief too, that I'd read him right. That for once, thank God, I hadn't been wrong.

'It makes sense, you moving in here,' he'd said softly, stroking a wisp of hair out of my eyes, peeling off my T-shirt, then unfastening the zipper on my shorts.

He was right. He had a narrow, terraced house, while my place was small – and shared with Robin, who had got snide on the rare occasions I had guys over. I'd tried not to let it get to me. Robin was jealous, but girls often were, I found. Of how I looked, that I was always meeting different men. Even when I was moving out, Robin was a bitch.

I'd tried, really hard, to make things right. 'You must come over and see our place! Maybe we can double date . . . It'll be fun!'

But Robin's eyes narrowed. 'You really are nuts, aren't you?'

I shook my head and looked at her, puzzled. 'I don't know why you're being like this. We're friends.'

She flipped her hair over her shoulder. 'Yeah. Right.' She stared at me. 'Friends. Such good friends you take my clothes. And trash them. And don't tell me.'

I coloured. 'I borrowed them. But you said I could. And your clothes are so much nicer than mine. If I've upset you, let me pay you.' I fetched my wallet, pulling out a wad of notes.

'If it had just been the clothes.' Her voice was level, as she pushed the money away. 'But you didn't know where to stop, did you? My clothes first, then my flat, my friends, my family, just about my entire life, Casey.'

'That's not true.' My wounded cry was genuine. Her family and friends had made me welcome. 'I thought we were friends. I thought your friends liked me.'

But Robin shook her head. 'Christ. You're good.'

I looked at her, bewildered, as she went on.

'You really think some of your latest boyfriend's money will fix it and we can all pretend everything's fine.'

I felt myself tense. I hated confrontation. What was the point? It was far better to resolve things amicably. 'I'm sorry,' I said, avoiding her gaze. 'I really didn't mean to upset you.'

She ran her hands through her hair. 'Casey. I don't get you. It's the coming in at all hours, the drinking, the drugs . . . Then acting as if you've done nothing wrong.'

'But I'm not doing drugs,' I protested hotly. 'OK, maybe now and then, but I'm not now, I swear.'

'It's not just that.' Robin paused. 'You think I don't know what you do when you go out? It's not my business, but people talk, Casey. Everyone says you're fucking a different guy every night.'

'I'm not . . .' She was right. It was none of her business, but it was so unfair. I'd changed. I was telling the truth. 'I might have been, but now, I swear I'm not.'

'Whatever.' She sounded disgusted.

I could feel my cheeks flame. 'If I were you, I'd feel the same. I'm really sorry. You should have said. I was on the rebound. It was just a thing I did for a while, but not any more.'

Robin was silent for a moment.

'I'm not like you,' I said. 'I'm not good on my own. And it didn't

259

mean anything. It was just sex. There's nothing wrong with that. They all knew.'

'Except Liam.' Robin's voice was dangerously quiet. 'He was in love with you, Casey. You really screwed him up.'

'Liam was so bloody needy it wasn't true.' It was out before I could stop myself. I hadn't known about the ex-wife that made his every day a misery or the depression that plagued him. 'That's hardly my fault, is it?'

Robin's expression was disbelieving. 'What about compassion, Casey? Caring for other people? Caring what happens to them?'

'You're a fine one to talk,' I said, my temper flaring. 'You don't give a shit about me. Not really. You never did. I was just a convenient lodger who paid you rent.'

Robin whistled. 'Jesus. This is pointless. And to think, for a while, you almost convinced me.'

I watched her get up and walk across the room to the window. Silent, as she gazed out, her back to me.

'Look.' Robin turned round. 'We both know how it was. And it doesn't matter. You're moving out. It's for the best.' She hesitated. 'Just . . .'

'What?' I was impatient.

Robin folded her arms. 'He's a good guy, Casey. Be nice to him. Don't mess this up.'

'Oh, I get it.' I stood there, anger burning inside me. 'This isn't about me. It's about him, isn't it? You're jealous. You always have been, because guys like me. Loosen up, Robin. Have some fun – before it's too late.'

I'd wanted to leave as friends, but I couldn't help that she felt this way.

Robin's face turned white. 'Just get the fuck out.'

*

Losing Robin hadn't mattered to me. I was with someone who loved me, who knew how spiteful Robin had been, but who understood. He'd had friends who'd turned on him, too, but we had each other now. He appreciated me, lavished gifts on me.

When I found out I was pregnant, I was shocked. It was one of those freak cases – I'd always been careful, I was on the pill. The idea of motherhood had never entered my head before, but if it had been someone else it had happened to, I'd have laughed in their faces. It was a risk, wasn't it? If you had sex, it was always there. Nothing was a hundred per cent reliable.

People weren't, either. The fucked-up left a trail of carnage, I discovered. He loved me, but he was weak. I left it a couple of weeks before telling him, wanting to hold the knowledge tight to myself. To imagine a whole new world of possibilities; being part of a family that would be nothing like the one I'd grown up in. Life experience did that to you. You could choose not to repeat the pain, the dysfunction, to instead build a loving, nurturing home for a child to grow up in. Already I could see it – the carefully decorated bedroom, the family meals, the home that would always be a safe place, no matter what.

He didn't want a child, he told me. At least, not with me . . . But I didn't find that out until later. I hoped that because he loved me, love would change his mind. It didn't, of course. Since when had I got so stupid? So romantically naive, when everyone knew men were weak. They said all the right things, but didn't have the balls to see them through.

In the end, he didn't need to worry. After ten weeks, I felt the familiar hot stickiness between my legs as I lost the baby, and solved all his problems. That was when I felt it come back. The emptiness. Dissatisfaction. The deep, rotting hole inside my heart.

It was followed by the darkness. I hadn't meant to slip back into my old ways. I told myself that just once was forgivable. Twice, even.

Anyway, it was his fault he caught me. He'd lied to me about going away to meet a client. My heart almost stopped when I heard his key in the door. Fortunately, we were still dressed. I'd fabricated a story about how Oliver was a distant cousin who'd just happened to call me earlier that day.

But he didn't hold out a friendly hand. Nor did he smile. He didn't say anything, to either of us, not till later, when Oliver had gone. He didn't ask if it had happened before. It was worse than that. His look of hurt. The tears, which turned blood red for a moment in the reflection of car lights through the window.

'We need to talk.'

He took my hand and led me over to the sofa. There was sorrow in his eyes – such lovely, kind eyes – as he told me how he couldn't go on like this. Numbness descended on me, masking my pain. His words, bloody words, washing over me, leaving me untouched, as I forced a few of my own selfish tears. This wasn't my plan.

I didn't understand why he was being like this. Everyone knew happiness didn't last.

'I can't live like this,' he told me.

I'd reached forward to touch him, but he'd pulled away as if I'd shocked him.

'I know he's not the first. How could you? How could you?' His voice rose.

I flinched. It was so unfair. Only then did I work it out – how Robin must have warned him. He should have told me. Given me the chance to explain that Oliver, the other guys, they meant nothing. It was just sex.

He was just like the rest, I thought, feeling the shutters come down. I didn't have to explain myself to anyone. If that was how he felt, I was done.

★

You don't need to look for proof to see life for what it really is. To feel the hurt and grief; the bitterness. The bleakness and hopelessness which never leave.

All those stories about love, about sharing your heart, about the magic of connecting with someone, you find out the hard way, that's all they are. Fairy tales, waiting to be shattered, when you give your heart and it isn't enough.

I wasn't enough. But I'd always known that, even as a child. Not bright enough, pretty enough, smart enough. I'd simply forgotten. Nothing had changed. It was hardly surprising that he didn't want me enough.

I didn't matter. Ultimately, we all mean nothing. Our self-important lives have no significance, not really. In a thousand years, will anyone care? We're born, we live, we die – our lives a succession of eye-blinks on the timeline of a small planet, so at the end of time, the human race will have been meaningless. A cosmic joke, no more than specks of stardust, striving for survival, for greatness.

Greatness . . . What does it even mean? Is greatness measurable? Is it innovation, fame, your name written in history books? Or is there greatness in the man who saves the life of a small bird?

Everyone forgets we're small, so small that one day nature and the elements will reclaim their planet, rid it of its human blight, wipe away every last trace of us. Restore balance. Have you thought how a single tree benefits the planet more than a person?

People don't think about how nature's power is greater; how it's everywhere, in the height of the trees, the phase of the moon. In the weather – dull drizzle from saturated cloud that dampens scents and blurs the edges of footprints. In the seeds sown into ploughed fields, onto crumbly red soil, where they need light, warmth, water. The passing of time, before they're ready for harvest.

Timing is everything. But you can't leave things too long, because there's something that comes to all of us. When we least expect it, stealing out of the darkness. In our world of opportunity, death is our greatest certainty.

37

Charlotte

'I'm sorry I haven't been over for a few days. Man trouble.' I
hold up the bottle I'm carrying. 'I brought wine – if you're
allowed?'

Jen nods. 'Sounds good.' She opens one of the cupboards
and gets out two glasses.

'So what's been happening? Any news? No Detective
Inspector Abbie Rose?' I look around. 'Do you have a corkscrew?'

She opens a drawer without responding. When she turns
round, there are tears rolling down her face.

'What's happened, Evie? Tell me.'

'It's the police. The searches have stopped. They think I've
had a breakdown and Angel was my stillborn baby.' Her voice
cracks.

'They can't.' I'm shocked. Putting the bottle down, I walk
over and put my arms round her.

'I'm OK.' She pulls away, then turns back to the drawer and
hands me a corkscrew.

I open the bottle and pour the wine. 'Here. Drink this.' I

can't believe the police have done this. 'It's crazy,' I tell her. 'Completely. For Christ's sake, you're a mother. You know the truth. Just because you don't have photos, doesn't mean you made her up.' I pass one of the glasses to her.

She has a slug of wine. 'The police think I did.' Her voice breaks.

'Jesus.' I'm utterly shocked.

She stares at her glass. 'Jack thought the same as you.'

'Jack?' Then I remember. The guy who came when I found the body in the maize field was called Jack. Jack Bentley. I had a missed call from him.

'The policeman with the dog. He lost his son. He's the only person who really understands.'

'What did he say to you?'

'He said I should trust my gut.' She turns the wine glass between her fingers.

'Don't you agree with him?'

She looks at me, her eyes filled with fear. 'I want to. I really do. I've told them everything I remember, but you know how unlikely some of it sounds. Even Abbie didn't know what to believe. I can't trust myself.'

I imagine Abbie Rose, sitting at this same table, laboriously recording everything Evie says. 'It doesn't matter what Abbie Rose thinks. Jack's right. You're the only one who knows. Can you really give up?' I say, more gently.

'Right now, what else can I do?' She drains her glass and I top it up. 'I'm confused about so many things. Nick came to the cottage.'

'God.' He's the last person anyone needs.

She shrugs. 'I didn't want to see him, but it set off more

memories, which was something. And my mother's asked me to stay.'

'That could be really good for you.' I nod encouragingly. 'A change of scene and someone to fuss over you could be just what you need.'

Jen doesn't respond. 'We haven't really spoken for years. And . . .' She hesitates.

It's there, in her silence. The truth. She hasn't given up. A part of her still knows she has a daughter.

I'm probably over the limit after the wine but it doesn't stop me driving. When I get home, the lights are on in the house and loud music is playing. Inside, the place is a complete mess, with cupboards and drawers emptied onto the floor.

Rick's drunk – and stoned. At least he's an amiable drunk, rather than a nasty one. All traces of his anger seem to have gone.

'I'm looking,' he keeps saying to me. 'I know it's here, babe. Help me look.'

'It's a fucking mess, Rick. What are you playing at?'

'I can't find it,' he says mournfully. 'It's gone, babe. Where'd you put it?'

'Put what?' I snap, bending down to start picking up what he's strewn all over the floor.

'Dunno, babe, do I? Wouldn't have to ask if I did . . .'

By the time I've finished tidying, he's snoring on the sofa. I sit on the floor, watching him. This isn't working any more.

I catch him the next day, after he's seen off his hangover with an early morning surf. By the time I've waited for him to shower and change, I've worked out what I'm going to say.

When he comes downstairs, his hair still damp, neither of us mentions last night.

'Rick? This isn't working.'

He stares at me a moment, then sighs. 'I had a feeling you were going to say that.' He shrugs, cold again. 'So now what?'

'Are you still going to Portugal?' One of his surfing mates has a place there. Last I heard, a whole crowd of them were going in search of big waves.

'Not for another week. I could stay at Jimbo's,' he offers. 'It's out of season. He's got plenty of room.'

'No.' I shake my head. 'It's OK. There's no need. You get ready for your trip. I'll stay with a friend.'

He walks over and, leaning down, presses a kiss against my forehead. He smells of shampoo. Then he pulls back, looking into my eyes. 'Best thing,' he says quietly.

'Yes.' A pang of sadness hits me.

It doesn't take long to pack enough for a week. Only as I drive away do I realize what I'm losing. Not just a friend and companion. He was there when I needed him – my safety net.

38

Jack

He remembered that feeling of having no peace. Not in the quiet moments, or in the bittersweetness of memories, or the dead of night. Just a restlessness, a constant searching, clinging to the most fragile hope.

The police search had wound down. Jack had caught sight of Evie once or twice, walking through the woods alone, slightly lost-looking. Respecting her privacy, he'd kept his distance, until the morning he lost Beamer – and Evie found him.

As she walked towards him, he could see how thin she still was, just skin and bone, under the clothes that swamped her.

'Sorry.' He stopped as Beamer came bounding up to him. 'Once he gets on the trail of a rabbit, there's no stopping him.'

'I thought he might be lost.' She spoke quietly, her voice flat.

Jack hesitated before asking. 'How are you?'

'OK.' But her voice was trembling.

'Any news?' Kicking himself for asking, because if there was, the chances were he would know before she did. Anyway, he could tell from her demeanour there had been no good news. And if there had, whether he'd been to the police station or not, he would have heard.

'No.' She paused, before looking up at him, her eyes filled with tears. 'There are still these different versions of my life. So many people have told me things I don't recall. I still don't remember what happened to Leah – only what they've told me. But it's there. I remember being frantic with worry, the police coming to interview me . . .' She looked desperate.

Jack didn't know what to say to her. The focus had switched from a missing child to an attack on a woman suspected of having mental health problems; as if one precluded the other, that the two were mutually exclusive. They were no nearer finding out who had attacked Evie, meaning she still, at least, had a police guard.

'So, you're just walking,' he said.

'Yes.' Her voice wavered. 'I needed to get out of the house.'

He paused. 'Can I walk with you?'

She hesitated, then nodded.

Jack let her lead the way. However muddled her head, there were clearly places she wanted to seek out. Every so often Beamer lunged after a rabbit, or a squirrel gathering winter fodder, but he did so half-heartedly, for the most part trotting along with them.

'I might get a dog,' she said suddenly. 'Now I don't have a cat.'

'He hasn't come back?' A dog would be a good idea for her. Company, a pair of sharp ears.

'No.'

Thinking of the scream he'd heard in the woods near Evie's that night, Jack let the subject drop. For a while they didn't speak. Then, as the path widened enough for them to walk side by side, she said, 'I'm sorry about your son.'

Jack was taken by surprise. She had enough on her mind without worrying about him. Most people didn't know what to say, choosing instead to stay silent. But Evie wasn't most people. She understood.

'How do you cope?'

There was honest compassion in her voice. She wasn't prying, but it made Jack suspect that whatever she told him, a small part of her was holding on to hope.

'Day by day,' he said briefly. 'But also, you have no choice. When someone's life is taken so suddenly, especially a young person, it makes you want to make the most of every second you have. Not to waste it, because you're here and they're not. But, God – it'll never make sense. He was seventeen. Had everything to live for . . .' Familiar emotion overcame him. His voice cracked. There was more he wanted to say, like how he wanted to talk about Josh, all the time. It was other people who couldn't cope with it. You got fed up with the looks of pity and the platitudes. 'It takes time,' was a favourite. He'd lost count of how many times people had said that to him, as if they knew. They didn't, of course. It didn't matter how much time you gave it. You didn't get over the loss of your child.

She was quiet for a moment. 'I can understand,' she said at last. 'How it completely changes everything.'

They fell into silence as they kept walking, further than he normally went. Evie said little, her head moving now and then as she took in their surroundings. No matter what she said, she was still looking. It wouldn't take much for her to question what she'd been convinced of. Jack watched her, aware of the confusion that must be clouding her mind, wary also of making it worse for her.

Eventually the woods thinned out. Ahead of them were fields edged with stone walls, dozens of sheep grazing them. She looked unsure.

'We could keep going?' he suggested. 'Unless there's anywhere you need to be?'

She shook her head. 'Not really.'

'If we keep walking, we can pick up the coast path. Over there.' Jack pointed, and as her eyes followed, he saw them light up as she saw the sea in the distance, a shimmer of blue.

'It's a long way,' she said quietly.

He'd forgotten how frail she was. 'Maybe too far.'

'I think so.' She stood there, staring towards the horizon. 'I still haven't found any of her things.' As she whispered it, there was a blankness in her eyes. Jack frowned. He knew from experience how much clutter came with small children. You wouldn't have thought it was possible to remove everything a child left in its wake. Not just clothes, but the detritus of toys and tiny treasures children collect.

'What about photos?'

She shook her head, a sadness in her eyes.

Jack was silent, trying to imagine how she was feeling.

'I found a pebble,' she said suddenly. 'Under the sofa. All of a sudden, I felt hopeful, because I could remember the day Angel found it. We'd been planting bulbs last autumn, her little hands in the crumbling earth next to mine, when she'd pulled it out, brushing the soil off. I even remember our conversation.

'"It's a bone, Mummy."

'"Is it? Shall we wash it and see?"

'"It might be a dinosaur's." That's what she told me, as she turned it this way and that.'

She went on. 'It wasn't really a bone.' Her voice was distant again. 'Just shaped enough like one to spark her imagination in a hundred directions. She brought it inside. She had a collection of treasures – a black and white feather and the shell of a blackbird's egg which she kept on her windowsill, along with her hairclips and plastic bracelets and things. And they've all gone.' Her eyes were filled with tears. 'At least, that's what I remember. I guess I made it all up.'

'But surely . . .' Jack was confused. 'If your memories are that clear . . .'

She interrupted. 'You know what you said to me, about trusting my gut? I've really thought about that. I wish it worked for me.'

'It may yet.' Jack was still convinced she shouldn't give up.

She wiped her eyes, then turned to look at him. 'It's as though everything's there, in my head, but my brain puts the wrong things together. My memories are stories.' Her voice shook. 'Stories I want to believe, because they feel so real. I have to keep reminding myself they're not.'

'People often tell different versions of the same story,' Jack suggested. 'And yours aren't so very far apart.'

'They're far enough apart. And there's what happened with Leah. I've seen photos of her. In my head, she and Angel . . .' She looked scared. 'They're so alike. I don't know what to think.'

'No.' It was beyond anything he'd experienced. He knew that memory could be unreliable; that false memories could be implanted. But that wasn't what this was. He'd never seen anyone so confused.

'Everyone tells me I need time.' She was silent for a moment. 'But the more memories that come back to me, the fewer I trust.' She paused for a moment. 'I just want it all to go away.' There was anger in her voice. 'I wish I could go back to before. Don't you wish that? That you could go back?'

'Yes.' Of course he did. He'd give anything for Josh to still be here. His death had changed Jack. He wasn't the same person he used to be. It had changed his marriage too, in the worst way. Nothing was the same, but that was life.

Talking about Josh brought a wave of painful, nostalgic memories flooding back. It still got him, a melancholic yearning for something lost forever.

'It's no good just remembering, is it?' Anxiety flashed in her eyes. 'It's not enough – for the police and for me, too. If Angel's real, she's got to be there, Jack. In my brain. If only someone could splice it out, that sliver that holds her face, or a moment from her childhood, so that we had something tangible. And if it wasn't there, then we'd know.'

Sensing her desperation, her frustration, he could only nod.

'If I had her things,' Evie shook her head. 'You know how they make you think of a particular time – like I can remember the day I gave her Pony. And when she put on the little bracelet I gave her for her birthday . . .'

Suddenly Jack thought of something. He got out his phone, scrolling through the photos until he found what he was looking for. 'Do you recognize this?'

Evie stared at the photo of the pendant the bird dropped, the day he found Tamsyn's body, recognition dawning on her face. 'It's Tamsyn's.' She looked at Jack. 'I'm not making it up.'

274

He didn't think she was. He didn't tell Evie where he'd found it. 'You're sure?'

Her face was pale as she nodded. 'I gave it to her.'

'Evie befriended Tamsyn, by the sound of things.' Jack had called Abbie to let her know. 'She says she used to leave Angel with her occasionally, when she had to go out.'

'It could explain why no one saw her with a child.' Abbie was silent for a moment.

It explained a lot, Jack was thinking. Evie hadn't left her daughter alone. She'd timed her deliveries to the farm shop and any shopping she needed to do so that they coincided with Tamsyn's visits.

'According to Forensics, Tamsyn died around the same time as the attack on Evie,' Abbie told him. 'It fits with our theory about Tamsyn seeing what happened.'

'Maybe she was staying at Jessamine Cottage. And whoever is behind this needed her out of the way.' Jack was thinking how easy it would have been for the killer. Everyone was so used to Tamsyn disappearing that no one missed her.

39

That winter wasn't far away could be seen in the shortening days and the falling of the leaves; autumnal anti-cyclonic gloom giving way to night frosts and cold sunshine. Jack thought about Evie often, walking with her now and then, when he wasn't working. Her eyes would be pinned to the ground, hunting for anything that the searches may have missed, only occasionally flickering elsewhere, along hazy lines of long-ago planted trees, or upwards through the tangle of branches towards the sky.

He wished he could have given her some answers. Words of wisdom that would have helped her when she most needed it, but who was he to explain what the grand plan was? There were two certainties in this life. You were born and you died. The bit in between, either you embraced it and made the most of it, or you sat back and let it happen around you. Either way, it was brief.

He had a suspicion that Evie fell into the latter category. Life was too short to waste in the wrong places, in stifling situations with the wrong people. After leaving Nick, she hadn't been sure how she'd like living here, she told him. But as the months went by, the surroundings had crept under her skin and taken root. Or maybe it was the ghosts, she ventured, because she could almost feel them, the ghosts of the people who had been born and had died during the centuries that had passed while the woods had grown up. It made you wonder how many people had walked where they had, because an oak tree could live for a thousand years.

Jack thought of the stag. Then Josh.

They walked a different way every time, kicking through leaves, scanning low branches for a ripped shred of familiar fabric, finding none. During one of their walks, she told him that the isolation which she'd come to love was now her enemy, because there were too many places to hide.

A couple of days passed when he didn't see her. Then one grey, damp morning, from deep in the woods, he heard a scream. He broke into a run. There was another scream. Jack ran faster.

Somehow, he knew it was her. 'Evie?' His voice echoed through the trees, as beside him Beamer barked. 'Evie? Are you there?'

She was crashing through the woods, not far from them.

'Evie? Wait! Where are you?' Suddenly, Beamer ran off ahead. The crashing stopped and he heard her call him.

'Jack?'

He followed the sound of her voice, shocked when he caught up with her. Her eyes were wide and red with crying, her breath coming in gasps.

'I found something, quick, follow me . . .' He couldn't get a word in. 'This way, I need to show you.'

He followed her.

She stopped abruptly, turning round with a look of panic on her face. 'I can't find them. I don't know where we are.'

'Find what?' Jack had no idea what she was talking about.

'Graves, Jack. In amongst the trees. Two graves.'

A shiver ran down his spine. He could see why she was so upset. 'Think, Evie. Which way were you walking?' They were on one of the main paths that they both knew well.

'I – I'm not sure.' It wasn't just her voice that shook. Her whole body seemed to be shaking uncontrollably.

Jack took her arm. 'Come on. Let's keep going straight on.'

They walked only a few yards before she veered off to the left and took a different path. It was narrow and overhung by brambles, so that if you didn't know it was there, you'd walk straight past it.

'Are you sure this is right?' he asked, then watched the back of her head move as she nodded her reply. A few metres further on, she stopped, pointing directly ahead of them. 'There.'

He tried to see where she was looking, then walked past her to take a closer look. At first, under the covering of fallen leaves, it was hard to make them out, but as he focused, he could see what she'd found. Side by side, unmistakeably, were two graves. One of them filled in, scattered with a covering of leaves, the other empty. He got out his phone.

It took two hours for Miller and Evans to find them on one of the main paths, before they could lead them to where the graves were.

'Thanks for showing us. Forensics are on their way. Would you like me to escort Evie home?' Miller was clearly aware of how vulnerable Evie was.

'I'll go with her.' Jack wanted to stay, but he was worried about Evie. 'Call me when you know more,' he said to Miller. 'Evie? Shall we head back?'

He could see that she too was torn between staying and going. Between logic and fear that the daughter she wasn't sure she had might be lying under the mound of earth and fallen leaves. No way should she be here when they dug up the grave. 'Come on.' He took her arm. 'I'll walk you home.'

As they walked, she didn't speak. Jack could imagine the scenarios she was running through her head, in impossible turmoil – and limbo.

Who knew what was in the grave – or who the open one was intended for. Satanists came to mind again. The problem was, these groups kept themselves well hidden, by whatever means it took. When the occasional animal went missing, no one bothered too much. You could blame foxes or hit-and-run drivers. But not when it was a person. God, he hoped it was an animal in there.

Then he was thinking of Tamsyn again. It had become clear that she bunked off school and lived wild, sometimes for weeks at a time. He was reminded again of what his old boss used to say. *Feral children know where to hide.*

If Tamsyn had been feral, that was largely down to her mother. Having lost his own child, it incensed Jack all the more. Uncaring mothers were guilty of a multitude of sins. And now, at least in part because of Mrs Morgan's, Tamsyn was dead.

When they reached Jessamine Cottage, Evie barely said goodbye to him. Jack could see fear eating away at her. She'd seemed so accepting, but as he watched her, he realized that, like him, she hadn't given up on finding her daughter. Not deep inside.

'Will you be OK?' He was worried about her. The house was unlit, and it was too early for her police guard to be here. As far as he knew, she'd be alone.

She nodded, then turned to go in. He stood watching until she'd gone inside and closed the door.

Back at home, Jack couldn't get the image of her out of his mind, haunted by what she had probably been thinking since they found the graves. In the end, he decided to go back and check on her.

It was dark by the time he knocked on Evie's door, carrying a dish. Concerned that she might not be eating, on the spur of the moment he'd brought the casserole he'd made for his own dinner. There was no answer. She clearly had nothing left, not even a polite *hello* for whoever had come to intrude. Intrusions into your small, desolate world – that's what people became when they continually arrived without warning, especially when, like Evie, you were private. He pushed the door open and walked in.

'Hello? Evie? It's Jack.'

There was no reply. Placing the dish on the kitchen table, he carried on through to the sitting room. She was tiny, curled up on her sofa, as though finding the graves had somehow diminished her size. Looking around the room, he noticed it was untidy, clothes thrown over the back of a chair, dirty plates left on the low coffee tables. A manifestation of her life now.

'I hope you don't mind.' He paused. 'I thought you should eat.'

Her head came up as his voice startled her. Jack stood there awkwardly. 'I brought you food. I hope you don't mind . . .' He hedged, suddenly unsure how she felt about him letting himself into her house like this. 'It's just a casserole.'

'Thank you,' she replied, her response automatic. Her eyes drifted away from him.

'I hope you don't mind – I let myself in . . .' He was repeating himself, trying to get her attention, but she seemed out of it. 'The door was unlocked. Your police guard's outside – he saw me come in.' Recognizing Miller in the car, Jack had knocked on the car window but hadn't stopped. Miller had been talking on his phone. Jack hesitated. 'I'll put some on a plate, shall I? It's chicken – home-made.'

The gesture of kindness was lost in what was already an unnavigable landscape of loss and uncertainty, where familiarity was absent, where uninvited people came and went at will. Jack remembered it all too well. Evie didn't move and he realized, after the events of the day, how exhausted she must be. Her body was so slight, her mind so stretched, that she had no reserves, no capacity for the extraordinary.

'Are you coming with me?' He made his voice matter-of-fact. It seemed to stir her. Sitting up, she slid her feet to the floor and followed him to the kitchen.

'Where are your plates?'

Walking over to a cupboard, Evie bent down and reached for two, handing them over before sitting down. It was clearly too much effort for her.

'You didn't have to.'

After hunting around for cutlery, he dished up the casserole and placed a plate on the table in front of her. 'I know what it's like. How much effort it takes.' Placing his own plate on the table, he sat down.

After a couple of mouthfuls, she pushed her plate away. 'I'm sorry. It's good, I'm just not hungry.'

Jack didn't say anything, just carried on eating, noticing out of the corner of his eye as she picked up her fork again, toying with what was on her plate.

'Does your wife mind you coming here?'

Her question took him by surprise. He thought he'd told her. 'My wife doesn't live with me. She left me a couple of months ago.'

She stopped, her fork poised midway to her mouth. 'I'm sorry. I didn't know.'

'Don't be. She'd been having an affair. To be honest, our marriage was falling apart long before Josh died. I think we were already falling out of love, only then the accident happened. Josh's death kept us together – for the wrong reasons. We had grief in common. Nothing else.'

Evie didn't comment.

Jack wasn't used to talking about his marriage. Suddenly he was awkward. 'I should go.' She was clearly tired and he didn't want to outstay his welcome.

Evie got up. 'Thank you. It was really kind.' Her eyes held his.

He left her the rest of the casserole. As he walked down the path to his car, he could feel drizzle on his face. A reminder that the seemingly endless rain of winter was ahead. He didn't look forward to it.

Further down the track, he could make out the shape of a police car, dimly lit from inside, reassured to know that someone was watching out for Evie. As he drove away, he couldn't help wondering what the future held for her. He supposed, at some point, her memory would come back. But maybe it wouldn't.

That night, he couldn't sleep, lying awake as he went over what he'd seen that day. He wondered who the empty grave Evie had found was destined for; and who or what had already been buried there.

Evie was at the centre of everything, he was convinced of it. His gut was telling him loud and clear that this was far from over.

If he was right and this was linked to some occult group, there would be another killing in a matter of days, in observance of Halloween. The victim might already be held captive somewhere. A woman, a girl – even a child. He knew who he needed to talk to.

40

At the station the next day, he bumped into Abbie again. She might not be spending her days with Evie any more, but this case was far from resolved.

'Any news about the graves?' It was too soon, Jack knew, but sometimes, if the identity of the remains was obvious, Forensics would give them a heads-up.

'They're at the site in the woods now. It shouldn't be long before we know what we're looking at.'

'So they've found something.'

'They're confident they have remains in there, but they haven't been any more specific.'

Jack had worked with Underwood about three years ago, on a case near Bude. He knew him well enough to know he trusted him. Something in his head was telling him not to take chances.

'Hello?' He stuck his head round the door to the office where Underwood sat at a desk, frowning at the screen in front of him.

'Hi. Come in.'

Jack closed the door firmly and took a seat. He cleared his throat. 'This is unofficial – for now.' His eyes met Underwood's, who was leaning forward, intently. 'Right now, we have four unsolved crimes. We're trying to find whoever attacked Evie Sherman and killed Tamsyn Morgan. That may or may not be the same person, but I know we've established several links between the cases. I know it's slightly controversial, but I believe Evie's daughter is still missing. Then there's three-year-old Leah Danning's disappearance, fifteen years ago, which was never solved.'

'You think all four are related?'

Jack went on. 'Possibly. There's one person we need to talk to – Xander Pascoe. The police suspected he was involved with Leah Danning's disappearance, but he had an alibi. We know he was involved with Leah's older sister, Casey, and according to Charlotte Harrison, Xander was involved with all kinds of stuff. People didn't want to cross him. Then we're back to Evie, who used to babysit Leah. The only way Tamsyn fits into this, is if she saw something.' Jack sighed. 'I'd like you to come to the Pascoes' farm with me. I want to talk to Xander.'

Underwood shook his head. 'I've already tried. Twice. Both times, there was no sign of him.'

'I know. No warning, this time. We'll just drive up there. If he's not around, we'll talk to his mother.'

Underwood frowned. 'Is there something going on I should know about?'

Jack's answer was evasive. 'Right now, I don't know any more than you do.'

★

The drive to Chicken's Farm, where the Pascoes lived, took thirty minutes along winding lanes edged with stone walls overgrown with grass and bracken. A grey morning had turned to drizzle. From previous experience, Jack wasn't expecting Janna Pascoe to be welcoming.

He was right. As they drew up in the farmyard, a light flickered on inside the house and he saw a face pressed against a window. After ringing the doorbell, they stood there for several minutes before hearing the sound of a heavy bolt being pulled back.

'Yes?'

The woman in front of them was in a wheelchair. 'Janna Pascoe?' Jack held out his police badge. 'Detective Chief Inspector Jack Bentley.' Jack didn't often use his full rank, but dealing with Janna Pascoe merited it. 'This is Detective Sergeant Underwood. May we come in?'

The woman glowered at them. 'If you must.' Leaving the door open, she spun her wheelchair round and disappeared inside.

Once they were inside, Pete closed the front door behind them, the sound echoing throughout the cavernous hallway. Looking around, Jack studied the paintings.

He tried to strike up conversation. It wasn't likely to work with someone like Janna Pascoe, but it was worth a try. 'Are these your family?' He nodded towards the ornately framed paintings on the walls.

'You didn't come here to talk about my paintings.' She had a heavy West Country accent. Her eyes bored into Jack. 'What do you want?'

'A word with your son.' Jack stopped looking at the

paintings. He'd dealt with the likes of Janna more times than he could remember.

'Xander?' Janna seemed to smirk. 'Sorry. He isn't here.'

'Could you tell me when he'll be back?' Jack kept his calm.

'I haven't a bleeding clue. He's a grown man. Comes and goes as he pleases. Now, if that's all . . .' Turning her back on them, she started propelling herself towards a doorway.

'Actually, that's not all. Can you tell us where your son was on the night of twenty-fourth September?' Jack paused briefly. 'Or how about eighteenth of June, fifteen years ago?'

Janna Pascoe's head came up and her hands froze on the wheels of her chair. When she turned round, she wore an expression of pure malice. 'Now what makes you think I can?' she said icily. 'I can't remember last week, let alone fifteen years ago. The accident affected my head. Haven't been the same since.'

'We're not here about your accident, Mrs Pascoe.' Jack held the woman's hostile gaze. 'We just want to know about your son.'

'And I can't help you.'

It was a stand-off. Nothing to be gained by trying to push her further. Jack reached into his pocket for a card, holding it out to her. 'Perhaps you'd be kind enough to ask him to call me?'

When she refused to take it, Jack walked over and left it on top of a large oak chest. Glancing at Underwood, he started walking towards the front door.

'You can see yourselves out,' Janna Pascoe shouted after them. Neither of them replied.

They were still standing outside the closed door when they heard the heavy clunk of the bolt sliding back into place.

'Makes you wonder who she's afraid of.' Underwood glanced at Jack, but he was looking across the yard at some farm buildings.

'Shall we check them out?'

Side by side they walked towards the old stable block. The doors were all closed, with the exception of one top door, which was missing. The building looked unused, neglected even, and had a corrugated roof which had lifted round the edges where the wind had caught it.

'It doesn't look like they do much farming.' Jack peered in through the missing door, where dead leaves were scattered on top of the filthy floor.

'They're empty.' Underwood was checking out each of the stables in turn. 'They don't look like they've been used in a while. Hang on . . . not this one though.'

'What have you found?' Jack looked inside, then immediately stepped back when met with the sight of the slaughtered deer strung up by its hind legs. 'If someone around here's a deer hunter, I'm guessing it's not Janna . . .'

They stared at the carcass until someone spoke behind them.

'Looking for something?'

It was a cold, calculating voice. They turned round. It was Xander Pascoe. It had to be. He had Janna's eyes, full of hostility.

'That's yours, is it, Mr Pascoe?' Jack nodded towards the deer.

'So what if it is? It's not a crime to shoot deer on your own farm, officer. Bloody nuisance, they are.'

So it was him. 'Xander Pascoe?'

'Yes. And what the fuck are you doing nosing around my

farm? Got a warrant?' His manner was as aggressive as his words.

So he knew they were the police. He'd obviously been there all along, while they were talking to his mother.

'I thought I heard a cry coming from one of these stables.' Jack spoke calmly, frowning slightly as he looked at Pascoe. 'A woman, I think. Or maybe it was a child. I'm not sure.' He stared at Xander, watching for the smallest giveaway.

Xander didn't say anything. Then he threw back his head and laughed, an evil sound that gave Jack the chills, reminding him of the laugh he'd heard in the woods.

'You *think*? Well, I'll tell you what I think. It's dangerous out here. First a murder, then an attack . . . It would be safest if you got in your car and left.'

'Before we go, I'd like to ask you one or two questions.' It took all Jack had to ignore Xander's poorly concealed threat. 'Can you tell us where you were on the night of twenty-fourth September?'

'Probably in the pub with my mates. Any one of them will vouch for me – as will the landlord. The Smuggler's Rest – I'll even give you their number. Next question?' He hooked his phone out of the back pocket of his jeans and started scrolling down the screen.

'We have their number.' Jack stared at him. 'Where were you on eighteenth June, fifteen years ago?'

Xander's mouth dropped open, then he pulled himself together. 'How do you expect me to remember fifteen bleeding years ago?'

'Oh, but you do.' Jack's voice was dangerously quiet. 'Remember little Leah Danning, Xander? She was three years old when she disappeared from her garden. The police talked to you about her, only funnily enough, you had a whole load of mates who'd vouch for your whereabouts. You were in a pub, if I remember correctly. The Smuggler's Rest. Like I said, we have their number.'

Xander's eyes narrowed. 'I'd be very careful about what you say if I were you, or you'll end up looking as stupid as the last cop who tried to pin that kid's disappearance on me. I had nothing to do with Leah Danning and I had nothing to do with whatever went on last month. Will that be all?'

'For now,' Jack said brusquely. 'If we need to talk to you again, we'll be in touch.'

As they drove away, neither of them spoke.

'He knows something,' Jack said at last. God, he was relieved to be away from the man. 'He knows we know, too. We need to watch him, see where he goes, who he's with. I've a feeling Xander Pascoe's guilty as hell.'

'But why? Why would he be?'

'Charlotte Harrison told Abbie he had his own Cornish mafia. And because he's obviously a psychopath. He has no feelings. Who knows what his motivation is – or even if he needs one.'

'Money,' Underwood said briefly.

'I was thinking that, too. But did you see those paintings in the farmhouse? I'm no expert, but I'm pretty sure there was a Turner amongst them.'

'Blimey.' Underwood sounded shocked.

Jack's gut feeling was growing stronger. 'So, if it's not money, what the hell is it? People trafficking?' He didn't want to consider the alternative, which was fast approaching – the Satanic practice of ritual sacrifice on Halloween.

41

When Jack got back to the station, Abbie was waiting for him with the forensic results for the blood they'd found on the leaves in the woods.

'Forensics had a load of stuff to work through from the Morgan scene and somehow this got shuffled to the bottom of the pile. They've only just got to it. It was animal, not human. Thank God. After what you told me, I was worried you'd witnessed a murder.' She paused. 'There's nothing more on the remains from the grave,' she added. 'It's taken forever to get all their kit out into the woods, so they've barely got started.'

'How about the results for the fabric I sent off?'

She shook her head. 'They haven't come back yet.'

It shouldn't take much longer, Jack was thinking. 'We didn't get anything out of Xander Pascoe.'

'I didn't think you would. Maybe I should talk to Charlotte again – and Evie, too. There has to be something we're missing.'

'If you talk to Charlotte, I'll go round to see Evie,' Jack

offered. It made sense. He'd do it on his way home. 'I've been thinking about Miller.'

'What about him?'

'I don't trust him. There's the fact that he didn't report the incident in the woods. And have you noticed how often he's at Evie's?' Jack had certainly noticed. More often than not, it was Miller parked outside overnight.

'Spending the night shift in a car isn't exactly popular,' Abbie told him.

'That's my point. Evans has been there a couple of times, that's all. Check the rosters.'

Then Jack had another thought. It was a long shot, but it could make all the difference in the world.

He saw Abbie again briefly later on, just before he left the station.

'I tried Charlotte,' she told him. 'But it went to voicemail. I left a message, but she hasn't called back.'

'Keep trying her.' Jack could sense they were on the verge of something. And if Xander was involved, after his visit, time wasn't on their side. 'I'm going to call in on Evie on my way home.' He knew she was going to ask about the graves.

'Hopefully by tomorrow, we'll have something more from Forensics.'

'Would you like to come in?'

Jack nodded. 'Thank you. How are you? You look better.'

'I'm OK.' Evie sounded wary. 'I seem to be stuck where I was when you were last here. A few more things have come back, but not much.'

'I'm sorry.' He'd hoped for more. 'I've been to see Xander Pascoe. Do you remember him?'

Evie shrugged. 'Vaguely. From school.'

'He and Casey were an item for a while. Do you remember that?'

Evie paused. 'All I can tell you about Xander is that when you mention his name, for some reason I feel embarrassed. I feel ashamed, too. I also know I don't want to talk about him – it makes me uncomfortable. And I have no idea why.'

Jack frowned. 'There must be a reason.'

'You know more about me than I do.' Evie shrugged. 'Yes, there probably is, buried with everything else some place I can't get to.'

He had to ask. 'Has anything at all come back to you, about when Leah went missing?'

Evie frowned. 'There are things that don't make sense. I couldn't begin to tell you why.' She looked at him. 'I'm no help, Jack.'

'You know what I think?' He fixed his eyes on her. 'It makes sense that you came here to get away from Nick and your old life. And if you hadn't moved into your aunt's old house, you might have gone unnoticed, but I think either someone saw you or you saw them. Either that, or you know something that could harm them. And the mostly likely explanation is that it's linked to Leah.'

'Why?' Evie frowned at him. 'How can you say that?'

'I'm still working it out. I'm sure it's to do with Xander Pascoe, too. We have other leads we're following up.' Jack didn't want to tell her about how hostile Xander was, or about what he'd seen and heard, or the traces of blood in the woods. He changed the subject. 'Have you seen Charlotte recently?'

Evie shook her head. 'She came round the other night. She said something about man trouble, but she didn't say what.'

As Jack drove away, he was deep in thought. Evie had told him nothing new. He was pretty sure she wasn't intentionally hiding anything. In spite of what Nick had said, she didn't strike him as devious. He was halfway down the drive when his mobile buzzed. He glanced at the screen. It was PC Evans.

'Hi, Sara.'

'Jack, Abbie thought you'd want to know. It's about the graves. They've dug one up and found a cat buried there. I'll forward you the email – it's not good reading, but I thought you'd want to know. The cat's throat was cut and it was mutilated in various ways.'

Jack felt sick. It was like the dog he'd found last year. Who were these sickos who enjoyed torturing innocent animals? Then another thought occurred to him. That night in the woods, when he'd heard an animal being slaughtered, that terrible cry. Thinking of Evie's missing cat, his blood ran cold.

But Sara interrupted his thoughts. 'Oh God, Jack. That's not all. There's more. They found a third grave. It was further in than the other two. It's been there a long time. They're digging it up now, as we speak.'

'OK. Thanks, Sara.' Jack was filled with dread. *Please, God, it's not a small child.* As soon as he'd hung up, Jack called Abbie. 'Sara just told me about the third grave.'

'Thank God they spotted it. I hope there aren't more.'

'You know they found a mutilated cat?' Jack paused.

'You're thinking of Evie's cat. Is it still missing?'

'As far as I know.' Jack wasn't looking forward to potentially having to tell Evie what had happened to it.

'Can you check with her? I still haven't spoken to Charlotte. I'm on my way over to her house. I'll let you know when I've spoken to her.'

Casey, 2015

It's always there, the knowledge that you can end it. End the pain, the suffering, the unfairness, because whatever you try, there isn't always a cure.

From the moment you're born, you're moulded into something you have no control over. Forget what people say about how you can change. The best you can hope for is the ability to fool them all, so that they leave you alone and go away.

I no longer wanted anyone in my life. But to be alone was unbearable in a world where each day was bleaker than the previous one, growing darker, heavier, until I couldn't think, couldn't move. It was worse, this time. Months passed in which I barely ate, just drank myself into unconsciousness, until there was only one thing I could do.

Did you know there is beauty in the tides? In their ever-changing colour, their ebb and flow; in the pull of the moon, the power of the swell. Forces that we can't control, that at best we can only harness to our own advantage. Take big-wave surfers. Scientists, athletes, philosophers, who know their element, know their own limits, yet know also just how much they can push them, balancing courage with restraint, science with instinct, in the quest to catch a wave and stay alive.

They know, also, there is no margin for error. That the sea is unforgiving. But most people don't think how the same knowledge, of storms, rip currents, swell, can help you another way.

At the right time, when no one's watching, they can carry you away. A single act of insignificance by just one worthless person who wouldn't be missed, exerting their right to decide their own fate, to end their unhappiness forever.

To die.

42

Charlotte

As I turn down the drive to the house, I'm reminded how easy living with Rick was. I take in the view I've seen dozens of times – the rocky coastline, the expanse of sea that stretches into the distance, towards the horizon. At this time of year, you get the full benefit of the elements up here – the wind and rain, the sound of the waves crashing against the rocks below – perilous, but always breathtakingly beautiful.

As I get closer, I see Abbie Rose's car parked outside the house, next to Rick's. She's still sitting in it, talking on her phone. Hanging back just out of sight, I wait for her to get out, watching as she tries the front door, then walks round to the back of the house, peering in through the windows. There's an offshore wind and the tide is midway – I checked. Rick will be surfing.

Leaving the car where it is, I walk up to the house, letting myself in through the front door. I've only come back for a couple of things. The house is definitely empty. Going over to the window, I watch Abbie Rose walk across the garden towards the beach. Then I turn my attention to the view, drinking it in, photographing it into my memory. It really is idyllic. *Idyllic* . . . I savour the word. To be this close to the sea, to have this uninterrupted view, is close to heaven.

I look across the garden. To my amazement, Abbie Rose is climbing down the rocks to the beach. This I have to see. Running outside, staying out of her sight, I cross the garden, crouching down where it reaches the cliff edge, looking at the lone figure on the sand, sitting meditatively on a surfboard, gazing out to sea. Rick.

In her stuffy clothes and leather shoes, Abbie Rose makes it down the last of the rocks and onto the shore. It must be important. I can't imagine why she wants to talk to Rick. I laugh quietly as I watch her shoes start to sink into the wet sand. She slips them off, leaving them on a rock, before she makes her way towards Rick.

From where I am, I can just about make out her '*Hello?*' Lost in his own world, Rick doesn't hear her. As she gets nearer, she tries again. 'Hello?'

The figure turns round. It's definitely Rick. I see his lips move. 'Hi.' He doesn't move.

Carefully, noiselessly, I creep down the slope, hidden by fallen boulders and underbrush. Something tells me I need to hear what they're saying. 'It's Rick, isn't it?'

I've forgotten they haven't met. Then she adds, 'I'm Detective Inspector Abbie Rose. I'm looking for Charlotte.'

A faraway look comes into his eyes. 'Let me know if you find her, Abbie Rose.'

'What do you mean?'

'She's gone, man. Packed up and cleared out.'

Abbie's shaking her head. 'I don't understand. Why would she leave her house like that?'

Rick looks at her. 'Is that what she told you?' He has a sad half-smile on his face. 'It isn't her house. It never was. It's mine.'

'*Yours?*' The look of astonishment on Abbie Rose's face is comical.

'Even surfers can buy houses, lady.'

'I'm sorry. I didn't mean it like that. She seemed so at home. I assumed it was hers.'

'I always told her to treat it like it's hers, right from the start. When we met, she didn't have anywhere else to go. I offered her a bed. We got on.' He turns his head and continues staring out to sea.

'You miss her.' Abbie thinks he's upset. There's sympathy all over her face.

'Kind of. It was the way we met. I felt it was destiny, somehow. There aren't that many girls who get into surfing the way she did.'

'How did you meet?'

Why doesn't Abbie Rose leave him alone? Suddenly I feel protective towards him. Rick goes to the beach to meditate or surf, not to talk to people like her.

'I came down to the beach one day, after a storm. I'd dreamed about a mermaid, Abbie Rose. A beautiful mermaid washed up on the shore. And the next morning, there she was.'

'What? Here?' Abbie Rose looks puzzled.

'See that last rock where the seagull's sitting?' He points at the rocks to the left of them. 'And that crack in the rock over there, which centuries from now, when the waves have battered it long enough, will be a cave?' He points to the other side of the tiny beach, where there's a vertical crack that's just beginning to be eroded away. 'Draw a line between the two of them. Halfway along it, that's where I found her. Right here.'

He places his hands on the sand in front of his surfboard. Suddenly I'm choked. He's reliving the moment he found me.

Abbie Rose doesn't give up. 'Where is she, Rick?'

He shrugs. 'Gone.' He shrugs again. 'Don't know where. Not sure why, either.' He shakes his head slowly. 'All I can think of is this guy came to the house the other night. Big bloke. Really upset her. I got back and there was all this yelling going on. I asked him to go. Man, I thought he was going to punch me. When he'd gone, she drank a whole load of wine and went off on one. Ripped me to shreds, then drove after him. She came back the next day, but it's over. She's gone.' As I look at him, I know what he's hoping. That one of his big waves will wash his mermaid up again. 'Maybe she'll come back,' he says, but he doesn't sound like he believes it.

'I hate to ask when you're upset . . .' She trails off.

Rick looks flummoxed. 'Jeez, I'm not upset. It's not like that.'

Abbie Rose looks dumbfounded. She thinks the heartbroken surfer is mourning the loss of his mermaid.

Rick's silent, trying to choose the right words. 'It's just not right,' he says finally. 'Karma, man. She shouldn't have gone. She owes me.'

Before Abbie can say anything, he's on his feet, his board under his arm, jogging towards the sea.

'Why?' she calls after him. The wind carries the word to me. 'What does she owe you, Rick?'

From above the beach, I think I hear him say '*I kept her secret.*' Then he's in the water, the crashing of the waves drowning out Abbie Rose's voice. The philosopher and his element. Like Charlotte, gone.

43

Jack

Jack had been waiting for Abbie's call.

'I'm still at her house. Apparently, Charlotte's gone. Rick doesn't know where. All he could say was that this man had come to the house. He'd upset Charlotte and threatened Rick. A big bloke, was how he described him.'

'Xander?'

'I was thinking the same thing. Rick's surfing. I thought I'd wait until he's finished. Try and have a proper conversation with him.'

'I saw Evie a little while ago. She couldn't really tell me anything new.' Jack paused. 'The mention of Xander's name really disturbed her – but she couldn't say why. Maybe—'

But Abbie interrupted him. 'Jack, I have to go. I think Rick's just come back. I'll call you when I leave here.'

Just as Jack got home, Sara Evans called him again.

'Forensics want to talk to you or Abbie. They've found something in the third grave.' She hesitated. 'Jack, they've found human remains.'

'I'll go over there.' He was already turning his car round. 'If I park near Evie's house, can you get them to send someone to meet me? I'll be there in ten minutes.'

It took him only eight minutes, but a familiar uniformed policeman was already standing there, waiting for him. Jack felt a flicker of unease. It was Miller.

He got out of his car. 'Dan. Thanks for coming. Which way?'

'I'll show you.'

Jack had thought he knew where they were going. They'd been walking for a good ten minutes, snaking further into the woods, when he started to get an odd feeling. It was his gut again. Something wasn't right.

'How long before we get there?' he asked.

'Not much further.'

The feeling intensified. He'd spoken to Sara just ten minutes before he'd arrived here. It would have taken Sara another minute or two to contact the team in the woods, then however long for someone to walk back down to the road to meet him – the graves were deep among the trees. Yet Miller had been standing there, cool as a cucumber. He hadn't even been out of breath.

The numbers didn't add up. He didn't know where Miller was taking him, but he was almost certain it wasn't to the graves. Glancing around, Jack noticed a dense area of bushes a few metres away. Miller was striding ahead of him, not looking back, as Jack picked his moment and ran, as quietly as he could.

Jack didn't think he was going to make it to the bushes without being seen. Then he was there, flinging himself down, half expecting Miller to have followed him. But instead Miller was standing further down the path, looking around frantically and talking on his phone. Jack had no idea who to.

Jack needed to find out what was going on. But it wasn't over yet. To the side of Miller, he could see a familiar looming shape. It was Xander Pascoe, he was sure of it. Then he heard him arguing with Miller. He strained his ears to listen, but he was too far away to make out what they were saying.

Slowly, having no idea where he was going, he crept further off the path, until the crack of a twig underfoot gave him away. Without turning to see if they were following, he broke into a run, trying to work out where he was as he crashed through the undergrowth. He could hear them catching up, he was sure of it.

In his pocket, Jack's phone vibrated. Still running, he reached for it. Abbie's name was displayed on the screen.

'Abbie?' He spoke as loudly as he dared.

'Where are you, Jack? I'm on my way to the graves.' But her voice was breaking up.

'Go back to your car, Abbie. It isn't safe.' But he couldn't be sure she'd heard him. He hung up. He needed to find her before Miller and Pascoe did. Then, in the distance, he heard her voice. Following it, he ran faster. Then up ahead, through the trees, he saw her on the path.

Relief filled him. 'We have to get out of here.' Jack was so out of breath, talking was painful.

'Why? What's happened?'

'I was on my way to the graves. We were right about Miller. He's with Xander. Miller tried to lead me to him. I ran and they were following me. Abbie, come on – we need to keep moving.' Grabbing her hand, he pulled her after him.

The path narrowed and he jogged ahead of her, glancing over his shoulder to make sure she was keeping up, then they hit a wider path. Suddenly Jack knew where he was, but Abbie was falling behind. He heard a crashing sound from the two men, not far behind them.

'The graves are this way.' His voice was low.

The thought of more police not far away gave them the impetus to keep going, as Jack turned off the main path again. Up ahead they could see the familiar police tape, behind which Forensics were at work.

Jack stopped. 'Thank God.'

Abbie couldn't speak. They both knew that here, surrounded by other police officers, they were safe enough. Once either of them was alone again, Xander would be waiting for them.

'Look.' Jack hesitated. 'This is building to something.' Even without Halloween, which was only days away.

Getting out her phone, Abbie nodded. 'I'm worried about Evie. She called me earlier. She told me there's something that doesn't make sense to her. She wasn't talking about her lack of memory. It was something someone had said to her that didn't ring true.' She called the police station. 'Sara? I'm with Jack. We need backup down here.' She looked at Jack. 'Yes, we're at the graves.'

She turned back to Jack. 'We need to arrest Pascoe. Even if we hold him for twenty-four hours, it buys us time.' But time for what? To find Charlotte? For Evie to remember something else that might not be reliable?

Jack nodded. 'You should stay here and wait for backup. Then someone needs to get over to the Pascoe farm.'

'What about you? Where are you going?'

'To Evie's. I don't trust Pascoe.'

'Be careful, Jack.'

Jack knew what he was doing. They were up against something that didn't play by the rules – that had its own rules, and possibly dates, the next of which was fast approaching. He should wait, Jack knew that. But there were lives at risk and when you couldn't trust your fellow officers, it wasn't your typical investigation.

Whatever was going on, Jack would bet his life that Xander Pascoe was behind it.

44

When Jack got to Evie's, the house was quiet. Peering through the windows, he spotted her curled up and asleep on the sofa, but there was no sign of her police guard. Not wanting to disturb her, he made his way down the track to where his car was, then as soon as he was inside, called PC Sara Evans.

Jack didn't give her a chance to talk. 'Who did you speak to when I asked you to arrange someone to meet me?'

Sara sounded baffled. 'One of Forensics? I'm not sure. It's been non-stop today. You wouldn't believe—'

Jack interrupted her. 'Was it Miller?'

Sara's shocked silence echoed down the phone. 'Yes, it was actually. How did you know? Come to think of it, I was on the phone to him when you called. I put him on hold and then he asked what was going on. I told him how busy I was. He said he had to call Forensics anyway – he'd pass on your message. I was just grateful for some help. Honestly, Sir, all kinds of shit has been going on. You've no idea . . .'

Jack tuned her out. He'd always suspected Sara's inability to deal with pressure. Today, she'd proved him right – she'd inadvertently made the biggest mistake of her career. He wondered what other evidence Miller had withheld from them.

'Sara? Can you get on to Forensics and ask them to resend their reports from Evie's house?'

What if Miller had somehow prevented them from seeing any references to the presence of a child? Jack was kicking himself. He should have thought of this before. But it was done now. The question was, what next.

'Do you know who's scheduled to be at Evie's the next few nights?' he asked.

'Hold on and I'll tell you . . .' He could hear her typing. 'Miller, for the next couple of nights, then Cambourne are supposed to be sending someone over.'

Miller again. 'Get someone over to Evie's now, Sara. And I want them to stay with her. Twenty-four-hour protection – anyone except Miller. I don't want him anywhere near.' Not that Miller would volunteer. Now that he knew they were on to him, he'd be keeping away.

It had never been Jack's job to oversee this case, but no longer sure who he could trust, he wasn't taking chances. He went on. 'Sara, I want you to have someone ready to go with Abbie to the Pascoes' farm. Phone round though – don't put it on the radio. More than one person.'

'There isn't anyone. They're all out.'

'Then call Newquay. Tell them we need backup.' Jack was raising his voice. Sara knew the drill. He shouldn't have to tell her, least of all now, when time was running out.

'Underwood's just walked in.'

'Perfect,' Jack said. 'Tell him about Miller. Tell him I told

you to tell him. And find someone else to go to the Pascoes'.'
Then he hung up.

The uneasy feeling was back. Not just letting him know
something was wrong, but twisting, screaming at him. What
if more police were involved? How did he know Miller didn't
have an accomplice? Like Underwood? What if Sara was
involved too? What if she hadn't called for backup, if Abbie
was on her way to the Pascoes' farm alone and Xander was
waiting for her?

His hands were sweaty as he tried to tell himself he was
being paranoid, that Underwood was a good officer. But it
wasn't helping. Right now, he couldn't trust anyone.

Just then, his phone buzzed. Jack glanced at it, wondering
if it was Abbie, but it was Sara again. 'Yes?'

'Sir, I've just had a call from the Forensics team at the site
in the woods. It's about that third grave. The remains have
been there a long time. They're not saying how long exactly,
but it's more than a few years.'

'Did they say any more about the victim?'

Sara's words seemed to fill the car. 'Only that it's a child.'

'Thank you, Sara.' Jack's mind was racing. 'Let me know if
you hear anything else.' Thank God the remains had been
there too long to belong to Evie's daughter. Was it possible
that, after all this time, they'd at last found the body of Leah
Danning?

45

Evie

She'd had the strangest dream. She'd been walking, along a stony farm track. It was definitely winter, the sky overcast, the trees bare, when she'd noticed a honeysuckle flowering at the roadside, not the isolated sprig you might expect at this time of year, but a swathe of it, tumbling over the hedge. A splash of colour and scent against the stark landscape.

As she looked around, suddenly it was as though it was spring. Either side of her, tiny flowers were emerging through the straggly autumn grass – little stars of white wood anemones and yellow celandine, primroses, mayflower, tiny scabious, daisies – their buds slowly opening until they formed an avenue of colour either side of her. It was extraordinary, magical; it made no sense.

Then she'd heard the birds, to her amazement seeing the hedges full of them, their song deafening.

It was late afternoon when she woke up and saw the crow. Its presence unnerved her. She'd wandered into the kitchen to make a cup of tea when she noticed it just outside the back door. Pausing to admire the oily sheen on its feathers, she watched it fly up and try to perch on the windowsill. Unable to get a grip, fluttering its wings to hold itself there, it pecked at the glass, its round eyes staring sharply into hers.

It was most un-birdlike behaviour. Then she noticed it was holding something in its beak.

There was a churning feeling in her stomach as, grabbing a slice of bread, she hurried outside and sat on the doorstep. But before she could tear off a piece of bread and toss it in the direction of the bird, it hopped over and dropped something in front of her.

It was tiny. She picked it up, holding the small stone between her fingers, noticing it wasn't a stone at all. It was a bead. The crow had brought her a bead.

'Thank you.' She lobbed a piece of the bread towards it, but the bird ignored it, turned round and flew away.

She looked at the bead more closely, rubbing away the light dusting of dried mud and making out the letter on it. In pink. An E.

Her mind froze. For several minutes, she sat there, staring at it, as more birds came into the garden. She threw the remaining bread for them, then went back inside to fetch the rest of the loaf.

As she sat on the doorstep again, another crow landed on the grass then hopped towards her, not the slightest bit afraid. The same crow? Her heart missed a beat as it dropped another bead in front of her. An L. It was pushed aside by another crow carrying another bead. This time an A.

Slowly, she realized she recognized the beads. They were from one of those little bracelets made of thin stretchy elastic and bearing a name, that small children wear sometimes. She needed an N and a G. She willed the crows to bring them to her, tears pouring down her cheeks, the outpouring of weeks of uncertainty, of not trusting herself, as she tore up the remaining slices of bread, scattering the pieces for the birds as more flew down from the trees. There were dozens of them – blackbirds, thrushes, sparrows, finches and the crows, of course – their sounds combining to create an orchestra of birdsong.

Suddenly, she was aware of all their eyes on her. Getting up, she ran inside to find her phone. Instead of sharing her excitement that, at last, she had tangible proof that Angel was real, Abbie sounded flustered when Evie told her about the beads.

'Is anyone with you?' Abbie asked.

'No.'

'Someone's on their way over. Stay in the house, Evie. Don't let anyone in.'

'Why? What's happened, Abbie?' The DI sounded worried. Evie needed to know what was going on.

But Abbie cut her short. 'I'm really sorry, Evie. I can't talk now. I have to be somewhere.'

Then she was gone, leaving Evie shaking with disappointment and fear. Why was someone on their way over? Was she in danger? Or had there been another murder? She'd never heard Abbie talk like that.

But she knew she couldn't stay in the house. The beads meant something, she was sure of it. It was possible they weren't Angel's. With a sinking feeling she realized that it could be an H that was missing. They could be Leah's.

Suddenly her head felt like it was spinning. She must know who took Leah all those years ago. All the pieces were there, floating in her head, just out of reach. Then she heard a car coming up the track towards her house. From what Abbie had said, once the police had arrived, they weren't going to let her go anywhere.

She had to get out, right now. Grabbing her jacket, she put the beads in her pocket, along with her phone, then closing the door quietly behind her, ran down the garden into the woods.

Walking fast, she chose the opposite direction from where she'd found the graves. She didn't want to think about them. Instead, she needed to follow this sixth sense that seemed to have taken her mind over; telling her to keep going, along this path, until it met open fields, where, if you looked into the distance, you could see the sea.

So often the woods were quiet, but today they were alive with birds, rabbits, squirrels. Through the trees, she saw a group of deer, all of them raising their heads to watch her, instead of turning to run away. And all the time, there was a voice whispering to her. The same voice that so often had told her to trust no one, was telling her to *keep going*. Somewhere behind her, she heard a dog bark. Beamer? She wished he was with her, running at her side. If she'd had time, she'd have asked Jack if she could borrow him. But she hadn't.

She knew something about Leah Danning. The day the little girl had disappeared, she had seen something. Reaching the fields, she climbed the stile and dropped down onto the grass. It was damp, the ground soft underfoot from all the rain they'd had. Across the field, the sheep ignored her, as she started striding along the footpath. Then she heard her phone ring.

Pulling it out of her pocket, Abbie's number was displayed on the screen.

'Hello?'

'Evie? Are you all right? Where are you?'

'I'm fine. I had to go out, Abbie. It's the beads. They mean something. I'm sure of it.'

'Evie . . .' Abbie hesitated. 'I wasn't going to tell you, but Forensics found a third grave. It's years old – but they've found a child's body. You need to go home and stay there, Evie. You'll be safe there . . .'

'I'm not going, Abbie. I've listened to what everyone's said for too long. I'm making my own decisions now.'

'Please go back to the house. Jack's there and PC Evans is on her way.'

She hadn't taken to PC Evans – Sara. The officer had no feelings, no empathy.

'I can't, Abbie. I'm sorry.'

'Evie, you're in danger. We think Xander Pascoe's after you.'

'*Why?*' She screamed down the phone. '*What have I done?*'

'You know something—' Evie hung up, turning her phone to silent as she walked faster, her optimism tainted by Abbie's call. She looked towards the greying skies, the distant sea, which was a murky colour rather than its usual clear blue.

Whatever she knew about Leah was connected to Xander. Why the feelings of shame when she thought of him? She pictured his mean eyes and his cruel mouth. Remembered his hands on her, his lips on hers. Felt herself shudder. Did that happen? If it did, when?

As she reached the other side of the field, she climbed another stile onto a narrow lane. Which way? A robin flew past her and, without thinking, she followed it, until it darted off to the side. She kept walking, focused on the lane ahead of her, until a splash of colour caught her eye.

Bluebells? It couldn't be. They never flowered in October, and certainly not in open grass at the side of a lane. A breath of their hyacinth scent reached her. There was no mistaking them.

Suddenly she was reminded of her dream. She'd been walking somewhere – not dissimilar to this. Walking more slowly, she scrutinized the roadside for more out-of-season flowers, but this wasn't the dream. It was Cornwall in October.

The lane sloped uphill, then went round a corner, where she came to a crossroads. There were no signposts. Unsure which road to take, she walked straight ahead for a few yards before the same instinct that had brought her this far forced her back.

As she stood in the middle of the crossroads, she noticed some twigs in bud. Then a robin swooped past her again, followed by another, making the decision for her. She broke into a run.

The track was like the one in her dream. Stony, fit only for tractors and farm vehicles. She had no idea where she was. She must have been walking for two hours. The sky had got darker, more menacing. In her head, thoughts were pushing to the forefront, then vanishing before she could give them words.

Leah and Angel. Were they the same person? Were her memories of Angel just the dreams she'd had for the baby she lost, or had she been right all along and someone had taken her child? She still didn't have the answers, but they were getting closer.

She wasn't questioning what she was doing here. Instead,

she was thinking about the attack. Was it to do with Leah's disappearance? It would explain what Abbie had just said, why someone was still after her.

She should call someone. Taking out her phone, she saw a list of missed calls from Abbie. But it wasn't Abbie whom Evie wanted to speak to. She found his number.

'Jack?'

'Where are you Evie?' He sounded worried. 'I can hardly hear you. Abbie's been trying to call you. Are you all right?'

'I'm fine. It's the birds, Jack – hundreds of birds. You should see them . . .' It was true. There was a whole flock of them, circling above her.

'Tell me where you are.'

'I don't know. I walked across the field we came to the first time we walked together – do you remember? Where you could see the sea?'

'Yes.'

'It comes to a lane. I turned right and followed it to a cross-roads, then I turned right again. I'm on a farm track now.'

'I think I know where you are. Evie?' Jack paused. 'Has your cat come back?'

Why was he asking about her cat? 'Not yet. Why?'

'It doesn't matter. Can you stay where you are? At least till I get there.'

'Don't tell Abbie . . .' she started, but he'd already gone.

Ignoring his instructions to wait for him, she kept walking. She hoped he wouldn't tell Abbie. Abbie would make her go home and wait in that house that had become a prison. She stopped. The track had come to an end. Ahead, there was a rusted farm gate. On the other side there was a collection of derelict farm buildings. Looking around and seeing no sign of anyone, she climbed over.

It was as if she'd crossed over to a place where there were no birds. Not a single out-of-season flower. It was deathly quiet, the air heavy with expectation and menace. Her skin prickled as she thought of what Abbie had said, imagining Xander Pascoe somehow waiting for her. She took a tentative step forward, as quietly as she could on the loose stones.

As she made for the first of the buildings, her unease was building. There was an air of decay, menace. The first building she came to was filled with rusting farm machinery that looked as though it hadn't been used in years. She moved on to the next, a smaller barn, tentatively pushing the heavy door open and peering inside, but it was empty.

There were a couple of loose animal boxes, their doors swung open, the bedding left from when they were last occupied. Then she came to another barn, but this time it was locked.

Her hands were tingling, her nerves on edge. The sound of footsteps reached her ears, some distance away, coming closer. Looking around for somewhere to hide, she saw only an old water butt buried in a patch of weeds.

Crouched behind it, she watched as a man's figure came into sight – then breathed a sigh of relief. It was Jack.

Slowly she stood up. He saw her, an expression of relief washing over his face as he hurried towards her.

'God, Evie. Are you all right?'

Before she could answer, his arms were round her. As the tension left her body, she could feel the warmth of his, and for the first time in as long as she could remember, she was aware that she was safe. But she pulled away.

'Jack, there's a barn. It's locked. We need to look inside. There's something weird going on here.'

But he took her arm. 'Evie, I think the strain has got to you. Let me give you a lift home. My car's over there.' He nodded towards the rusty gate she'd climbed over.

'Not yet.' She couldn't go until she'd checked the barn. 'It's locked. I need you to help me.'

He didn't say anything, just stood there, looking worried. 'I'm not breaking into any barn, Evie. I've come to take you home.'

Then she remembered the beads, and, fishing in her pocket, pulled them out one by one.

'Look.' She was desperate for him to understand. She was terrified of what the beads could mean, but she couldn't ignore them.

'A, E, L.' He held them in the palm of his hand, then he looked at her.

'If I don't look inside this barn, I'll never know,' she pleaded. 'Just this one, and then we'll go.'

He hesitated, then nodded. 'OK.'

Jack inspected the padlock, then looked around and found a metal bar, which he used to force the door open. 'I can't find my phone.' He looked worried. 'I probably left it in my car. Wait here, Evie. Don't go in until I'm back.'

But she couldn't wait. She knew, as she watched him disappear out of sight, that even minutes could mean the difference between life and death.

Other than the strip of dim light where the door was open, it was completely dark inside the barn. Using the torch on her phone, she shone the beam around. Mostly it was empty space, the old timbers hanging with cobwebs, but at one end there was a crudely built wall, with a door.

She was walking towards it when she became aware of someone walking behind her. Spinning round, she expected to see Jack, not this person. This was someone who didn't belong here. She heard herself gasp.

'Hello, Jen.'

It was as if she was caught in another of her dreams. What was Charlotte doing here? She looked different, not at all like the cool, confident Charlotte who'd been to her house. There was a wild, manic look in her eyes, as they darted around the barn. As she took a step nearer, from the strip of light at the door, Evie saw she was holding a knife.

Evie took a step back. 'What are you doing?' Her voice was shaking, but she needed to keep Charlotte talking, buy herself time, until Jack came back.

'You can't be surprised. Or have you really forgotten?' Charlotte's eyes were vicious, her words like venom as she spat them out. 'How could you, Jen? How could you be so happy, in your pretty house with your pretty little daughter, when it was your fault that Leah died.'

'I didn't hurt Leah.' Edging away, Evie was shaking her head.

'Liar!' The word pierced the darkness. 'If you hadn't been there, it wouldn't have happened. I told everyone, but no one believed me. They believed *you*.'

'But you weren't there, don't you remember?' Or had she been? Something in Charlotte's voice triggered a memory, and in that split second, Evie knew this wasn't Charlotte Harrison.

'It wasn't my fault.' Evie tried to keep her voice calm as the memories came flooding back, a tidal wave of them, hitting her all at once. 'Someone else took Leah. I was distracted – I shouldn't have been, I know that.' It had been a set-up, Evie knew that now. Xander Pascoe had been at the Dannings' house that morning. She could remember being flattered by the way he was flirting with her. How she'd flirted back, when she should have been keeping her eyes on Leah. How shocked she was when he kissed her. That awful, terrifying moment when she'd realized Leah was gone, she'd never forget it again.

Hearing another movement from outside, praying it was Jack, she stood her ground. 'You always needed someone else to blame, didn't you, for the way your parents treated you, for the way you behaved. But that wasn't anyone else's fault, Casey. It was yours.'

As Evie spoke her name, Casey's eyes glittered. Evie could remember them now. Casey and Charley, both with long dark hair and a disregard for everything and everyone. At the time, she'd disliked both of them. She should have seen her mistake, but so much time had passed they'd become entwined in her head, confusion compounding her memory loss.

'You gave yourself away. It was you who helped Sophie with her French homework, not Charlotte. That's the thing that didn't ring true, that I couldn't make sense of.' More and more was falling into place. Evie stared at her, aghast. 'You were there. The day Leah disappeared. You were supposed to be away, but you came back.' Her mouth fell open. 'I saw you.'

On that day, Mrs Danning had looked troubled, the shadows under her eyes darker than usual. Casey wasn't at all well, she'd told Evie. Evie had asked her what was wrong. She'd hesitated, then told her that Casey had attacked her. Evie had been shocked, even more so when Mrs Danning told her about Casey's venomous outburst, her hatred, her jealousy of her sister. Casey had gone to stay with an old friend for a while. Mrs Danning had been unable to hide her worry. Evie could remember the forced smile that had been too bright when Leah came in. But Casey had been there that day. Evie had glimpsed her face, framed in an upstairs window; their eyes meeting for a moment. All this time, the memory had been blocked out, but Evie knew, with certainty, it was true.

'It was you.' Evie didn't know where her courage had come from, but suddenly she wasn't frightened. 'You were jealous of Leah. So jealous you wanted to kill her, and you've convinced yourself it's my fault.'

If she didn't know first-hand how malleable the human mind was, Evie would never have believed it was possible. Now, as she watched the expression on Casey's face, she knew it was true. She was so disturbed, her mind so twisted, she was completely convinced of her own lies.

'Or did Xander do it? How did you bribe him, Casey?' Evie watched the fear in Casey's eyes when she mentioned Xander. 'What about Tamsyn? Did you kill her too?' As Casey's eyes flickered, Evie took a shot in the dark. 'Or was that Xander, too? Picking off the unloved, the unnoticed, thinking he'd get away with it . . . Aren't you worried he'll take you, too?'

'It's lies.' Casey tried to compose herself, but her voice gave her away, each word pitched higher than the previous one. 'You're a liar.'

'You got Xander to attack me.' Evie stared at Casey. 'Where's Angel? *Where's my daughter?*'

She'd pushed Casey too far. Screaming, Casey ran at her, the knife raised. Suddenly Evie was frozen, riveted to the floor, seconds from death, when Jack burst in through the open door. In two strides he reached Casey, catching her, bringing her crashing to the floor.

'Evie, are you all right?'

But Evie was screaming at Casey. '*Why? Why did you take her?*'

A horrible laugh came from Casey. 'Stupid fucking bitch . . . You should have died, Jen. Why should you live? But you ruined it, like you ruin everything. Poor little Jen, always the victim . . .' she mocked, as Jack pulled her to her feet, then wrenched the knife from her hand and threw it out of reach.

'Can you call Abbie?' Evie's voice was shaking, her body trembling, as she watched him twist one of Casey's arms firmly behind her back.

'I already have. In fact, that's probably her, right now.' There was the sound of cars pulling up outside.

Evie was shaking. 'Tell her you've found Casey Danning.'

Casey

Nothing is ever by chance. When you came back, the future shifted. But I'd known it would. My bones held the knowledge of what no one else would ever know; secrets to take to my watery grave. Even when my flesh rotted away and left them exposed on the floor of the seabed, they would never tell my story. The only person who can do that is you.

It's in your bones, too.

I remember you at school, the essence of an unfair universe, because you had it all – grades, looks, friends, clothes, talent. A career mapped out – I heard you tell one of your friends you were going to work in television. As if you had no doubt – for girls like you, there was only certainty.

You didn't know who I was, beyond the dimmest kind of recognition. Not at first. I was someone you'd seen around. One of the invisible, who blend into the background of other people's lives. They're the most dangerous. Did you know that? Always hovering close by, but you never see them.

Your life was full of promise. Not mine, though. Promise implies the prospect of a positive, exciting future. It wasn't everyone's right, though. How could it be? I knew the universe was fucked up when it contrived to give my cheating father a roof over his head, when so many innocent people had nothing. The suffering of the innocent, of the millions, for the security of the few.

But nothing in life is fair. There is no justice, only a construct manipulated by people with letters after their names. The rest of us make it up, under the guise of so-called morality; the most meaningless word, as subjective and malleable as we want it to be.

Human beings are good at that, though. Twisting words to mean what they want, dressing up unpalatable truths into something more wholesome. What happened to honesty? Does it, like justice, depend on where you look at it from? One man's truth is another man's lie, just as one man's victory is another man's failure. Think about it. A killer succeeds, their victim dies. A court case is won, a murderer walks free. That's justice for you.

You were the brightest summer day with cornfield hair and eyes the colour of the cloudless skies, while I was the deepest, blackest night. That was before, of course. Before your summer turned to autumn overnight, making you a dark, tormented shadow of yourself. Ghosts sucking the happiness out of you; your prettiness, your laughter, even your friends, devoured by guilt. Oh, you knew who I was by then. Your guilt and misery and ugliness were a just punishment – or so it seemed at the time. They weren't, though. Not if you knew what I'd gone through. Not when, much later, you managed to shake them off and be so happy.

It isn't right. And I've waited, always wanting to believe the moment would come when our paths would cross. It seemed inevitable, that the past would be redressed, injustice rectified. A matter of balance, that at last would make sense of it all.

They're fleeting, those moments. Easily missed, like that one a few years ago. I was ready to seize it, but you were too busy talking to the man you were with. A few seconds either way would have changed the course of the future – for both of us. I glanced away and when I looked back, you'd gone. I knew then that it wasn't the right time. There was so much more that fate had in store for you.

You are the last person in the world to deserve happiness, though you're probably one of those people who think it's your right. How can you, of all people, believe that? When you alone are responsible for so much misery. When there are innocent, tortured souls in the world, what right have you not to join them?

I came here to hide from a world that judged so harshly; cruelly. I thought this place had saved me. A year ago, when I arrived, I was dying, but you don't know how it feels to drown in blackness. To exist in a place where there's no sunrise, just a perpetual night filled with hatred and jeering voices. You don't know what it's like, to fight each day, for every breath, when it would be so much easier not to. Seeing you, now, brings it all back, hypodermic-sharp. You were too fragile, even in your new-found happiness, to put yourself through what haunts me every day.

There's no love – not for people like me. Not everyone is loved – you don't know that, do you? But in the long run, it makes it easier, because from the outset, when you know it isn't a caring world, there is no harsh awakening to reality.

The police weren't interested in what you'd done. Didn't look past your pretty hair and your tears. Nobody could. Even you didn't know you'd killed my family. You didn't see the rift you'd caused, which became a chasm, into which each of us fell, spinning, deeper and deeper until we'd gone. You fooled everyone. In a world that favours beauty, each and every one of them was taken in.

Not me, though. My razor-sharp eyes saw straight through you. It's why I've kept breathing. There was a moment, out in the future, spiralling towards us, when the truth would be exposed and everyone would know.

Rick hadn't needed to teach me to surf. Or about swell and rips and storm surges. The universe brings us what we need. The day I stood on the beach as the waves powered in, the rain lashing the shore, I saw the telltale signs of the rip.

It had always been there when I needed it. The knowledge that I could disappear for good. I was calm, resolute, ready to die, if it was my time, throwing myself at the mercy of the elements. Their choice if I lived or not. The prospect of death didn't frighten me. After years of pain, I envisaged uncomfortable minutes in cold water, as it filled my lungs, stopped me breathing. Minutes that after a lifetime of hurting, would seem like nothing. Then, blessed, eternal release.

As I waded out, I didn't falter. The storm had given the rip a force I hadn't felt before, that sent a strange euphoria coursing through me as it swept me out to sea. It was the ride of my life, one that there was no turning back from, as I was lost amongst the might of the waves.

It's life's greatest certainty – death. Our strongest instinct is to keep it at bay, so that it takes inhuman strength to invite it in – or maybe desperation. I'd known today would come. Counted down as the blackness grew more dense, more suffocating. No one would miss me. In a matter of minutes, Casey Danning would be gone forever.

I was ready. I let my board go. Felt myself choking on the seawater, then the sudden quiet as I submerged myself, then felt the current dragging me down; panic building as my lungs wanted to explode, my last thoughts about how long it would take to stop breathing, how long until I drowned.

*

Does the manner of your death define your arrival in the next life? I hadn't expected to come round on a small sandy beach, blinded by sunlight. Was this death? Thrown up on a shoreline? The most gentle rebirth into whatever came next?

Aching as I tried to move, flashes of the storm came back to me; the height of the waves, watching my surfboard blown away as if made of paper. Disappointed, all of a sudden, because after a life in which I'd achieved nothing, I'd failed in death too.

As I lay there, I waited for the darkness to return, but I could only feel the sun warm my skin. For the first time I could remember, I felt peaceful. The universe had granted me a second chance: it must believe I was worth something.

Above the beach, I glimpsed a single, white-painted house and the brilliant, hopeful beginning that follows the darkest, most bitter end.

'You OK?' The voice startled me. 'You must be crazy to have been out there. You could have killed yourself.'

Dragging myself up so that I was leaning on my elbows, I saw a guy in a wetsuit.

'I'm Rick.'

'Hi.' I stared at him, at his friendly eyes, as I realized. I'd been granted a fresh start. 'I'm Charlotte.'

The easiest place to hide – behind a name.

I was only borrowing the name. I saw it as repayment of a karmic debt. After betraying me and moving with her parents to California, Charlotte Harrison owed me.

'Whatever happened to you, Charlotte?' Rick sounded bemused.

'A narrow escape,' I told him. 'In more ways than you'll ever know.'

As he helped me climb the rocks, then showed me along the path towards his garden, suddenly I knew there was a reason I'd been spared. One I could see, that was crystal clear. In the bright sunlight after the violent storm, everything was falling into place.

I'd thought it was my time, but it wasn't. I could see that, from the way Rick ran me a bath, then after cooking breakfast, told me to stay as long as I wanted to. The darkness was nowhere to be seen. It had been laid to rest with Casey Danning.

Later that day, I sat in the garden, looking out across the bay. What a difference a day could make. How much life could change. It didn't matter how much you tried to control things. Sometimes the universe had its own ideas.

You thought you were hidden, didn't you? But no one can hide forever, can they, Jen? When I saw you a few weeks ago, I knew that finally it had come. The moment our eyes would meet. When you remembered what you'd done. The first time in all these years you actually saw me.

People, cats, children . . . everyone dies. Does it matter when? You were lucky, weren't you? You weren't supposed to be found. Xander laughed when he heard you'd been taken to hospital. You weren't supposed to survive his attack.

Some things just are – like Einstein's laws, or Newton's, or the regularity of the tides, or the predetermined length of a lifespan. Wrongs be put right. Karmic debts repaid. Balance redressed.

An eye for an eye; a life for a life.

46

Evie

As Jack led Casey out of the barn, Evie's heart was thudding. As she reached the door in the makeshift wall, she turned the handle, expecting to find the door locked, gasping as it came open and she saw what was behind it. This couldn't be right. She was hallucinating. Angel's things were piled up against the far wall. Her little bed with the pink duvet. Her wall-hanging, crumpled on the floor. All her clothes; shades of pink piled messily in a corner. Crying out, Evie's hands went to her mouth. Even one-eared Pony was here on the floor in front of her. Her mind was playing the ultimate, cruellest trick.

Suddenly she was light-headed, the room spinning round, her legs feeling as though they couldn't take her weight. Jack was right. She needed to go home.

She called out to him. But before they left, she wanted him to see this. '*Jack* . . .' A plaintive, desperate cry for help.

A voice answered. It was a voice she'd know anywhere; a husky, gravelly voice, from a little girl with tangled hair and chameleon eyes who she knew from the depths of her soul, emerging, terrified, from the shadows.

'*Mummy* . . .'

EPILOGUE

As they walked along the beach, Angel held on tightly to her mother's hand. The abduction had left scars. It would take more time to come to terms with than the few weeks since Evie had found her.

He'd driven them all to Rock, thinking the change of scene would be good for both Evie and Angel. It was a glorious winter's day, the kind Jack loved. The sky was blue and in the curve of Daymer Bay the sand dunes sheltered them from the biting wind.

'It's the best time to come here,' he said to Evie. It was true. No one else had braved the wind and they had the whole expanse of golden sand to themselves.

He reached into his pocket for Beamer's ball and threw it. The dog chased after it, bringing it back and dropping it at Jack's feet. He did it again, then, picking it up, he had an idea. 'You try.' He passed the ball to Angel.

She took it, a guarded expression on her face, then threw it a few feet, giggling when Beamer obligingly brought it back to her. Letting go of Evie's hand, she threw it again, running after the dog.

Evie started after her, but Jack stopped her. 'Let her. No harm can come to her here.'

'I suppose . . .' But she sounded reluctant. Jack could understand. After everything that had happened, it wouldn't be easy to put it behind her.

They stood together, watching Angel. 'How is she?'

'Fragile.' Evie shook her head, her eyes not leaving her daughter even for a second. 'She's been having nightmares. But she's surprising, too. Like this, now, with Beamer . . .' They watched as Angel grabbed the dog's collar and trotted along beside him.

'I've never asked you how you found the graves.' Jack was curious. They'd remained undiscovered for so long.

Evie frowned. 'With all the searches that had been carried out, I knew I had to look further afield. It was by chance, really. I saw the open grave first. It was only when I looked more closely that I noticed the second. I keep thinking about Tamsyn.' Evie's voice faltered. 'She must have seen the attack.'

'It looks that way,' Jack said gently. 'Either that, or she saw Casey take Angel.'

'I still don't understand.' She stopped walking. 'About Casey, I mean. Why she did this.'

Jack wasn't sure he understood, either. But when you were as damaged as Casey was, you couldn't apply normal thought processes. 'Casey hated her little sister, for being everything she wasn't – pretty, loved by their mother . . . You've always known that on the day Leah disappeared, Casey shouldn't have been there, but she was. You saw her, but with everything that followed, you simply forgot. In Casey's mind, you represented a risk. When she tried to start a new life here as Charlotte, seeing you back here too must have tipped her over

332

the edge. You weren't supposed to survive the attack. Maybe somewhere in Casey's warped mind she'd convinced herself that you were guilty of her sister's death and her revenge was taking Angel. If you'd died, she'd have got away with it. The way you've been living, no one would have known you had a daughter.'

Evie shook her head.

'Pascoe told us that Casey was insane and tried to blackmail him.' *Fucking mad*, had been Xander's exact words. 'Apparently she told him she'd tell the police he killed her little sister if he didn't help her . . . She told him she had evidence. We're fairly sure Pascoe has links to a Satanist group, but of course, they're very good at blending into the background.' He didn't want to tell her what he really thought, that there was an active group of Satanists which included Xander, and that Angel may have been held as a potential sacrifice. There were some things she didn't need to know. At least, not just yet.

'I want to get a dog.' Evie's voice was distant as she watched Angel and Beamer, still engrossed in their game. 'It would be good for Angel. And I might feel safer. I really don't . . .' her voice shook, 'feel safe.'

'It's hardly surprising.' Jack spoke gently. 'It's going to take time to get over what you've been through. But if you're ever worried, you can always call me – I mean, not as in calling the police, but more as a friend.'

She was quiet. He wondered if he'd overstepped the mark. After everything that had happened, it must be almost impossible to trust anyone.

'Thank you.' She sounded hesitant. Then she turned to face him. When she spoke, she sounded more confident. 'Would you help me? Find a dog like Beamer?'

'Of course.'

There was hope in her voice, he noticed. Over weeks, months, it would get easier, he knew that, but she had to find her own way. 'Come on.' He nodded towards Angel, still hanging on to Beamer. 'Let's catch her up before she completely wears him out.'

Evie nodded, slipping her hands into her pockets, her arm brushing against his as they walked together towards her daughter.

AUTHOR'S NOTE

A couple of years ago, I read about a little girl who fed the birds in her garden. In return, they brought her gifts – coloured glass, buttons, even beads. There are other accounts of birds, usually crows, bringing similar gifts to people they often interact with.

Who knows why some birds do this, whether they reward the person who feeds them, or are rewarded with food for bringing gifts. Either way, the story of the little girl stayed with me, eventually finding a home in this book.

There is much online about Satanism, its practice and rituals. If you believe what's there, it's more commonplace than most people think. There are images and descriptions, and there's also a calendar.

The Satanic calendar lists the dates of holidays throughout the year when a sacrifice is required to take place. One of those is the September equinox; it's closely followed by the days of preparation in the run-up to Halloween.

ACKNOWLEDGEMENTS

As always, I owe a huge thanks to the wonderful team behind my books. To my brilliant, insightful editors – Trisha Jackson at Pan Macmillan and Alicia Condon at Kensington – I'm blessed to work with you both. To everyone in the editorial, art, sales and marketing teams, for all your work getting my books out there, and to Alice Dewing, my fabulous publicist. To my superstar of agents, Juliet Mushens, who has, quite simply, changed my life – a heartfelt thank you, for everything you do. Thank you also to everyone who buys my books. I wouldn't be doing what I love without you.

One of the themes of this book is loss and how life changes forever when you lose someone too soon: in particular, if you're a parent who loses a child. While writing this, I've been somewhere in my head I'm grateful never to have visited in real life, but to those who've shared your stories with me, much love. They will stay with me always.

Again, thank you and huge love to my sisters, Sarah, Anna and Freddie, and also to my friends, for your support, this last year more than ever, especially Clare, Lindsay, Katie,

Heather . . . You know why. XXXX. Fred and Callum, thank you isn't enough – I owe you both so much, for your generosity and for being my port in a storm. Much of this book was written on your beautiful island.

So, lastly, Georgie and Tom. You are my world. This one's for you, with love.